THE BODY IN THE
MARINE BUILDINGS

_____

Richard Hernaman Allen

30127 08708403 9

For information, or to order additional copies, please contact:

Beacon Publishing Group
P.O. Box 41573 Charleston, S.C. 29423
800.817.8480| beaconpublishinggroup.com

Publisher's catalog available by request.

ISBN-13: 978-1-949472-60-8

ISBN-10: 1-949472-60-4

Published in 2019. New York, NY 10001.

First Edition. Printed in the USA.

INTRODUCTION

As I was close to finishing "Death on the Volga", I was wondering whether this was finally the time when I would part company with Nick and Rosemary Storey. I have enjoyed writing about the "sleuthing" they got up to during their careers, all placed within the context of HM Customs & Excise, and after their retirement, in more conventional crime-solving mode. But I felt I could not get into the habit of them being involved in a crime mystery every holiday they took. In any case, ensuring that their involvement has a fair degree of plausibility limited my choice – and I remain keen to write about matters where I have some personal experience.

But a weekend in our flat in Deal revealed one or two tales about the building. Our flat is in a terrace on five floors, built in late Georgian or early Victorian times, on or close to the site of a gallows. At the time it was built, it must have been about mid-way between Lower Deal and Sandown Castle, subsequently demolished. The only nearby building might have been one of those creepy Victorian Gothic houses that remind one of witches, Norman Bates's mother's abode in "Psycho", etc – though I reckon it was built a little later than the terrace which contains our flat. It has had a long history being, at times, a school, boarding rooms for the Marines who used to be stationed in Deal, rented to alcoholics and junkies, etc.

It seemed to me that if a body that had been concealed in a flat, say, fifty years or so earlier, but without interesting any "cold case" unit, I might be able to weave a crime mystery around Nick and Rosemary being authorised to investigate. It would enable me to dig more into the history of Deal, while making use of direct local knowledge which I already possess. Deal is a unique town: a naval port without any quays or docks; a sheltered bay behind the treacherous Goodwin Sands; a long history of smuggling (indeed, you can even see France from our flat on a clear day).

As usual, I started with some circumstances and a few characters, to see what story I could develop from them. What emerged wasn't entirely what was in my head at the start, but the limitations of records and archive material added to the usual way in which the story seemed to develop its own course.

I have included a short glossary of initials or possibly unfamiliar terms. I also should make the usual disclaimer about the names of people or organisations mentioned in this book. No reference is intended to any person or organisation with those names in real life. They are entirely the product of my imagination and there is no suggestion that anyone or organisation of that name has been or is involved in anything of the nature described.

I have delved somewhat into the history of Deal, but I make no claims to detailed accuracy. I am, however, indebted to David Coles of Defra for his identification of the age of "the Marine Buildings"; to Mr. McConnell, the owner of "the Golden Hind" for several invaluable details which I hope have made this story more credible to any resident of Deal who reads this; and to various publications which we've collected during our time in Deal. I am also grateful as ever to Vanessa for her encouragement, support and love – but in this instance also, for her knowledge about genealogy. And also to Jo and Kat for their continuing support and love.

Richard Hernaman Allen
January 2014

1. MARINE BUILDINGS, DEAL

It was Spring 1998. I had recently celebrated my 60th birthday in modest style in a restaurant in the West End, but, perhaps understandably, without immense enthusiasm. Though my birthday announced to the world I was sixty, I didn't feel sixty. Sixty was the start of old age, as far as I was concerned. But I didn't feel old. I continued to feel like me – not young, I reluctantly accepted: but certainly not old. However, as Rosemary had remarked when I'd given rein to these thoughts, there was more silver than black on the top of my head. At least it wasn't mainly pink!

My birthday meal was purely a family occasion: Rosemary and me, with Emily and her partner Greg along with Sarah and her partner Adam. It was an enjoyable occasion. Rosemary and I liked Greg and Adam, without ever feeling particularly close to them. I suppose the sort of people who work in the fields of art and design or music tend to have little in common with an older generation from the world of law enforcement, taxation and fraud. Their sporting interests were limited to the gym and playing badminton, a sport which I'd always considered - undoubtedly utterly incorrectly – as bourgeois and sissy. We couldn't even share good-natured abuse about football teams – and Rosemary and I continued to play squash once or twice a week, Rosemary swam and I continued to jog a few miles, at least as often.

Nevertheless, the evening went well. It was worth while, just to see how happy Rosemary was and to appreciate what pleasant, sensible, decent young women Emily and Sarah had become. But Emily had a surprise for us.

"You know we did a big project for one of the big insurance companies?" she began.

"Yes," replied Rosemary, before I could display my ignorance or possible forgetfulness... perhaps I was getting old?

"Well, they gave us a whopping great bonus. We thought about moving to somewhere bigger, but our flat is so convenient for the centre of town – and we don't really want to move until we start a family..."

"Which evidently isn't yet," said her mother.

"Not for a year or two... But we thought property was the best thing to invest in... So we thought we'd copy you two and get a flat by the seaside. But we haven't got so much cash to splash, so we've been looking around and we've seen this place right on the seafront in Deal. It's going really cheap... mainly because it takes hours to get to Deal by rail from London and almost as long by car… But before we actually put any money down on it, could you come and have a look at it?"

"When?" asked Rosemary.

"Next Tuesday. We're going to take the day off and drive. We could call in at Beckenham and pick you up on the way… It's a bit of a way from the station and the centre of Deal, so if we're going to put in an offer, we'll need to be whizzing around from one place to another, so the car seems more sensible."

"Perhaps you might park your little Fiat in our drive and we'll take the Escort. It may not be all that big, but at least no-one's knees will bang their chins in the back," I suggested.

So it was settled. In the intervening days, Rosemary and I looked at our road map to see which was the most straightforward way of getting to Deal and realised almost immediately that unless we went a rather long way round, most of the journey from Canterbury on would be on the equivalent of B roads.

On the Tuesday, Emily and Greg arrived around 9 am and we set off immediately, as we'd decided to do the journey there and back in a day. Slow-moving traffic on the A20, M20 and M2 reminded us why property in Deal was relatively cheap, because it took an age to get there. After navigating Canterbury, the roads to Deal were narrower and slower, but through pleasant Kentish countryside, the remains of one of the East Kent coalmines which I'd completely forgotten about, the handsome church of Upper Deal and then a rather ordinary suburban road into the centre of the town.

"What do you want to do first?" asked Rosemary.

"When I phoned the estate agents, I said we'd pick up the key at midday," replied Emily. "So we could find somewhere to have a coffee and use the loo."

Rosemary drove up to the sea-front and we parked just beyond the Royal Hotel.

"It's just ten past eleven," she said. "Do you know where the estate agents are?"

"In Broad Street. I think it's the road we just drove up. It's almost opposite the pier according to the map book."

"There looks like a café at the end of the pier," I suggested. "Why don't we see if we can get a coffee there?"

So we walked along the pier. It was a cool day and a strong breeze blew across our faces.

"This is the North Sea, of course," remarked Rosemary. "I reckon you'll need some thick overcoats when you come here in winter."

The pier had several shelters on either side. In them, there were gathered one or two fishermen, with fishing rods leaning over the parapet and the lines stretched out into the waves pounding below. They were all well wrapped up, and several had bags of various sorts and thermos flasks. In between them, several small birds alternately stopped and pecked at something on the ground or raced – perhaps more accurately, skittered – at surprising speed away from us as we approached.

"I wonder what those skitterers are called?" asked Rosemary. "They're rather sweet."

"There must be a bookshop or a library here where we could check," I suggested.

The café at the end of the pier seemed a little the worse for wear, with some cracked panes of glass and an air of having put up with several batterings too many by the nautical elements. But it was cosy enough inside, in the way of traditional British seaside "caffs". It had no pretensions and strictly non-uniform furniture and fittings. But it had an extensive and remarkably cheap menu.

"I think after we've seen this flat, this would a good place to come back to for lunch," I remarked.

We were served by an ancient, tiny lady with a south-east London accent and a large, plump young man with straight black hair. As he called her "Nan", I guessed he must be her grandson. I caught glimpses of the intervening generation working in the kitchen area. We waited while a couple of fishermen got a pie, chips and mushy peas each and then ordered four coffees and slices of fruit cake. The cake was home-made and delicious. The coffee was instant and quite milky, but perfectly drinkable. We sat by one of the uncracked windows and looked out at the grey sea with waves beating themselves against the pier, the gulls dipping and diving through the grey sky, a couple of white-sailed yachts beating their way against the wind and half a dozen grey shapes of large ships – presumably tankers, container ships or ferries – just visible on the horizon.

"Somewhere over there, to the north-east of us a bit, are the Goodwin Sands," explained Greg. He was slightly shorter than me, with dark, straight hair and gold-rimmed glasses. I always forgot how posh his voice sounded, though from what I remembered, he'd been to an ordinary grammar school in Reading and his parents were both teachers. "I guess that's probably where you can see the waves breaking as though it was the shore."

"It certainly seems like the sort of unusual place it'd be interesting to get to know better," observed Rosemary.

As we walked back down the pier we could see lots of attractive eighteenth and nineteenth century houses all along the front – and a curious tower with a sort of metal spire and large ball at the base of it. We walked the short distance into Broad Street, and Rosemary and I looked in the estate agents' windows while Emily and Greg went inside. There seemed to be any number of attractive old houses and flats in larger houses for sale at prices that seemed incredibly cheap compared to London prices.

Emily and Greg emerged with an estate agent in tow, holding keys in his right hand.

"We'll go to the flat in Mr Barton's car," explained Emily. "He says if you keep going in the direction we were going when we parked, the Marine Buildings are the large terrace almost immediately after you pass the Coast Guard station. You can park outside, apparently. The flats we're looking at are in number 42. We'll wait for you outside."

We walked back to our car and drove along the front northwards. Ahead of us I could see what I guessed must be Ramsgate, with a ferry nearing the terminal there. On our right was the sea, with a promenade and sea-wall between it and the road, along with a few vaguely modernistic shelters. The houses on our left were mostly rather elegant eighteenth or nineteenth century houses, with the occasional twentieth-century addition, some of which seemed completely out of place. The Coast Guard station was a modern excrescence, but well enough away from the older houses not to stick out too much like a sore thumb. Immediately behind it was a Victorian house which could've been the abode of Norman Bates and his mother. But immediately beyond it was a five-storey terrace of considerable elegance. It certainly looked Georgian. The southern end was rounded and must have had some lovely large rooms which would see the sun for most of the day. The terrace itself seemed typically Georgian, with the two end houses having additions, like these rounded rooms at the southern end and a rather more ramshackle oblong affair at the northern end – which, unlike the southern end, looked like a possible later addition. Between them, there were three houses with what looked like basements, the whole making up a large and elegant terrace. Typically, the ground and first floors had large floor-to-ceiling windows and the upper floors had smaller square windows.

Emily, Greg and the estate agent were waiting outside number 42, the middle of the terrace. The front garden was composed of paving slabs round a large expanse of pebbles, presumably gathered from the beach at some stage.

"We're looking at flats B and C," explained Emily. "They're the first and second floor ones."

"Hi, I'm Steve," added the estate agent, a man of around forty, with a face and manner that reminded me of a squirrel.

"I see the first floor flat has a balcony... of sorts," observed Rosemary, looking upwards.

The balcony was about four feet wide and stretched across the whole of the front of number 42, joining up with similar balconies on the other houses. But the balcony on number 42 seemed to have been chipped away in places by the elements and there were definite signs of rust coming from the cast-iron balcony rail. The others looked in somewhat better shape.

The front door was reached up a short flight of stone steps. Steve opened the front door and we went inside. It was quite gloomy, with walls painted yellow and old-fashioned light switches on the walls.

"This is the communal part of the house," explained Steve. "You and the other tenants have to sort out between you keeping it clean, redecorated and carry out any other work – other than major structural stuff."

"Would that cover rewiring?" asked Emily, asking the sort of question which would undoubtedly not have been asked by her sister in a month of Sundays.

"I don't know. You'd need to check the details of the lease."

"You're renting?" asked Rosemary.

"No. It's leasehold. I think both flats are on about 95 years, aren't they?" replied Emily, looking at Steve.

"Yes, just under 95. But you can negotiate with the landlord to increase the length. Of course, there'd be a charge. You might even be able to negotiate for the freehold, but you'd need all the other tenants to come in on something like that."

"Who's responsible for the outside of the house?" asked Emily.

"As with the communal bits inside, the tenants are jointly responsible for repainting and general refurbishment – unless it's a serious structural matter. Then it's down to the landlord," replied Steve. "Shall we go upstairs and see Flat B?"

We followed him up the stairs, past what looked like a broom cupboard half-way up, and into the first floor flat. Immediately we could see a well-finished room. It had tall ceilings, and the large Georgian windows looked even more impressive from inside. The ceiling had various moulded decorations round the lights and by the walls. It was all painted – evidently very recently – in matte white. Right in front of us was a cooking area, furnished with plenty of cupboards, a cooker, sink, fridge-freezer and washing machine. The cupboards were in a sort of light marine blue – a bit as though the original light blue had been over-painted with a light coat of white. It looked very suitable for the marine location of the flat.

Steve pointed out the various items in the kitchen, demonstrating that the cupboards and units all opened and closed satisfactorily. Then he led us forward into the lounge area. It was certainly large and already carpeted with a light blue carpet. It felt like a very elegant space, the sort of room a Captain of Marines might've used as his lodgings when ashore. There was also an old fireplace with a fake coal fire in it. It too was well-proportioned and suited the room down to the ground.

"This really is rather fab!" exclaimed Emily, who was rarely given to excesses of emotion.

Steve led us on to a narrow hall, off which led a small bathroom/toilet with a shower and all the necessary fixtures and fittings. It was stylish without being showy or too plush. Beyond was a bedroom, where you could easily fit a double bed and a couple of cupboards or wardrobes. It looked out to the landward side through a large window.

"There's a garden below," Steve pointed out. "It's divided into two. The ground floor has half and the basement the other half. Apart from a share of the front garden and your balcony, that's all you own outside."

"That's a good thing," replied Emily. "As we're planning to use it as a weekend and holiday home, we wouldn't want to have to pay someone to look after a garden for us… and we wouldn't want to feel we had to come just because the garden needed something done on it."

"You can see a fair amount of the town from here… and the countryside beyond… including what looks like the remnants of a coal tip," remarked Rosemary.

"There's a big project to deal with the coal tip," explained Steve instantly. "It's going to be levelled and grassed over, with trees and shrubs planted and turned into a country park with a cycle track, I believe. In a year or two, you won't even know it was ever there."

Though it was undoubtedly sensible to get rid of something of an eyesore, I hoped that there would be some memorial of a lost part of Kent's industrial past. It was too easy to forget where we'd come from. I could remember the docks of my childhood in Woolwich – now full of snazzy towers of offices and plush flats for bankers and consultants of various sorts.

"This looks OK too," said Emily.

"There's one other room... and you've actually already walked past it," continued Steve. "Just down the stairs at the back there's what is known on the deeds as a box room. At the moment it's empty, but the owner has done it up and, at a pinch, it could serve as a second bedroom or guest room. Of course, whoever was using it would have to go upstairs to go to the WC, but it has various possibilities."

We all went downstairs to have a look. The room had a couple of smallish windows and wasn't particularly large, but you could certainly fit a fold-up couch/bed in there, along with a cupboard. Or it could be a study, I supposed.

"Shall we see flat C?" suggested Steve.

We followed him up another two flights of stairs, past another box room, and up a further flight to what looked like the top of the staircase.

"On your right is a small cupboard, under the stairs that go up to flat D," said Steve. "It's got a fair amount of storage space – but I'd be a bit discreet about when you use it. The chap who owns flat D apparently thought it belonged to him and had been using it for several years. But the present owner of flat C dug out the deeds, which appeared to show it belonged to flat C. So the chap in flat D has had to give it up. But you'd do well to try to avoid rubbing salt into the wound."

"He's not likely to be unpleasant about it, is he?" asked Emily.

"No. he's a very decent chap. But he was surprised and disappointed… Not least because the owner of flat C didn't tell him until he'd got everything signed, sealed and delivered by his solicitors… Shall we go in?"

The door to flat C was in the back corner of the lounge. It too seemed very pleasant. The ceilings were lower and less ornate and the windows were smaller, with window-sills a couple of feet from the floor. It, too, was painted in white, but this flat had a beige carpet in the lounge with black tiles in the kitchen area which was around the corner from the front door. The kitchen had all the cupboards and cooker, etc. The cupboards were in light "pine-effect", with a couple with glass fronts. There was a large fridge-freezer and a washing machine. The bathroom/toilet and bedroom at the back differed little from those below, though perhaps the fittings in the bathroom were a little more functional and a little less stylish. But the view was better – though I noticed that the rear of the house seemed to me to need a fair amount of maintenance, which at some point Emily and Greg would have to contribute to.

"How do the tenants arrange things like maintenance?" I asked Steve.

"I'm not certain, to be honest. I think they just sort things out informally between themselves. There's detailed information in the contract about what's the tenants' responsibility and the landlord's."

"Is the box room we came past between the first and second floors part of this flat?" asked Emily.

"Yes," replied Steve, "It's very similar. I'll show it you on our way down if you like."

Which he did.

Slightly to my surprise, he didn't try to press Emily and Greg about what they thought of the two flats.

"We need to think a bit and talk about it," said Greg as we stood in the front garden. "Shall we get back to you this afternoon?"

"There has been some interest," replied Steve. "But they've only just come on the market and I'd expect more people looking round at the weekend."

He put his brochures back into his folder, putting the folder into a metal briefcase, and got into his car. As he drove off, Emily put the copies of the details into her handbag.

"I think we should take a brisk walk back to the café on the pier and think while we walk," she suggested.

So we strode along the promenade, the wind beating against our faces. The waves pounded the pebble beach with growls of fury and seagulls stood around or perched on groynes or other poles sticking out of the water, occasionally floating overhead without apparent effort. Unsurprisingly, the café was busier at lunchtime, but we got pies and chips or whatever with plenty of peas, HP sauce and vinegar, washed down with a strong mug of tea soon enough.

"So what did you think, Mum?" asked Emily, putting Rosemary right on the spot.

"I assume the second floor flat is a bit cheaper than the first floor one?"

"About five k."

"You're the ones who are buying it and will be using it. So what I say is how I look at it as if I was going to buy it. The first floor flat is very handsome, but it has some drawbacks. Those higher ceilings mean it'll be more expensive to heat – and you won't be able to leave the heating off all the time during the winter. Those big doors to the balcony are lovely – but they'll need quite a lot of maintenance. And you'll need to make sure they're completely secure. People are likely to know you're away a lot of the time and those doors could be the best way in, as I reckon you could climb up to that balcony without too much difficulty. Finally – the balcony. It's a nice idea – but it's going to need replacing… some of the ironwork quite soon. And though it's on the outside of the house and I imagine it's supposedly the responsibility of all the tenants, I think you'll have problems getting them to pay up for something which can only be used by one flat. On the other hand, the second floor flat isn't so elegant, but it's more secure and will cost you less to run. The only disadvantage I could see is that its box room has the roof on top. So if that bit of the roof leaked, the water would almost certainly end up in the box room."

"So you'd go for the second floor flat? What do you think Dad?"

"Rosemary's already said what I'd say. It'd feel swisher in the first floor flat, but there are more complications with it and when you're not living there all the time, you don't really want to add extra complications to your lives," I replied.

Emily's face gave nothing away. She was very much her father's daughter in that. If Sarah had been pleased or disappointed in what we'd said, we'd've known about it instantly, without her saying a word.

"Let's talk about it," said Greg.

Perhaps he'd spotted something that we hadn't – or perhaps Emily felt he wanted the first floor flat, while she preferred the second floor one. At any rate, they both got up and went outside. We could see them walking round the outside of the café, talking – but not animatedly.

"I wonder who wants the first floor and who wants the second floor?" I asked.

"Don't you know your own daughter?" replied Rosemary. "Emily wants the second floor flat. She wants somewhere to get away to, not somewhere more elegant which is going to be a lot of hassle. When they have a baby... if they have a baby... she doesn't want to be worrying about having to sort out problems down here."

"So they are thinking about having a baby?"

"Yes. But not yet... Not that Emily has said anything. But she talks most things through with Sarah and Sarah was on the phone the other day."

"So presumably Greg would like the first floor flat."

"It's the one with style. You could imagine a flat like that looking really stylish with the right furniture. They're all very modern in their flat. I guess he'd like a bit of Regency style here."

"So that's why Emily got us down here! I'm surprised Greg didn't drag his parents along to support him."

"But Emily played it quite cleverly. She didn't tell us which one she preferred… and Greg's parents moved to the Dordogne a couple of years ago, if you remember."

"I'd forgotten. I think I've only met them once or twice, so it hadn't really registered."

"Well… They seem to have reached an agreement… Up, down or neither, I wonder?"

Not to my surprise, we learnt they'd chosen to buy the second floor flat, but would make an offer in an attempt to shade a few thousand – or 'k', as they put it – off the price.

Indeed, as they were paying cash, their offer was accepted and the flat was theirs within a couple of months.

Initially, they went to Deal most weekends and took a couple of long weekends there to buy furniture and get it delivered. On a couple of occasions, we drove to the flat to be there when an item of furniture was delivered. We had an invitation to stay there whenever we wanted and planned to take them up on it. But, of course, we already had our holiday flat in Budleigh Salterton and over the last few years we had got used to the town, knowing the shops, places to eat, places to walk. So we didn't really plan to spend more than a couple of weekends in Deal, mainly to find out a bit more about what seemed to be an unusual and interesting town.

So the idea that Deal might come to dominate our lives for the next few months would have been something of a surprise to us.

2. A BODY ENTOMBED IN AN ATTIC

It started with a phone call from Emily, which Rosemary answered. Though it was a longer conversation than usual, I barely paid it much attention. I was writing about one of the incidents earlier in our marriage and was trying to remember certain names of people attending a series of meetings in the Cabinet Office some thirty years earlier – in the guise of a committee called MISC 38 (67).

"That's certainly something they hadn't bargained on!" exclaimed Rosemary after she'd put the phone down and sat down next to me on the couch.

"In regards to what?"

"Emily's flat in Deal…"

"A leak? A seagull down the chimney? A Victorian poltergeist?"

"You're getting warmer. The man in the flat above has just found a dead body walled up in his attic!"

"A form of early loft insulation?"

"Very droll! It sounds as if it came as a great shock to him. After all, he's been living with it there for more than a year."

"Perhaps you could start at the beginning?"

"Only if you don't interrupt me with supposedly witty comments."

"OK. Fire away."

"Emily and Greg have been in the flat for a long weekend. Emily said they'd met the man in the flat above a couple of times and had had tea with him once – mainly because he's an electrician and she reckoned it's always handy to know where you can lay your hands on an electrician. His name is Bill Joyner... and don't make the obvious comment, please! Apparently he worked as an electrician in the big Japanese car plant near Sunderland for a while... is that Toyota? Well, I suppose it doesn't really matter. He was doing quite well and decided to put his savings into property. He'd already got a house somewhere near Sunderland and decided to buy the top floor flat in the Marine Buildings in Deal because his parents rented somewhere in Dover and he thought they'd prefer living in Deal. But all at the same time, he had a bust-up with his fiancée, got into an argument with his boss and his father was diagnosed with Parkinson's disease, so his father couldn't live in the flat. So he moved south and into the flat about a year ago, getting a job with BT which means he's home about half of the time.

"He told Emily that not long after he'd moved in he realised there were several damp patches appearing that the previous owner had painted over and, he reckons, must've used some industrial dryer to dry out, so the surveyor who surveyed the flat before he bought it didn't spot anything. Also when he came to do the survey, it was a very windy day and he wasn't prepared to check out the roof... At that height I doubt many people would fancy it! But anyway, he discovered that there were several leaks in the roof and he's having to strip back the walls to the original brickwork and relay most of the floors, including re-wiring and re-plumbing. He's doing most of it himself in his spare time. Plainly, he needed to start with the roof and sort that out so that there were no more leaks.

"Though you can't see it from below, his flat is actually on two floors – the third floor isn't all that different from Emily's flat, but above is much more like an attic – and evidently has just been used as a store room for years. There was nothing in it, other than a water tank, some pipes and loads of cobwebs. But being an intelligent artisan, he began to realise that the length of the attic was shorter than the ceiling of the floor below – not just a bit shorter, which might be explicable, but three feet shorter, at least. So he did a bit of measuring and reckoned that one of the end walls concealed some sort of cavity... which might, of course, be the source of some of the leaks. So he started to test the wall that seemed most likely to be the front of this cavity and he'd knocked about a third of it down – not unnoticed by Emily and Greg two floors below – when he realised there was a cavity and something in it, which, on a quick examination, appeared to be a skeleton still covered in some remnants of clothes and other things which he didn't really take in at that stage.

"In fact, he told Emily he reeled back in shock, twisting his ankle and falling over, bashing his elbow on the floor. Emily and Greg probably wouldn't've known much about it for a while, but evidently he hasn't got a phone fitted yet… what'd you expect from a BT engineer! So he knocked on Emily and Greg's door to ask them to phone the police. He was plainly in considerable shock - and pain from his ankle and elbow – so while Greg phoned the local police, Emily bandaged him up as best she could and gave him tea and sympathy and listened to his account of what'd happened."

"It's a good thing it's Emily who's in that flat. If it'd been Sarah, she'd be convinced there was a ghost around and probably wouldn't set foot in the place again!"

"Either that or she'd adopt it – like the two lost kittens that now live in their flat."

"Had the police been in when Emily phoned?"

"Been and gone. She said she thought it best to wait until she got the full story. A uniformed PC and a plain clothes detective, as she put it, appeared. Despite his ankle, they insisted that Bill Joyner accompanied them to where he'd discovered the body – and, following years of watching her parents being nosy, Emily accompanied them. Knowing her, she just did it with such authority, no-one questioned why she was there."

"How old is this Bill Joyner? Perhaps they thought she was his wife?"

"I don't know. I suppose that's possible… Anyway, they went up and had a look and gave their opinion that the body had been there 'for a long time', which, as Emily remarked, was stating the blindingly obvious. While the PC stood guard, the detective went downstairs to use his radio to get a pathologist and a couple of SOCOs. When he returned, he had another look at the corpse and told everyone except the PC to get downstairs – to Emily and Greg's flat where he asked Bill Joyner to give him the full account of how he'd found the body again – plus such history of the flat that he knew. But he'd only had it a couple of years and all he knew was the name of the man who sold it to him – Kenneth Bartle – and the landlord – East Weald and Thanet Estates Ltd. Emily said that from the brief glance she'd had at the corpse, she reckoned it was a lot older than a couple of years. It was so covered in dust and cobwebs it could've been there a century or more, perhaps bricked up there when the Marine Buildings were first built."

"And?"

"When the pathologist and the SOC team arrived, the detective – DC Wernham apparently – went upstairs, taking Bill Joyner with them. They left just now, just before Emily rang. She said she's going to try and find out more…"

The phone rang. I picked it up. It was Emily.

"Hi Dad. Has Mum told you what's been going on here…? We're in Deal…"

"Yes."

"Just to say, the corpse has been taken away in an ambulance and the police have all left. Bill Joyner just popped his head in to say he's going to spend a few days in a hotel as they're treating his flat as a crime scene. So that's all we're going to find out for now… I wonder why they take corpses away in an ambulance? Isn't it a bit late?"

"I suppose it's going to a hospital for the pathologist to carry out a post-mortem…"

"Of course! How silly of me! Anyway – must dash! We booked a restaurant and we're already five minutes late!"

I passed on the news to Rosemary.

"It seems a bit odd to me," she remarked. "You'd've thought someone owning that top flat would've noticed that the attic room was smaller than it should be before now."

"And why would you brick a corpse up in the wall like that? Wouldn't it be easier to throw them in the sea? After all it's near enough there."

"I suppose if you didn't want the person to be recognised because they'd connect to you immediately. But perhaps they weren't dead. Perhaps they were bound and gagged and just left there?"

"That seems a particularly horrible way to die. If someone had done that to me, I guess I might hope that there were things like ghosts, so I could come back and get my revenge."

"It sounds as though it was a fair time ago. Otherwise I doubt you'd get many people wanting to live in that top flat. It must feel a bit weird for Emily and Greg being there... If it'd been Sarah, I bet she'd've been spending tonight in a hotel too."

But we received no phone calls the next day and largely forgot about the incident. We were in the throes of getting a largish conservatory added to the back of our house and, to save money, we were doing as much clearing of the area as possible before the workmen came to make the concrete foundations. Also, a slightly larger and much more open garden than our previous one meant that we felt we needed to keep it tidier. We both found it therapeutic – while remembering that too much bending could make playing squash a day or two later more problematical. And though we realised it was unlikely we'd be able to keep on playing squash – even at a pace we would have regarded as snail-like twenty years earlier – our doctor hadn't yet advised against it. So we'd agreed to keep on going as long as we could.

I'd actually gotten to the point where I expected to hear little or nothing about the 'corpse in the attic' as Rosemary referred to it. But there was a ring at our doorbell early on Tuesday evening, and Emily and Greg appeared, evidently on their way back from Deal.

"Hi Dad," said Emily. "Can I use your loo?"

"Of course," I replied, noting to myself how much Greg appeared to have 'gentrified' my daughter. At home it'd been known as the toilet... or 'bog' when Rosemary wasn't within earshot.

"Would you like some tea or coffee?" asked Rosemary.

"A break would be nice, thank you," said Greg. "The M20 was very slow – and it always seems to be more tiring driving in a traffic jam than on an open road."

"We're going to look and see whether there aren't better routes," added Emily, emerging from the "loo".

"There's always the train," I observed.

"It takes two hours from Charing Cross," replied Emily.

"But you can just sit in the train and read a book or listen to music," I suggested. "And I'll bet you get there and back feeling a lot fresher."

"Talking of being fresh," said Rosemary. "Have you heard any more about the body they found in the flat above yours? How old was it?"

"The police came over for a little while earlier today. Apparently, the body is at least fifty years old and even if he was murdered in the most horrible manner, they're not going to treat it as a crime. They've taken a lot of pictures and they said they'd be getting someone to look at old files of missing persons, but they've lots of more important things to be dealing with."

"I can understand that. But couldn't the pathologist be more accurate than that?"

"The policeman said that once the pathologist had confirmed the body was at least fifty years old, they told him to stop doing any more work on it. Apparently there've been a couple of murders in Dover and they wanted the pathologist to get to work on them."

"Seems a bit odd. You'd think they'd want to get a reasonably accurate date of death. Otherwise whoever has been asked to check out missing persons would presumably have to go back as far as when the buildings were originally built... When was that?"

"Nobody seems to know exactly. It could be as early as 1820 or as late as 1850."

"A lot of missing persons to look for – even if you only look in Deal and thereabouts... So did they tell you what they're going to do with the body?"

"No. Do they just bury it?"

"I'd expect the pathologist to store it somewhere and do a proper assessment of the date of death when they've got the time to do it. Unlike a recent corpse, this one is unlikely to start deteriorating. If I was a pathologist, I'd find it quite interesting trying to work out not just when the man died and how, but also what else was left around there that might tell you more about him... Did the police take away any of the other stuff you said was lying in the walled-up chamber?"

"I don't think they did… I suppose Bill Joyner will arrange to get it all removed… and if I was him, I'd get someone else to knock down the rest of the wall and renovate the whole attic without me going anywhere near it… But I suppose if you lived there, you'd see it as an excuse to do some of your sleuthing…"

"At least there'd be no one likely to menace us with guns," I said. "Though I guess we might be plagued by poltergeists."

"Perhaps the building will never be at peace until someone finds out who that man was and why he was killed," added Rosemary. "I don't mean that in the sense that the place will be haunted or that there is some sort of 'spirit of place'. But unless you can give some sort of explanation, you may find it hard to sell your flat when the time comes that you want to… and this Bill Joyner is even less likely to be able to sell his… So you may find an empty flat above you for the next few years…"

"Just you… and an unquiet spirit!" I continued.

"Well – perhaps you'd better see whether the police will let you do some of your sleuthing then," replied Emily. "After all – you've got plenty of time… and you could always stay in our flat while you were on the trail of the long-dead murderer… If the corpse is old enough, you could pretend you were Sherlock

Holmes or that detective in 'The Woman in White'…
and judging by all this hilarity, you plainly aren't
bothered by the thought of dead bodies having been
in the attic above your heads."

"But I already know who the murderer was," I
said, with a smirk to rival Rosemary's. "As Deal is a
seaside town it was plainly Jack the Kipper!"

Everyone laughed… out of politeness's sake as
much as anything else.

"But that is an interesting idea. I've been starting
to look at doing some family history, so looking back
over old records and seeing what we might find could
be quite fun… and we'd get a holiday at a different
part of the coast into the bargain," said Rosemary.
"But what do you think, Nick?"

"I suppose we wouldn't need to be there all the
time anyway. We could do some of the checking from
here or even Budleigh Salterton. It'd be interesting to
know Deal better, anyway."

"But we'd need the local police to be completely
happy about what we were doing… and I'd want to
try and encourage their pathologist or another
pathologist to examine the corpse properly. We could
waste a lot of time trying to find out who was in the
building in 1945, say, when the man was actually
murdered in 1914 or 1875."

"Then I suppose we need to get in touch with the police pronto, to make sure they don't tell the pathologist to get rid of the remains."

"Actually, I've not been thinking properly. They can't get rid of the body just like that. There'll have to be a coroner's inquest. Though it'll almost certainly be an open verdict – presumably murder by person or persons unknown – the coroner would almost certainly allow the body to be buried or however they want to get rid of it… After all, it'd be difficult, though not impossible, I suppose, to wall yourself in. But then you'd expect to see a suitable implement in the cavity… unless this man was some sort of unfortunate Houdini…"

"So that gives us a bit of time…"

"Not a lot. We need to get a look at the murder scene and lay our hands on anything there that might be relevant. For instance, might the bricks used to wall the man in tell us something about the date it was done?"

"If we're going to be using your flat doing all this, what plans have you got for staying there?" I asked Emily.

"We're just about to start on a new contract, so really we've been using the last couple of weeks to get everything straight in Deal, so we don't have to go down there for a month or more… Apart from getting the meters read and checking everything was OK, we weren't really planning to go for more than an odd weekend until August," she replied.

"I hope we'll have finished whatever we needed to do there well before then. We're due to go to Brittany in August," said Rosemary. "I assume you've got a spare set of keys?"

"Of course."

One of the advantages about being retired – but without the responsibilities of grandchildren – was that we could pack what we needed and set off at short notice. So we gathered together what we reckoned we'd need for a week or two and set off for Deal the following day. We drove – mainly because we realised that using public transport in and around Deal might slow us down quite a bit.

Going into Emily and Greg's flat seemed a little strange. The whole building appeared silent and still – almost as though everyone, indeed all signs of life, had been chased away by the unquiet ghost of the dead man. Of course, as far as we were aware, no ghost had been reported as haunting the building before the body had been discovered. It'd seem rather odd if a ghost only started to appear after its former 'mortal coil' had been found. Nevertheless, entering the flat gave me an eerie sensation. But once we'd stowed our stuff away, put on the radio for some music and made ourselves a mug of tea, it seemed more like somewhere where we'd be happy to spend some time.

"I must say they've made the place very comfortable," remarked Rosemary. "I thought they might've preferred style to comfort... You know what designers are like!"

"If they'd gone for the first floor flat, there'd probably been a chaise longue and other Regency-style artefacts, if Greg had had his way," I suggested. "But I guess up here, the rooms are more ordinary... Though the view across the English Channel is magnificent."

"I reckon it'd be nice to leave the windows open a bit at night if it isn't too cold. I'd really like to hear the waves coming up the beach as we go to sleep. It's a pity we're a bit too far from the beach in Budleigh Salterton to hear them..."

"What are you going to do about the police... and getting into the flat upstairs?"

"I thought now we'd settled in, we could ring them. That'll be better than just dropping in. If we make an appointment to see someone, they can check up on us in advance. Otherwise it'll just delay things while they note everything down and then check it all out."

"Sounds OK to me. I think we can safely say that you'd better take the lead. I know some of the provincial forces probably don't like the Met all that much, but I can pretty well guarantee that Kentish coast police like C&E even less."

So Rosemary rang the local police station. It was credit to the sensible Emily that she already had a "Yellow Pages" for the local area. They suggested we come into Deal police station the following morning and took down various details about us.

"Let's hope their contacts in New Scotland Yard are with people who I got on with," remarked Rosemary. "Even when I retired, there were still men around who evidently didn't think I was up to my job and that I'd probably got it by sleeping with the Commissioner."

"I'm glad you encouraged them to try to contact someone in London about me. The last Collector Dover and I weren't the best of friends. He was one of those who needed a move, but didn't want early retirement and had the strongest claim to be Collector down here. But he was an arrogant twerp, one of those who thought he should've been made Director Outfield when I got the job... At least he didn't get it when I retired, even though he'd been licking Peter Somerset's boots for the previous couple of years. I doubt he'd say too many kind things about me – certainly not after his pretensions forced me to remind people at my last Higher Management Conference that taxpayers and Ministers expected our staff to be used to catch smugglers and collect taxes not have a so-called culture change unit of fifteen staff."

"Somerset was that very smooth man who, once he'd said hello at one of those dreadful Epiphany parties, used to look over my head to see if there was someone more high-powered to talk to?"

"Got him in one. He was a bit less smooth than he used to let on. I was told that when he got in a temper, he used to charge out of his room and start kicking the metal filing cabinets in his outer office, cussing away as he did so."

"That's where you need a strategically-placed video camera."

"It feels like a long time ago… Almost another world… and as we've not been to the Epiphany parties since I left, it feels even stranger… Though I do meet up with some colleagues from time to time, of course."

"I'm just sorry that Jacob Foulkes never seemed to want to make it to the ones before you retired. He was rather fun."

"I don't think he ever really saw himself as being a C&E person – just someone brought in to sort us out."

We slept with one of the lounge windows slightly open so we could hear the sound of the waves pounding the beach below. It was extremely relaxing – and the alternative would probably have been an eerily silent building, with the occasional ghostly creaking.

According to the town map, which Emily had thoughtfully left behind in a bookcase, Deal police station was in the London Road beyond the railway station. Nevertheless, we decided to walk. It was a breezy day. Indeed, we began to wonder whether every day wasn't a breezy day - at a minimum – in Deal. We walked along the promenade and then down one of the side streets away from the beach into an elegant small square – Alfred Square – with two pubs at opposite corners. Then we found ourselves in the High Street, which we followed as far as Queen Street, where we turned right and headed past the Post Office and a variety of shops that looked like a former cinema, solicitors' and accountants' offices and a pub curiously named "the hole in the roof" – though the hole wasn't visible from where we were! Then we went over the railway bridge close to the station and past a row of elegant Georgian-style houses and some less stylish modern houses until we reached the police station, which was opposite some nice Victorian houses built in classical style, but was itself in what looked like a converted 1930s semi-detached house.

There was a youngish WPC .at the reception desk. She gave us a slightly quizzical look. Perhaps she knew who we were – or perhaps we were unlike the people who normally came in there. Rosemary explained that we had an appointment at 10 am – and that we were Mr. and Mrs. Storey. The WPC picked up the phone and turned away from us to speak to her colleague on the other end of the line.

"DC Nelson will be out in two ticks," said the WPC, with a distinctly Scottish accent, which seemed out of place so far in the south-east.

Within a couple of minutes, a man in his late thirties emerged from a side door. He was only an inch or two taller than Rosemary, quite slight, with a round head and dark, quite penetrating eyes in an otherwise unremarkable face.

"Please be coming through," he said, in the South London accent that seemed to prevail over much of Kent. "When you phoned yesterday, you said that you wanted to speak about the dead body they found in the Marine Buildings recently. I understand that you're a former Chief Inspector in the Met and you were a Commissioner in Customs and Excise. It's not clear to me what your interest is. Perhaps you could inform me?"

"One of our daughters has recently bought the flat below the one where the dead body was found," replied Rosemary. "She told us that, as the body had been there at least fifty years, quite reasonably you weren't going to carry out any investigation. So, presumably, there'll be a coroner's inquest which'll give an open verdict and that'll be the end of it. As you'll know, we're both retired. I spent most of my career working in the Fraud Squad and Nick did a lot of different jobs, but he was in charge of the Customs Investigation Division for five years. We also got caught up from time to time in other things, including being asked to assist in investigating the deaths of a young man in a hotel near Riga and two people on a cruise ship on the River Volga in Russia. We were wondering whether we might be allowed to investigate the circumstances of the death of the man found in the Marine Buildings. Of course, we wouldn't want to step on anyone's toes or cause any difficulties for the police here – and if we came across anything that was likely to interest you, we'd get in touch straight away… The only thing we'd ask would be to see if we could find a pathologist who could carry out a sufficiently detailed examination to give us a rough idea when the man died. We understand at the moment, it could be anything from fifty years ago to whenever the Marine Buildings were built… and no-one seems to be too sure about that."

"What's your interest?"

"I suppose academic and nosiness. We thought it'd be interesting to try and find out what we could about who lived in the Marine Building at around the time the man was killed and what information there might still be about them. As I said, we don't even know when the Marine Buildings were built. So finding out things like that would be an interesting challenge. During our careers, we've also been concerned about following up details and tying up loose ends. I suppose this is a rather large loose end we'd like to see if we could tie it up."

"As you may expect, we've been doing a bit of checking up on you and what we got was positive. So we haven't got any problems about you looking at this case. Our problem is really about whether you'll suddenly dig something up that means we'd have to put men on to it… and also the call you're bound to make on the time of a pathologist. Obviously, you wouldn't want to be trying to investigate a death that might've taken place any time over a hundred years or more. I guess you'd need a ten- or, at most, twenty-year slot. Doing the sort of investigation to get to that would necessarily take some time. The remains are a skeleton and a few rags. Unfortunately, if the corpse had a newspaper or diary with him, they failed to survive. So it'd be a matter of quite detailed analysis. Forensic pathologists with the skill and experience to do this are thin on the ground and in great demand. What concerns us is that this body could easily grab the enthusiasm of one of our pathologists, just as it grabbed your interest. Then when we need something done urgently, they're too busy on your case to work on ours."

"Couldn't we work something out on that?" suggested Rosemary. "Couldn't we do it only on condition that any police work always gets priority? After all, it doesn't need to be done urgently and presumably the body isn't going to deteriorate suddenly and make the pathology work harder?"

"You probably won't have come across too many pathologists in the fraud line of work. They're often men and women who have a strong attachment to their work... After all, why would you be a forensic pathologist otherwise? And bodies like this one are out of the ordinary – exactly the sort of thing that's likely to stir their enthusiasm. Whatever we agree in theory may run into a brick wall in practice... and though I know virtually nothing about bodies this old, it may be that some of the tests can't just be halted at a few minutes' notice."

"So?"

"We're certainly prepared to let you have a look at this case. You can view the crime scene and see where that gets you. We'll have a word with our pathologists and see what might be possible. A lot may well depend on whether they can drop any tests they're carrying out on this body pretty well at a moment's notice."

"Fair enough."

"At least we can start along this path," said Rosemary, once we'd got outside, as she placed the keys to flat D into her handbag.

3. THE SECRETS OF AN ATTIC ROOM

We walked back to the Marine Buildings, stopping for a cup of decent coffee in the town's department store, called Laughtons. It was quite a bit smaller than most department stores we'd come across, but seemed to stock pretty well everything we could think we might need. We went up a side road from there, thinking to walk back along the promenade, but we found ourselves in Middle Street, a narrow street which seemed unchanged from a century earlier, full of handsome cottages and larger houses, most Victorian or earlier. It was almost as if we'd entered the film set for "Pride and Prejudice" or "Great Expectations". There was no single building that stood out, but, as a whole, the street had an unusual and unexpected magic that took quite a strong hold over us.

Middle Street ended in Alfred Square and became Sandown Road. We continued along it, past a building that we assumed must've been some sort or workshop or small factory at some stage because of the tall, misshapen and apparently somewhat perilous chimney. After a couple of hundred yards past old, but less distinguished cottages, we saw the back of the Marine Buildings. Unlike the handsome front, the back was mostly grimy brick – and even from fifty yards away looked in need of some renovation.

Indeed, I assumed from the griminess of the bricks that no renovation had been undertaken at least since well before the Clean Air Act and possibly never.

We made our way up Albion Road and went in through the heavy front door of no. 42, fighting against the wind to close it behind us.

"I hope Bill Joyner hasn't decided to return to his flat unexpectedly," I remarked. "Otherwise we're going to give him a bit of a shock... something I guess he could well do without."

But after we'd knocked several times on the door to flat D and got no answer, we concluded that the flat remained empty, unlocked the door and went in. The staircase was quite steep and felt dark and narrow.

"I guess these were the servants' quarters," remarked Rosemary. "Do naval officers have batmen?"

"I've no idea... I was what the Navy called 'a brown job'. Perhaps they were called stewards, like the male servants were called on the cruise... But I'm not even sure the Royal Navy had a base here. I've a feeling I read somewhere it was just the Marines – but perhaps that was just more recently... I've a feeling I read somewhere in the flat that Nelson stayed here with Lady Hamilton. So I guess the Navy may have been stationed here at some point."

We entered the main rooms of the flat. Much was evidently in the throes of renovation and redecoration. The floorboards were up in about a quarter of the room, with a rug covering about half of the remaining floorboards, with (sensibly) an elderly couch and chair, along with a small table and an old TV. We made our way gingerly past them and up an open staircase to the attic rooms. The most obvious thing there was the contrast between the recently removed and carefully sealed ceiling and the rough brick of the walls, where the plaster had been scraped off. The floorboards were largely down, but there were a few up, presumably where Bill Joyner had been working on the electrics or the plumbing.

At the southern end was the small chamber where the body had been found. About a third of the wall had been knocked down, with bricks – both broken and intact – lying in a heap near the open part. Next to them was a coal hammer and a large chisel.

Cautiously, we peered into the chamber, switching on the torches which we'd bought in Laughtons on our way back from the police station. It was about two feet wide and ran the whole depth of the room – perhaps ten feet. On the far side was the real external wall of the flat – between number 42 and number 41. It was bare brick.

"That's interesting," remarked Rosemary. "The wall on the outside of this secret chamber was evidently plastered. But the real wall was just brick. I wonder whether this room was originally an attic and had brick walls and someone plastered them later? Or whether they were plastered when the building was originally built? Which'd mean this chamber was built at the time the building was originally constructed."

"I wonder whether you could find any records that could tell you anything like that?" I said.

We shone our torches along the walls. Apart from, some ancient spiders' webs and damp patches, there was nothing other than the bare brick.

"If you look at the mortar," I observed, "you'll see that it's not very good on the inside of the attic wall. It's regular and looks good on the outside, but the inside looks to me as though the wall was put up in a great hurry and from this side, obviously... the dead man didn't brick himself in... Of course, I'm not an expert in bricklaying, but that's what it looks like to me... It may be that the backs of brick walls where you can't see them are always like that. But it looks rather sloppy."

"Perhaps we can find a bricklayer and ask."

Inevitably, what was lying on the floor of the secret chamber was more interesting. There were, of course, old spiders' webs and a few lumps of mortar, which must've fallen there when the wall was built. Because Bill Joyner hadn't been sure whether it was

47

the dividing wall with number 41, he'd been pulling the bricks out towards him. There were a few shards of brick and mortar on the floor immediately next to the opening that were evidently his handiwork, but the rest looked more like blobs of mortar that had fallen when the bricks were placed on top of it.

"I wonder if there's any way you could date this mortar?" I remarked, thinking out loud.

"Possibly," replied Rosemary. "But unless what goes into mortar has changed much, you might get a very wide range of dates, I suppose. We might think about it… You'd better add that to your notes in your notebook… along with finding a bricklayer to talk to about mortar… and we ought to take samples of the mortar and the old bricks"

More interesting were various pieces of dry, dust rags and what looked like pieces of paper.

"We're going to have to deal with these very carefully," said Rosemary. "I guess the police haven't touched them because they thought they might disintegrate… and when they learnt the corpse was at least fifty years old, they decided to leave them where they were… We need plastic envelopes and large tweezers and something like a cooking spatula to get all this stuff safely where we can look at it properly… We should also take a few photos of exactly what it looked like before we move anything."

"I can get a camera from downstairs."

So I made my way down to the flat below and got Rosemary's fairly new camera, which had an excellent flash. I handed it to her and she took a dozen photos, both of the debris on the floor from several angles, but also the rest of the chamber and the opening.

"We should try to get this off for processing today," I remarked.

"There isn't any more we can do here at the moment," replied Rosemary. "We've got to find a stationers' or somewhere like that which sells plastic envelopes. So we might as well go into town and get the film processed and see what we can find… and perhaps get an early lunch?"

So, we locked up flat D and went off into the town, finding a Boots that could process the film quickly for an additional charge and a stationers' that sold plastic envelopes in various sizes. We got twenty, mostly in larger sizes and found a very pleasant small café at the southern end of the High Street on the corner with Wellington Road. The owners seemed to be Italian, but the food varied from typical Italian dishes to cheese on toast and baked potatoes, etc. The service was friendly, helpful and quick and we told ourselves we should go there often.

The photos wouldn't be ready until the following morning, but we decided to ignore the slight risk that they might not have come out all right and return to the chamber where the body had been found and collect the debris and put it into the plastic envelopes. On the way, we stopped off in a hardware shop and bought some washing-up gloves and found some handy wooden cooking tongs in Laughtons.

"I doubt whether the debris will tell us much," said Rosemary. "But if we've got it bagged up, hopefully it won't deteriorate and we might be able to get a forensic scientist interested in it... Not that I know any, I'm afraid... and certainly not in this part of the world... Of course it'd be best if it was left where it is. But if the local police regard this case as closed, Bill Joyner will be able to do whatever he wants with the secret chamber and whatever was in it. If I was him I'd get rid of the lot of it and get the whole place redecorated as fast as I could... and double the size of the windows in that room, if I could."

We were walking along the road, close to the Marine Buildings.

"You realise you can't see the attic rooms from the road at all," I remarked. "There are the third-floor windows, above Emily and Greg's flat, but the balustrade hides the upper floor completely... I wonder if you can see it from the beach?"

"I doubt it. You're going down and away, so your angle of sight must be even worse. I reckon the only place you could see the attic from would be well out to sea."

I scrambled down to have a look, merely confirming that Rosemary was correct... and that the beach had some steep inclines of moving pebbles, which made getting back a lot harder than getting down the beach... and that there seemed to be a sort of fossilised – or at least bleached and dried – seaweed all over the place.

We went back up to the attic and while I held a torch, Rosemary put on the washing up gloves and sifted through the debris with great care, mostly using the wooden tongs, placing what she thought seemed best into one plastic envelope after another.

"At this stage, all I can reasonably say is that some of this looks like what was once clothing or perhaps some fabric the body was wrapped in - and some seems to be bits of paper, but I can't really tell what it is in this light," she remarked.

"We can have a closer look at it downstairs."

"If Bill Joyner does decide to get rid of all of this stuff, I think we should ask him to let us sift through it in daylight, just in case there's anything significant that I might've missed."

"Of course, he may not come back until it's all been cleared out and renovated… But on the other hand, it strikes me that he seems to be doing all this himself. Which suggests he may not have a lot of money to spare to get someone else to do this for him."

"If he's got any sense, he'll have a word with his local TV or radio station. There must be a few hundred in it for him at least… a body in the attic that might've been there for over a hundred years… I'd've thought that'd rate as much as that."

"All he'd need to do is to hint that he'd had bad dreams when he wondered whether he'd seen a ghost… and he'd probably double his money…"

"And the next thing you know, Emily and Greg would have ghouls and ghost-hunters trying to wander around the building. If you see him, please don't put that idea into his head."

"Certainly not. I was just speculating… or perhaps spookulating would be a better word."

"I hope you're going to take this seriously…"

We gathered the envelopes and other stuff and returned to flat C.

"Well, I guess these gloves and cooking tongs can be put to more common uses," I said, washing them under the taps in the kitchen area, using plenty of washing-up liquid.

"Just as long as you don't tell Emily what they were used for first."

I made us each a mug of tea, saying a mental thank you to Emily for maintaining a Storey family tradition of drinking tea and coffee from mugs, rather than cups and saucers.

"These mugs are nice," said Rosemary. "I like the old scenes of Deal on them. That was clever of Emily to get some like that."

We finished the tea and then sat at the breakfast table Emily and Greg had put in the kitchen area by the window and looked at the plastic envelopes.

"Let's look at the fabric ones first," suggested Rosemary. "I doubt they'll tell amateurs like us much. But you never know."

"That piece looks like a piece of carpet... All those strands look like what you see under a carpet... I don't know whether that was the original colour, but what I remember about getting the carpets laid in Manor Way, the colour of the backing was that sort of washed-out sepia... But that stuff seems quite tough, so you'd think more of it might've survived..."

"I suppose if it was wet, it might've rotted away... But that can't've been from the roof. If there'd been a leak in that part of the roof, Bill Joyner – or whoever was in his flat before him – would've had to repair it and surely they'd've noticed the secret chamber then?"

"I suppose it could've been the dead man's bodily fluids?"

"I guess so... What's that on this bit... Looks like tar or oil to me."

"That piece looks quite strong... perhaps it was some kind of canvas or sailcloth?"

The other pieces of cloth told us little. They were off-white or a pallid sepia, mostly some sort of canvas or something like that. There was no visible pattern or any marks on them.

"That wasn't much of a start," commented Rosemary. "Let's hope the bits of paper tell us a bit more."

The first fragment of paper had very faint writing on it. The ink had faded so badly it was impossible to see what was written on it.

"We're going to need a magnifying glass," said Rosemary. "And don't say anything about Sherlock Holmes!"

"The next piece looks as if it's printed," I continued, resisting the temptation to be flippant. "But whether it's a newspaper or something else, it's difficult to tell… I can make out a few words, but they don't really tell me anything."

"The next bit is larger… It's printed too… There are a few words here… it looks like 'ioners of excis' and then on the next line 'resents shall' and then 'oyal and trust' and finally, I think it's 'ake accou'. Pity there's not any more… Must've been quite good ink… but I guess time and dampness got to it…"

"Did you say 'oyal and trust'? That sounds like my Commission from the Queen as a Board member… I was 'loyal and trustworthy'… in my own fashion, at any rate. And if that's actually 'loyal and trustworthy', it might well be some sort of royal commission… 'ioners of excis' must be 'Commissioners of Excise'. But the commission always said something like "*To all to whom theses presents shall come, greetings, We, the Commissioners of Customs and Excise appoint X…*" and nothing about being loyal or trustworthy… or any fine characteristics. And if it is an Excise Commission, this bloke was killed between when the building was constructed and the middle of the nineteenth century, because the Excise was combined with Inland Revenue until the merger with Customs in 1909… I suppose it could be a bit later, as someone could've hung on to an excise commission after the merger. I've no idea whether the excise officers would've had to get new commissions after the merger."

"It'll be an interesting check on what the pathologist says about the body... Always assuming we're able to get a pathologist to look at it."

"Perhaps it'll turn out to be a C&E case after all... An exciseman murdered by smugglers... I bet Deal was a smuggler's haven in the eighteenth and nineteenth centuries!"

"I believe we might need a little more evidence than a scrap of paper to get that far. It could just as easily be an exciseman who was cheating on his wife with the wife of a marine and he found them at it and killed the exciseman in a fit of rage."

"Point taken. What else have we got?"

"Another scrap of paper with illegible scrawl on it... One of the love letters between the exciseman and his mistress perhaps?"

"It'd certainly show he was an exciseman. If he'd been a customs officer, chances are he wouldn't've been able to read or write... That's certainly what the old OCXs would've said about the old Waterguard."

"There's a bit more printing on this one... But that looks more like a newspaper or something like that… There's even a bit of a headline… 'zette'… Gazette, possibly?"

"Perhaps it's the 'London Gazette'? Pity there isn't a date on it."

"The other bits all have this scrawl on it… I don't think it's all the same handwriting… But until we get a magnifying glass, we won't be able to make head or tail of it… And probably not even then… So – where do we get a magnifying glass?"

"Laughtons. They seem to sell practically everything else."

"I was hoping to have a cup of tea before we went out, but as we don't know when Laughtons closes, perhaps we'd better go there now."

So, we set off again out of the Marine Buildings and along the promenade as far as Golden Street which took us into Middle Street, which we followed until we got to the back of Laughtons. Inside, we wandered around until we found the right section and then spotted a very Sherlock Holmes style of magnifying glass at a remarkably low price. So we bought it and – resisting the temptation of having a cup of tea and a cake in their café – returned to the flat and made ourselves a mug of tea there.

"If we start eating cake and not getting any proper exercise, you're going to have to start running along the promenade and I'll have to see if there's a swimming pool anywhere around here. I'm not, repeat not, swimming in that sea. It may look quite blue when the sun is out and there are no clouds, but it's the North Sea," said Rosemary firmly.

"I wouldn't mind running along the promenade," I replied. "I could run from Sandown Castle to Walmer Castle and see Deal Castle somewhere in-between. At least it'd be flat, unlike Beckenham Place Park."

"I'm surprised we haven't been able to see Sandown Castle as we approach the Marine Buildings… According to the street map… Oh! I see… It says 'remains of'… Evidently, there's not much left… And there's a leisure centre with a swimming pool over towards Walmer… Perhaps we might explore that tomorrow sometime?"

"OK. But we haven't got any suitable gear here… But I suppose there must be a sports shop around here somewhere… or…"

"…we could get it in Laughtons," we said together, and cackled like a pair of demented geese.

"But we ought to see the castles while we're here anyway," said Rosemary after the mirth had subsided.

"Yes… Too much sleuthing and no sightseeing makes Holmes's brain sherlocked…"

"Good grief! How long have you been working on that one?"

Rosemary started to put the plastic envelopes in a box file, which she'd also got in the stationers. Suddenly she stopped.

"What idiots!" she exclaimed. "We really haven't thought this through at all!"

"Go on."

"We've been assuming that this stuff was placed with the body when it was left in the secret chamber. But there's actually no reason why it should've been. Indeed, if I was concealing a dead body, why would I place with it a whole lot of things that might enable the police to come along later and work out when the body was placed there? Though it may be fifty or even a hundred years since the body was left there, why should the murderer assume that? He'd have to take into account the possibility that the body might be discovered within a few years. So why would you leave with it letters that might incriminate you? Although it looks as though the brick wall was put in a bit of a hurry, he must've had enough time to think about making sure he didn't leave any incriminating evidence around. So, all we can realistically say about the bits of paper is that the body was placed there no earlier than they were written – and possibly some time later. They might just have been debris that

happened to be on the floor in that part of the attic…
But the fabric may be linked more closely to the dead
man."

"You've just said something else that we hadn't
thought about either. That brick wall used dozens of
bricks. Where did they come from? Were they already
in the attic – innocently? Or because the killer had
been planning the murder for some time? Or did he
bring them in and all the way up these stairs
afterwards? Wouldn't someone have noticed? Or
perhaps the body was placed there when the buildings
were being constructed?"

"The trouble with that is that unless several men
were involved in the murder, you could hardly just
build a little chamber like that without other people
on the site noticing… But from what I recall of the
wall, it didn't look as though it'd been put up by an
amateur. If I was putting up a wall like that, it'd look
irregular and probably wouldn't fit as neatly into that
space as it did. Indeed, if it hadn't looked as though it
was part of the wall built by whoever constructed
these buildings, someone would surely have been
curious and discovered it long before now."

"So we probably need to find out when the
Marine Buildings were built and then everyone who's
lived here – especially in the top flat - ever since…
And presumably it wasn't always flats. It looks like the
sort of place that was originally designed for someone

with servants. The first floor looks like the main rooms with this floor the bedrooms. The ground floor would've been kitchens and so on, with the attic and basement for the servants' quarters."

"Where could we find out about that? From the deeds? From the Public Record Office?"

"The Land Registry? There must be records somewhere of who lived here from the censuses and somewhere they must keep records of who's owned these buildings."

"But much as though I might like to trace the ownership of this building over the last century or more, I'd rather we had a rough date when the man died, so we can concentrate on that period."

We settled down to listen to some music or just look out of the window at the waves pounding the pebble beach. Beyond the yacht making its way southwards were the Goodwin Sands, partly visible because we could see the waves breaking on them. Still further out to sea were the grey shapes of container ships and ferries. Indeed, far to our left, we could see a white ferry departing from Ramsgate.

"Since these bits of debris are likely to be less relevant than we thought," Rosemary remarked, "and we've got enough stuff for possible evidence, I wonder whether we shouldn't just have one last poke around and see if there's anything underneath it that we might've missed… We could do it tomorrow, if you like?"

"No time like the present. Besides, we might find Bill Joyner has returned tomorrow morning."

So, we returned to the "scene of the crime" and Rosemary poked around through the debris on the floor while I held the torch. The light was fading outside, but that part of the room always seemed to be dark… I assumed that Bill Joyner was planning to put electricity up there and have proper electric lights. Indeed, it looked as though there had been electricity up there and he was in the throes of replacing it with modern wiring.

"There's a couple of old nails… and that looks like an old metal pen nib… But that seems to be about it," said Rosemary.

"It's a bit odd, if you think about it," I suggested. "You'd think you'd find the remnants of a belt… a buckle at least and you'd expect there'd be something left of his shoes… I suppose his shoes and belt… possibly all or most of his clothes must've been removed… otherwise there'd be buttons and things."

"I suppose anything that might help to identify him. Which suggests that even though he'd hidden the dead man in this chamber, whoever did it wasn't confident he wouldn't be found fairly soon…"

"Or he was intending to remain in the vicinity for quite a long time, but couldn't prevent other people having access to the attic, perhaps?"

"One thing you can always say when you've got virtually no evidence – the number of theories you can have is almost limitless."

Rosemary scooped up a sample of the ordinary debris – tiny pieces of paper, dust, fibres, etc – into the last of our plastic envelopes and brought the remaining bits and pieces down – placing them in an ordinary envelope, as that was the last of the plastic ones. All you could reasonably say about the nails and the pen nib were that they plainly weren't recent. But unless you possessed an expert knowledge of nails or pen nibs – which we didn't – that was all we could learn from them.

At this stage, we realised it was getting quite late and pangs of hunger were beginning to bite. So, we made a last foray into the town and found a Chinese takeaway in Broad Street which turned out to be extremely good – and noticeably cheaper than in the London suburbs.

Rosemary was lying on my shoulder as usual as we went to sleep.

"This is an unusual town," she murmured. "I don't think I've ever come across anywhere quite like it."

Within seconds she was asleep. On the other hand, I always found it hard to get to sleep right away when in an unfamiliar bed. I lay awake, thinking – mainly about what we'd got ourselves into. Would we find anything out? Would we get ourselves so deeply into it that we'd be disappointed if we couldn't find anything out? What would we do about it if we did get sufficient evidence to point to who the dead man was, who murdered him and why? Would we keep finding things like this to keep our sleuthing instincts up to speed? Or was there some time – perhaps after this – that we finally let go these curious adventures? But, as I tried to settle myself a little more comfortably without disturbing Rosemary, I realised that most of these affairs had come to us, rather than us seek them out. So there seemed to be no point wondering.

4. PATHOLOGIST AT WORK

I did get to sleep reasonably soon and slept the sleep of an untroubled soul… and apparently without snoring. I was just making tea when the phone rang. It sounded like a policeman's voice, asking for Rosemary. I handed the phone to her and listened to her largely monosyllabic replies. Her tone seemed positive, however, and she said "good" and "thank you" several times. She rang off.

"You'll be pleased to know that a pathologist is interested in looking at our body," she explained. "Dr. Julia Radford who is accredited to the Kent Constabulary and is based in the University of Kent in Canterbury is interested, because of the indeterminate date of death and the possibility it might be a very old body. Apparently they don't come up very often, so she's keen to get the experience. She's even content for us to observe, if we wish… and we do wish, don't we?"

"Of course. When will this event take place?"

"They're shipping the body to her later today. They've given her office our phone number so she can contact us directly."

"I can safely say I've never met a pathologist. They weren't anyone we ever came across in Customs work… and I don't count Dr. Berglund as such. He was just brought in by the Baltic Coast Hotel to make sure there were no problems for them if a guest died on their premises."

"I don't think I ever met one either in the course of my work. The first murder victim I saw was the body of that East German woman being taken out of our flat… and I didn't actually see her body. Other than the Grays on the river cruise, that's it. I can't think there can be many policewomen who've seen so few… and actually none in the line of duty."

"You were very good at what you did. I don't think any woman got to Chief Inspector in your day without being extremely good at your job… You were a round peg in a round hole…"

"I suppose so… I wish I'd had a chance to see whether I could do some of the other stuff though. When I was getting involved in your stuff – especially when we were working on our own – I always got more of a buzz."

"If people waving guns at you or you waving guns at them constitutes a buzz, I can understand. But if that sort of thing was happening regularly in your day job, I wouldn't have given much for your chances of reaching retirement age."

"There is that, of course. And Emily and Sarah certainly believed that whenever we got into any confrontation with crooks."

We ate breakfast. As we'd forgotten to bring our breakfast cereal with us, we had to make do with toast and marmalade, with tea and orange juice to wash it down.

"I hope you can leave messages on the phone here," said Rosemary, after we'd finished and washed up. "I don't want to spend the whole day waiting for it to ring. I thought we ought to go and have a look at one of these castles and see what the facilities are like at the sports centre."

"Knowing they're such busy people, I'm sure Emily and Greg have got that."

I confirmed that they had, so we went out and walked as far as Deal Castle, which was, roughly speaking, on the way to the sports centre. Brought up on older and more traditional castles, I found Deal castle unexpected – but also handsome and intriguing. We wandered around it for more than an hour, wondering whether we might get lost in some of the parallel corridors that ran behind the walls. The design, which seemed to be based on concentric circles, and designed to be effective in a time when cannon were used both on land and, more important in this case, at sea, was impressive. It lacked the dramatic splendour of Caernarvon Castle or the Tower of London, for instance, but it had an unusual charm of its own – something we were beginning to discover about Deal as a whole.

We walked on to the sports centre, which had a swimming pool, gym and a couple of squash courts. We decided to take up a temporary membership, which would last for a month, and was cheap. The young woman who sorted out our membership was also able to give us the name of a sports shop where we could get some kit.

"We could always take this stuff to Budleigh Salterton," said Rosemary, after we'd got what we felt we needed. "I'm sure if we looked, there must be a sports centre with a pool and squash courts within reasonable driving distance."

"Just as long as it isn't in Exeter. Whenever we've gone there, the traffic has been horrendous."

"It's all right for you. You can run virtually anywhere."

"If we haven't had a message from the pathologist, I might run a bit later… after my lunch has had time to settle. I quite fancy seeing what Walmer Castle looks like."

"If we were here permanently, I think I'd get a bike, then I could ride along beside you... But there may be somewhere we could hire them."

We had a salad in Laughton's café and went back to the flat to check for any messages, but there were none. We read for a while, then I changed and set off for my run, while Rosemary went to Boots to pick up our photos. There weren't many people around, so I could run at my normal speed. Oddly enough, though the ground was flat and the surface of the promenade even, it felt like quite hard work. I ran past the Royal Hotel, the pier, Deal castle, fishing boats pulled high up the shingle of the beach, the lifeboat station and a long green. Eventually I made out Walmer castle, which was evidently inhabited and looked rather larger and more impressive than its Deal counterpart. I continued on along the path until I reached a road with a few houses – looking much like the sort of houses by the sea you can see almost anywhere round the English coast. Eventually I reached a pebble beach, with white cliffs facing me a couple of miles away and a pub on my right. The first few yards running over a pebble beach persuaded me that this was a good point to head back. So I turned and retraced my steps – noticing all the different bushes, grasses and wild flowers growing along the edge of the shingle. It still seemed harder going than I'd expected for an almost completely flat run. But by the time I reached the Marine Buildings, I felt the urge to continue along the promenade, which was supposed to end at the ruins of Sandown Castle. However, when I reached the far end, I could see nothing that resembled the ruins of a castle of any description, just some steps up to a sea wall, with a heath extending northwards and what looked like a golf course beyond that. So I turned back and ran the few hundred yards back to the flat, where Rosemary was waiting.

"I saw you run past," she said. "I waved, but you didn't look up."

"I was feeling too knackered. It's further than you think... and it may be flat, but it didn't seem like it!"

"Well, I hope a shower will help you recover. The pathologist is going to start having a first look at the body at 4 pm. We won't be able to get there by then, but we should aim to make it as soon after as possible... But you definitely need a shower before we go... You smell like a wet dog!"

"I guess there are worse things to smell like."

However, about half an hour later, a clean and sweet-smelling jogger accompanied Rosemary to our car and set off for Canterbury. As usual, I did the map reading, while Rosemary drove. The pathology lab appeared to be in the campus of the University of Kent, to the north-west of the city centre. As we arrived in the city along the Sandwich road, we hit a slow-moving traffic jam which lasted until we were heading out of the city on the opposite side. Fortunately, the pathology lab was easy to find and there appeared to be parking which we could use, without usurping some professor's space.

We gave our names at the entrance and had to wait while we were escorted to the laboratory where Dr. Julia Radford was working. Of course, we weren't allowed to enter the lab, but could watch her working through large windows, which looked down on the lab, from perhaps four or five feet above floor level. There was a long, narrow table in front of us, with several chairs and headphones. We put on the headphones and – to no great surprise – heard Dr. Radford commenting on the skeleton she was examining.

Mostly it was – to me – unintelligible stuff about the various bones she was looking at. But after about ten minutes, she glanced up and presumably noticed us.

"Mr. and Mrs. Storey? I can tell you from my examination so far that this was a male, aged between thirty and forty-five. At this stage, I cannot say how he died or when. It was certainly not more recently that fifty years ago, but we're likely to have to run more detailed tests in the lab to get a better idea. But you should assume any date I give will have a confidence range of at least ten years either side. Indeed, if I were you, I'd assume more like fifteen...

"I examined his teeth before you arrived... In reasonable condition, but it strikes me that he wasn't a great one for eating vegetables and fruit... He was around five feet, eight or nine inches, tall... Quite a stocky man, with a big frame... A Caucasian, I should say... We could consider trying to reconstruct his face... But there are so many variables, you've really no idea how close you might've got to the real thing... and if he's much over fifty years dead, you aren't going to find anyone who might see some sort of resemblance... Similarly dental records... If you can find a dentist who's still got records of someone who's been dead for at least fifty years, I'll tell you whether this chap did the football pools...

"There are no signs that he ever broke any of his limbs... At least... nothing serious... It's possible he broke this little finger sometime... And it's definitely a pre-death wound... You can see it'd healed up... Just left its mark... But there's some odd wearing around the socket of his right shoulder... I wonder? ... And here on the socket of the right hip and again... right knee... Whatever he did, I'd say involved considerable effort almost entirely on his right side... Which probably suggests he was right-handed and involved in some form of manual labour for quite some time during his life… So, who knows – you might be lucky finding his dentist?

"Finally… All I can do before we carry out more detailed analysis of our samples… I reckon that he was almost certainly quite flat footed… and the wear and tear on his hip and knee would suggest he must've walked with a limp – not necessarily a particularly noticeable one… If you want to ask me any questions, we can have a word outside in a couple of minutes…"

We waited for five or six minutes and then Dr. Radford appeared without her mask and surgeon's cap. She was in her mid-forties, with curly, somewhat unruly hair, quite a wide face, with what I'd describe as a rosebud mouth and glasses.

"We brought a load of stuff we collected at the place where the body was discovered," explained Rosemary, after we'd introduced ourselves. "Mostly it's pieces of paper or fabric of various sorts, but we also picked up some nails and pen nibs and scooped up some of the miscellaneous debris in case it'd be of any use to you."

"Thank you. It'll be useful to have a look at that stuff… Do you mind if we go and have a cup of tea. I came straight here from giving a lecture and I'm completely parched." She spoke with a distinct

Yorkshire accent, which reminded me of Alison Dryden.

"Do you lecture in pathology?" asked Rosemary, as we made our way along a corridor to what turned out to be a small canteen.

"I do a couple of introductory lectures... But not today... My main subject here is medical ethics and a general introduction to the medical profession for first years... What would you like?"

"Tea for both of us, please... But as you're doing this for us, let us get them for you..."

"It's a faculty facility, so they probably wouldn't let you pay... But in any case, I volunteered to take this on. We don't get many old corpses like this chap. So it's the sort of challenge which, when it comes out of the blue like this, is really exciting. And unlike a recent death, we're under no pressure to get our work done quickly. We can examine this chap thoroughly and at a sensible pace... What you heard just now were my first impressions. It's only when I've got a better idea of when he died, I can start looking in more details for other things... and the microscopy, spectroscopy and chromatography may give us a lot more information... And the stuff you've brought will help too... I'm just hoping we might find the odd hair among this stuff..."

We collected our cups of tea and sat down at a small table. It was a modern, airy cafeteria, with a couple of other tables occupied – one by men in white coats, I noticed.

"What's the place like where the body was found?" asked Dr. Radford.

"It was a brick compartment built into the attic of a five-storey terrace house. The chamber was only a couple of feet wide and bricked up and subsequently plastered on the outside. The man who currently owns the flat where the body was found has had to renovate it because of water leaking in through the roof. So he'd had to strip back to the bricks and pull up the floorboards to re-wire and re-plumb. As far as we know, he realised that there was a discrepancy in the length of the attic room and knocked part of the wall down and found the corpse," explained Rosemary. "It'd seem that, in that part of the attic, the roof was quite sound, as there didn't seem any real evidence of damp."

"I assumed that. Though there's some effect of the bodily fluids, there didn't seem to be any other cause of damp. Do you know what sort of roof material it is there?"

"Slate tiles – on wooden beams, of course."

"Depending what comes out at the next stage, I might need to go over there and have a look for myself. Would there be any problem?"

"I think you might have to go over sooner than later. The owner has been staying in a local hotel. But as the police don't regard it as a crime scene any longer, he can go back any time and could clear everything out if he wanted to… and I guess he probably would."

"If you see him, perhaps you could encourage him not to do anything for a couple of days. Tomorrow would be an impossibility, but I should be able to shuffle things around the day after. Would you be able to show me where it is?"

"Yes. You've got our phone number. We're living in the flat below – It belongs to our elder daughter and her partner – while we try to find out as much as we can about the dead man. Once we know roughly when he died, we can start trying to find out who was living there at the time. We may not be able to get very far… But we're retired and we've been involved in a few investigations in our time and we thought it might be interesting to see what we could discover."

"I understand… A challenge, a bit like what I felt when I heard about the 'body in the attic' as it was described to me."

"Of course, though we keep describing it as an attic, it almost certainly may never have been that," I suggested. "Judging by the age of the building, I'd say that the top two floors – which are now flat D – were almost certainly servants' quarters. And I suspect that once the building was divided up into flats, it's been a bedroom or two for flat D. So, eerie as it may seem, there's quite possibly been someone sleeping in that room, right next to where the dead body has been lying… for decades presumably."

"You'd think someone might've noticed that the room was slightly smaller than the one directly below?" asked Dr. Radford.

"I'm not sure about that. I guess if you'd been measuring up very accurately to put furniture in, you might've felt it seemed a bit odd. But the ceiling is relatively low in the upper rooms of flat D and follows the contours of the roof, so I reckon you'd feel the rooms there were smaller anyway… And I suppose the plumbing and electric wiring didn't need to go that far into the room."

"So the man living there at present measured it up and found a discrepancy?"

"From what we were told, he had dreadful damp problems in his flat and had to strip back everything to the bare brick, as well as rewiring, re-plumbing and fixing the roof. I suppose that when you started to take up the floorboards you'd realise that the false wall was in a wrong place."

"It doesn't suggest that anyone has been doing much maintenance in that flat for quite a long time."

"Compared to the other flats, it's a bit pokey… presumably because it was originally intended as servants' quarters. I guess it may have been rented, along with the other flats, for quite a long time. I doubt whether Deal has been the centre of much interest or attention since the war… apart from the IRA bombing of the Marines… and the Marine Buildings are a fair way from the centre of the town, so I guess there's been little scope for spending much money there until recently. Now there are Londoners keen to buy second homes by the sea, I guess the value of places like that has gone up enough to make it worth people spending money to get the flats into a suitable condition to make money on them."

"And Deal wouldn't've been high up the list of seaside places where Londoners would be buying second homes," added Rosemary. "There must be plenty of places on the Kent coast where you could get there a lot faster, by car or train."

"I spent my childhood in Hull," replied Dr. Radford. "I'm perfectly happy not to live by the sea. I've never been sure why so many people persuade themselves to pay through the nose for properties by the sea… But each to his own…"

Having agreed that she'd keep us in touch with what she and her team found out, we departed. She said it was likely she'd come and look at the place where the body had been concealed the day after next, but that might depend on what they learnt in the meantime about the body from the skeleton and the samples we'd provided.

Though we felt we should take the opportunity while we were in the area to have a proper look at Canterbury, we decided it was too late in the day to do so now. So, we drove through the winding roads back to Deal and found a fish and chip place on our way. That was dinner sorted out. Afterwards we went for a walk along the promenade as far as the pier before turning back. The sky and sea seemed remarkably dark, with just a few lights out at sea, mostly pointing the safe channels round the Goodwin Sands, we assumed. There were a couple of ships much closer to shore than the Goodwins… One was a fishing vessel. The other struck me as being a Customs cutter, but I couldn't be sure. Certainly, from what little I knew about Deal, the town and Customs would've been well acquainted with each other over the centuries.

"We must try and buy a history of Deal tomorrow," I suggested to Rosemary. "It should give us some background about whenever this bloke was killed."

"I bet they've also got those books of old photos that seem to be becoming so popular everywhere," replied Rosemary. "If they've done one of Budleigh Salterton, I'm sure they must've done at least one of here… It's certainly a proper town, with much more history than Budleigh Salterton."

We walked along, holding hands, in a way we'd started to do again once we'd retired and felt that we were just a couple again. Though we saw a fair amount of our daughters and loved them dearly, it felt good to be just a couple again… until such time as grandparent duties caught up with us… though neither Emily nor Sarah were yet admitting to feelings of 'broodiness'.

As the telephone in the flat had a message facility, we decided there wasn't much we could do about the case the following morning, so we walked into Deal and bought a couple of books about Deal's history and another couple of old photographs. Sitting down to have a cup of coffee in Laughton's café, we looked through the books of photos. There were no direct photos of the Marine Buildings, though they appeared several times in the background of photos of the northern part of the promenade. All that they told us was something we were clear about already. They had definitely been in existence since 1898. But there were no earlier photos looking in that direction, which might've shown us a time before they'd been built.

After that, we walked along the front to Walmer Castle and spent a couple of hours visiting. Unlike Deal Castle, which was a well-preserved fortress, Walmer Castle was a residence, the residence of the Lord Warden of the Cinque Ports, one of whom had been Churchill, of course. So there was more history than fine furnishings – and a tea shop to quell the hunger of missing lunch. And we came away with the inevitable English Heritage booklet, which we'd leave next to its counterpart from Deal Castle in Emily and Greg's flat... along with the books about Deal.

We were walking back past the pier, when the pangs of hunger became too great. So, we hastened along the pier and had sausages and mash in the café at the end, along with a large mug of strong brown tea. Then, as we came back along the pier - trying not to disturb the "skitterers" as we called them – we spotted a strange house on the far side of the road, with what looked like a ship's figurehead fixed up between the windows of the first floor. When we got to it, we could see that it either was a real figurehead or a convincing replica. The cottage seemed old and rather small. But a little further along, there was a wonderful antique bookshop which also sold prints and maps. I confess to having been sorely tempted by a couple of maps of the coast round Deal and the sea around the Goodwins, both made in the later seventeenth or early eighteenth centuries, and two or three rather fine engravings of the town and the coast. If it'd been our flat there, I probably would've bought some. In the end, I settled for a nineteenth century engraving of a Customs cutter, "the Lively", which could go on the wall of my study-cum-guestroom in our house in Beckenham. Rosemary bought a nineteenth century guide to Leicestershire in a fine leather-bound volume.

"I'd like to know what some of those areas we've been in over the years were like at a time beyond anyone's memory," she said. "I'm not sure I feel like a Londoner, but I've spent over thirty years there now – more than half my life – so I suppose I feel it's more my home than anywhere else… but inevitably, I've still got some affection for my home county."

"You wouldn't want to retire somewhere like this – or Budleigh Salterton? We could get somewhere very fine in either place."

"No. I'm happy with the flat in Budleigh Salterton and I reckon we could always come down here from time to time too. But I like Beckenham. I like being able to go up to London for concerts and that sort of thing and feel we can get home the same day. I'd hate to be like those people who have to dash out before the end of a concert or a film because they've got to catch their last train home… Why, would you?"

"Some of me says it'd be nice to live in a really distinguished house somewhere like this. When you've been brought up in a council house and you see some of these really lovely houses on the front here or in Middle Street, it's an odd feeling... I can't really describe it... But I like going to town for films and concerts too... And wherever you're happy, I'm happy."

"In any case, as we've found in Budleigh Salterton, anywhere where there are quite a lot of weekend homes means that it's not very easy to make many friends, and I'm not the type to join the local churchwomen's guild or genteel ladies knitting circle... or a book club, for that matter. The great thing about London is that even if your friends are dispersed a bit, you can always meet up in the centre for a coffee or lunch. If we were based here or, even worse, in Budleigh Salterton, we'd never get up to London for coffee or lunch, it'd just take too long... Which doesn't mean that if you were desperate to move somewhere like this I wouldn't."

"I'm not. I like our house... and I'm quite happy to shove off to Budleigh Salterton and maybe here for a few days or a week or so. In many ways it's the best of both worlds."

"I'm certainly glad we never bought anywhere in Brittany. Those prices for some very nice houses looked really cheap, but it takes such a long time to get there, I think we'd've gone at most once or twice a year – and wasted our money."

We were woken early the following morning by a phone call from Dr. Radford. Rosemary answered it.

"I don't believe I need to visit the scene of the crime," Dr. Radford began. "The analysis of the bones and the samples you provided have pretty conclusively confirmed that the man died between 1880 and 1900. We might be a couple of years out at either end, but I doubt it. As yet, we don't know how he died – and we may never know. For instance, if he was strangled, the evidence would've disappeared long before now. There are no obvious marks of blows or stab wounds – nor of poison. But we've only just got started. And if he'd just been given some drug to knock him out and he was then bricked up in the cavity, in theory there'd be no evidence. But I think once he'd woken and found himself entombed, he'd've tried to get himself out. There's no evidence of that on the skeleton. You might want to check sometime that there aren't any marks on the wall that suggest he might've been alive in there for a while."

"I don't recall seeing anything, but we'll take a look just to be sure… Thank you for the information. We'll now see how we can find out who was living in the building at the time."

"Please keep me in touch with what you discover. It may help us with our research... For example, if you found there was an Italian or a Chinaman living there at that time, that might give us some helpful leads."

"Certainly."

"You heard?" asked Rosemary.

"Yes... Now our work begins in earnest."

"I confess I was hoping for a bit more from the pathologist. But I suppose if a corpse is a hundred years old or more, there's not going to be a lot left to provide many clues. And we've got some idea about his age, height and build and the fact that he probably walked with a limp."

"With all the strain on his right side... I wonder whether there are any doctors who specialise in workplace injuries who might be able to tell us the sort of work that might produce injuries like those Dr. Radford described to us?"

"I guess it's worth a try. But I'd have no idea where to start."

"There might even be a doctor around these parts. Don't forget, you can see the spoil tip from the Betteshanger colliery from the bedroom window at the back of the flat. Though I'm pretty certain mining didn't start there until the twentieth century, there may well be doctors around who would've treated injuries sustained by the miners. One of them could give us some ideas or suggest someone else we might talk to."

"And presumably we have to get hold of the census returns for the Marine Buildings at the appropriate time."

"The last time we filled in a census form was 1991 – and I think they're every ten years. So I suppose we want 1881, 1891 and 1901."

"And where would we get hold of them?"

"I guess the best place to ask might be the local library. They've usually got someone who knows about such things... if only for local history purposes."

"Well, I suppose if we got our stuff together to have a game of squash, we might see if we could find the library on the way."

"Let's look in the local street plan... Here it is... Just off Broad Street. It's only a few yards from the High Street... and pretty well on our way to the sports centre."

We gathered our squash gear together. We hadn't bought racquets, but we'd been informed that they were available for hire at the sports centre – and our standard of squash these days didn't require sophisticated modern racquets. Indeed, it wasn't so long since we noticed the younger, keener and fitter people at our squash club in Beckenham playing with strange elongated, pear-shaped racquets. Had we been thirty years younger, we might've decided to experiment with them, but as it was, we stuck with what we knew.

That was, I suppose, a fair description of what we were now setting out to do.

5. AMATEUR ARCHIVISTS AT WORK

Deal Library was a modern building right next to a large car park. We went to reception and were directed to a young woman with black jagged hair and a splash of vivid blue across the front. She had piercings in her ears and nose – and when she spoke I noticed also in her tongue. This was accompanied by several tattoos. She was dressed appropriately in a mixture of what I'd describe as "Goth" and "punk" styles – mostly black with a dash of 'shocking pink', as it was called when I was a teenager. She was practically the antithesis of what I'd expect a librarian and archivist to look like.

Rosemary whispered to her why we were there. She suggested a cup of coffee in the common and children's area.

"You want to know how to find out who was living at a particular address in the 1881 census?" she asked, in an extremely upper-class voice that didn't fit with her appearance at all. "Do you know the name of the person you're looking for?" In contrast to her appearance, the accent was very posh. A family rebel perhaps? But would you be a rebel and a librarian?

"No," replied Rosemary. "You might've seen something in the local paper about the body that was found in the Marine Buildings?"

"Oh yes. I did see something about it. As the police said it'd been there a long time, I didn't take much interest… rather a macabre story."

"Yes. But it was found in the flat above our daughter's flat and we said we'd try to see what might've happened. I used to work for the Metropolitan Police… and my husband was involved in investigation work too."

"And you know that the man died after the 1881 census?"

"The pathologist gave the time of death as between 1880 and 1900. So we thought we might see what was in the 1881 and 1891 censuses for a start. But we've no idea how we can get hold of information from the censuses – or even whether we can find it when we only know where the man was found. We wondered whether you might know?"

"Fortunately, you can get access to both censuses, as they're both over a hundred years ago. As you'll probably know, census information is collected on a geographical basis. So the forms were filled in by enumerators who'd have a specific area to cover. They filled out special books which were then copied on to the census records. The records – certainly of the older censuses – have mostly perished or been destroyed. But the books have all been filmed, because they were beginning to deteriorate too…

They're all kept in the PRO – the Public Record Office. Some of the records used to be in the Chancery Lane Building, but as of last year, they were all transferred to the office in Kew… Looking up an address rather than a name will be quite unusual. Generally, people looking at these records are genealogists, trying to put together their family tree."

"You seem very knowledgeable about it."

"There are quite a lot of retired people in Deal and Walmer. You'd be surprised how many want to find out as much about their ancestors as they can, and they generally start here… But I'm doing it as well… with a surname like Warnle, you have to try and find out where it originated."

"There was a merchant bank called Warnle and Garendon, wasn't there? Are you related to that Warnle?"

"Yes. Rather distantly. They're still going, though they're a subsidiary of one of the big banks these days. But a thought… before you go to Kew, you'd do well to check here or in the Kent County records office in Maidstone whether the Marine Buildings have always been called that… And though they're on the street called The Marina these days, I don't know whether that road has always been called by that name. It'd be worth checking that. Otherwise you may find nothing and have a wasted journey."

"Thank you. That's very helpful. Where should we look here to see?"

"There's a local history section over in the far corner there... You'll see there are several box files that may contain what you need – but you may find it quicker to look at a couple of the local history books. The ones by Morton and Lovelock are particularly detailed... which makes them virtually impossible to read, but if you're looking for pieces of detailed information, they're probably your best bet."

We went over to where she had directed us and pulled out a couple of histories of Deal. William Morton's *"Deal – Smugglers, Sailors and Marines"* was essentially a timeline of events in Deal's long history – going back to at least the Roman invasion. But it told us little we needed to know. Zephaniah Septimus Lovelock – a name which we felt had to have been a pseudonym for someone called something like John Brown – was more useful. From *"Deal – ancient and modern"*, we learnt that in the late nineteenth century, there was a considerable reduction in smuggling compared to earlier times. But not only the large "Bates house" next to the Marine Buildings belonged to a senior Coast Guard Officer, but also the terraced cottages behind – on what had been called "Rope Walk", now Sandown Road, belonged to Coast Guard officers. We also discovered something I should probably have learnt during my career in Customs &

Excise, that there had originally been the "Landguard" who tried to catch smugglers on land, the "Coastguard" who dealt with smugglers coming ashore and the "Waterguard" who tackled them at sea.

By and large, the Navy and, after they first arrived in the town in 1861, the Marines, were stationed at the southern side of the town, mostly in what would now be regarded as Walmer – with soldiers in the castles at both ends of the town. Though Sandown Castle still survived at the time the Marines came, it was sold by the War Office in 1863, so there was no obvious reason why any soldiers would've been using the Marine Buildings after that time. Indeed, it seemed that the Army left Deal at about that time. Though, as we hadn't found out when the buildings had been constructed, we had no idea whether they'd been built originally to house some of the soldiers from the castle. It also seemed that there had been at least one windmill in the vicinity. However, apart from fishing, a considerable business was provided by the regular wrecks on the Goodwin Sands, with apparently a bitter rivalry between the sailors of North Deal and South Deal over the salvage.

Generally, the town seems to have been regarded as not a particularly pleasant place, full of smugglers, rogues and mariners. Though the houses along the promenade, in Middle Street and the little roads running between them, seemed charming to us. We were looking at them from a very Twentieth Century perspective. Apart from the grander buildings south of the pier, closer to the naval and Marine establishments, they were often seen by visitors to the town as mean and commonplace – and the haunts of rogues and smugglers.

"There's an old Ordnance Survey map of the town from 1871," whispered Rosemary. "From what I can tell, the Marine Buildings must've been called Sandown Terrace then. But the road they're on has no name. There's "Rope Walk" running behind – but otherwise, it was either just the northern end of Beach Street or the mapmaker forgot to put in a street name…"

"Or there wasn't one… Doesn't it look odd! There's all that area where the Coast Guard buildings are… and the cottages behind… almost completely empty. Then there's Sandown Terrace – which is definitely the Marine Buildings… though the outbuildings at the back must've been knocked down at some stage as the properties at the back are all quite new… But then there's a windmill… then a pub… and then you get to the ruins of Sandown Castle… Why would anyone have built such a fine terrace practically in the middle of nowhere… and right on the outskirts of the town?"

"It does look rather strange, I agree… and perhaps only ten years before our man got killed… You do wonder who Sandown Terrace was built for? I wonder how we could find out?"

"The Land Registry, I guess… I don't know whether there'd be any local record."

Ms. Warnle, the archivist, suddenly appeared.

"There's something I should've mentioned," she whispered. "You may find that the records at Kew are indexed by name. So, unless you have names you can follow up, there'd be no point going there until you have. Otherwise you could be there for days, if not weeks. If you want to find out things on a street by street basis, the records that were copied from the census enumerators will be in the Kent County records… almost certainly in Canterbury, for this part of Kent."

"Thank you," replied Rosemary. "Do you know anyone we should contact there?"

"I'd try Adrienne Bishop, one of the archivists. I did my degree with her… I always said that with a name like 'A. Bishop', she'd end up somewhere like Canterbury… Tell her Rowena Warnle told you to get in touch with her."

We couldn't find anything else relevant in the Deal library so we made our way to the sports centre.

"She wasn't at all what I expected as a librarian," remarked Rosemary.

"I guess if you're from a merchant banking family and you want to rebel, that's the form it takes."

"I must say I didn't expect someone looking like that to be quite so helpful. It shows you shouldn't judge people on appearances."

"Quite so. One of the problems I always felt I was facing in C&E was the number of people who appeared to agree with me – because I was a Board member or whatever. I could never be really certain with many of them what they really thought. It was almost better when people disagreed. At least you knew where you stood… We never really got over the hierarchical mentality… It's a pity that the mentoring by junior staff of senior staff never really took off… Unfortunately, it required the belief and trust on both sides and we never got that in enough places."

"It wouldn't've got anywhere in the Met. If you thought Customs was hierarchical, you should've worked in the Met for a while!"

We played squash at the Sports centre, had a swim and a shower and found a small café that did sandwiches, soup and tea – all of which benefited from a menu designer who preferred simple food – like cheese and tomato sandwiches rather than exotic or over-complicated stuff, which increasingly seemed to be the way of things. And, of course, the more complicated or unusual, the higher the price that could be charged. Was that part of the world we lived in, becoming over-sophisticated and driven by the consumption of unnecessary gadgets and luxuries unknown a generation ago? Or was this the ghost of my long-dead father continuing to haunt me? Perhaps a bit of both.

"It looks like Canterbury first of all," observed Rosemary, when we got back to the flat – having paid rather greater attention than previously to the age of the various buildings on either side of what had been "Sandown Terrace".

"It's a pity neither of those books mentioned Sandown Terrace. It seems an odd building to put in this particular place at that time," I replied at something of a tangent. "If it was a single house, you might just think a rich bloke got some land fairly cheaply and decided to build himself a seaside residence. But the terrace seems evidently intended for five Victorian families, along with their servants. Why would you build it in such a relatively isolated spot? It's a long way from the station and everywhere else. According to the map, Sandown Castle was already ruined by 1871 and the only things nearby are the mill and a pub…"

"I wonder when it stopped being called Sandown Terrace… and why?"

It was too late to drive to Canterbury that day –
and we'd already been told that parking there was
likely to be difficult. So we had a take-away Chinese
meal again and went to bed quite early. Apart from
the sound of the waves pounding the beach, it
seemed remarkably quiet and still. Evidently, Bill
Joyner had decided not to return to his flat yet – and
the rest of the building seemed empty too – though
Emily had assured us there were people living in all of
the other flats. But perhaps they were 'week-enders'
like Emily and Greg? Or they went to bed extremely
early and never watched TV or played music? Not
that I minded just hearing the sound of the waves. It
was surprisingly restful –and I wished we were near
enough to the sea in our flat in Budleigh Salterton to
hear the waves there. Rosemary, her head resting on
my shoulder as usual, was already asleep, and after a
few moments thinking about the silent building, I
followed suit.

We rose very early and, after a quick mug of tea,
drove to Canterbury, promising ourselves breakfast
when we arrived. On the evidence of what we'd been
told, we parked in a 'park and ride' car park and got a
shuttle bus into the centre. Following previous
experience, we went into Fenwick's, the big
department store, and had a decent breakfast in the
restaurant there. Then we walked to the cathedral,
where the archives were located, in buildings which
looked old, but were, we'd been told, rebuilt in the

early fifties after the much older buildings had been bombed during the war. We were met by a receptionist who agreed to let Adrienne Bishop know we were there.

Adrienne Bishop turned out to be just about as unepiscopal as you could get. She was not much shorter than me, beefy, with short dark red hair and looked like my idea of an Olympic rower.

"Sent by Rowena Warnle!" she exclaimed with a guffaw, after Rosemary had explained why we'd asked to speak to her. "You'd never guess we used to do a Peter Cook and Dudley Moore impersonation together when we were at college. Regularly brought the house down! You want to look up information from the 1881 and 1891 censuses, but you only know the address, not the inhabitants?"

"That's right," replied Rosemary.

"It's not really my field of expertise, but I can certainly point you in the right direction."

She got us a daily reader's pass and led us through the reception area along a dark corridor into one of the rooms where the archives were evidently kept. It had books and box files in bookcases along the walls and tables with reading lamps and what looked like reasonably comfortable chairs in the middle of the room. The windows looked out on to what I guessed must be part of the cathedral grounds.

"It's probably worth reading this about the 1881 census," explained Adrienne Bishop in a loud whisper. "When you've read it, ask Maurice over there for the district. Then you'll have to work out which sub-districts are relevant... As I said, this isn't really my field..."

"Thank you," whispered Rosemary. "We're very grateful."

So we picked up a booklet about the 1881 census and read that it took place on 3 April 1881. The information required included: the full address, whether the house was inhabited, how many rooms were occupied, the names of all those spending the night of 3 April there, their relationship to the head of the household; each person's age, last birthday, marital status, and employment, place of birth; and whether they were deaf, dumb, blind and "imbecile or idiot or lunatic". A clever device was used rather than have a separate entry for sex – the age being put in one column for male and another for female.

"I wonder how the enumerator decided whether someone was 'an imbecile, idiot or lunatic'," I observed in a whisper. "It strikes me as a fine judgement to make. But you could hardly trust the word of someone who was an imbecile, idiot or lunatic, could you?"

"If you're not going to take this seriously," replied Rosemary, grinning, "just remember what happened to Thomas Becket a few yards from here."

"My impression was that he took things too seriously… But I'm deadly earnest…"

"That's probably who the murderer was… Deadly Ernest."

We nearly had to leave the room, but just about managed to stifle a fit of the giggles.

We read on. It appeared that the enumeration forms were distributed to all households a couple of days before census night and the complete forms were collected the next day. It reflected where people were that evening. So if they were travelling or living abroad, they were enumerated at the place where they spent that night. All of the details from the individual forms were later sorted and copied into enumerators' books, and the original householders' schedules from 1841 to 1901 were destroyed. The census returns were collected according to registration district. These returns were divided into sub-districts and assigned consecutive numbers – called piece numbers - for reference purposes. These piece numbers began in London with number one and worked roughly south to north. There could be hundreds of piece numbers within a county. As well as the piece number, each page of the returns included a folio number and/or a page number. The folio number was stamped onto every other page before the records were microfilmed and could be found in the upper right-hand corner of the image. The page number was part of the printed form and was located on every page in the upper right-hand corner. The page numbers started over at the beginning of every enumeration district. A full reference number for a record in the 1881 census would include the Public Record Office class number, the piece number, the folio number, and the page number.

"I didn't realise it'd be quite so complicated," murmured Rosemary.

"I suppose we just ask for Deal and see if we can work out its districts and sub-districts and go from there."

We went over to see Maurice at his desk in the corner of the room. He appeared to be working on some sort of catalogue. He was short and weedy. Adrienne Bishop could have made two of him. He had a very short, old-fashioned haircut, a narrow face with a pointed chin, and a habit of looking away when in conversation.

"We're looking for the 1881 census returns for Deal," said Rosemary quietly. "Can you help us please?"

"I'll dig them out. Where are you sitting?" His voice was south-eastern, ex-Grammar school: though whether he'd been to a grammar school was difficult to say, given that he was probably in his late twenties, despite looking about seventeen.

"Over by the window."

Within quarter of an hour or so, he came over to our table with several books containing the census information.

"Thank you," said Rosemary. "Do you also have the records for the 1871 and 1891 censuses for Deal? We'll be needing to look at them later."

"You should've said," he muttered and drifted away.

After a while, we found our way round the ordering of the records and found ourselves the records for Sandown Terrace. Plainly, our interest was mainly in number 3, which was the centre of the terrace.

The records were as follows:

3 Sandown Terrace					
Samuel Wheeler Rust	38	m	married	Chemist, apothecary	Whitechapel, London
Johanna Florence Rust (nee Prout)	31	f	married	Apothecary	Sandwich, Kent
Lionel Wheeler Rust	11	m		Scholar	Faversham, Kent

Susannah Myrtle Rust	8	f		Scholar	Deal, Kent
Edgar Prout Rust	6	m			Deal, Kent
Louisa Hephzibah Wellens	28	f	Single	Governess	Dover, Kent
John Horton	43	m	Single	Groom, servant	Ash, Kent
Clarissa Stoute	45	f	Single	Cook	Broadstairs, Kent
Maria Jane French	18	f	Single	Maid	Deal, Kent
Jacob George Dunne	16	m	Single	Servant	Walmer, Kent

In Number 1 Sandown Terrace lived Mr Joshua Walker Doughty, described as a retired bookseller from Canterbury, with his wife Winifred, and four servants. Number 2 Sandown Terrace was occupied by Gerard Jocelyn Culpeper and his wife, Clara, an author. The two of them had but a couple of servants – so they must have had plenty of space in a house of that size. Number 4 appeared to be unoccupied at the time – though the records didn't state why. Perhaps there was no-one living there? Or perhaps they were somewhere else on the night of the census? Number 5 contained Hubert Gordon

Horsfall, a marine chandler, along with his wife, Letitia and five children, plus four servants.

"Number 2 should've lent them some rooms," whispered Rosemary. "They must've been full to bursting in Number 5."

We sought and waited for the records for the 1871 and 1891 censuses. When they arrived, we decided to examine the 1871 census first.

Interestingly, Samuel Rust and his family were already living in the house – though, of course, at that time they only had one child, Lionel, still a baby. There was no requirement for a governess, so Louisa Wellens wasn't resident there. Nor were Maria French and Jacob Dunne – unsurprisingly, as they would've been eight and six at the time. However, John Horton and Clarissa Stoute were employed by the Rust family at that time, along with Elizabeth Coote, maid, and George Blenkinsop, servant. Both were single, local, and in their late teens.

Number 1 Sandown Terrace was occupied by Philip Carleton Wemyss, described as a 'gentleman', who resided there with his wife Henrietta and two sons, Flavius and Lucius – poor lads! – and five servants. Wemyss was in his late thirties, his wife a few years younger. Both children were less than ten years of age. Next door – at Number 2 – was Captain Francis Toller and his wife, with three servants. He was in his early sixties and described himself as a "retired ship's officer". Number 4 was occupied by Matthew Stowe, described as a "chemist and experimenter". He was 26 years of age. He appeared to have no family living there with him. But also living there were Peter Dent, 33 (maltster), and William Fernyhough, 38 (Excise officer), along with a cook and three servants. This suggested that Stowe, Dent and Fernyhough probably had the ground, first and second floors, one for each, with the servants living in the attics and the basement being used to prepare food, etc. If Number 4 had been used as a sort of lodging house, that might explain why it was empty in 1881, perhaps being converted to a family dwelling. And Hubert Horsfall was already in Number 5, but with only two children at this time.

We went straight on to the 1891 census. Yet again, the ownership of Number 1 Sandown Terrace had changed. It was now occupied by Dr. Henry Frederick Morley and his family, along with their servants. He described himself as a "surgeon practitioner" whatever that was and his wife, Elizabeth, as a matron. Number 2 appeared to have another family in residence – Charles Wilfred Culpeper, his wife and four children, as well as three servants. He stated his employment as "marine engineer". Presumably he was related in some way to the Gerard Culpeper who'd occupied number 2 in the 1881 census?

But Numbers 3 and 4 had undergone a dramatic transformation, apparently. It now seemed that they were some sort of school, called "Sandown Academy". Jerome Herrick Barfoot described himself as the "Master", with Percival Dromgoole and Lionel Blunt as "Assistant Masters". Barfoot had a wife, Margaret, living with him and an infant son. There were also four servants, including a cook. On the night of the census, there were even two "scholars" residing there – Horace Benskin, aged 11, and Alfred Spinks, aged 10. As they could hardly have been kept in detention overnight, it seemed the "Sandown Academy" had some boarders. Both gave their place of birth as Dover, so I supposed their fathers were perhaps seafaring men of some means.

Number 5 Sandown Terrace had also changed significantly. It was now evidently a boarding house with half a dozen single men aged between 26 and 49 living there, along with Mrs. Dorothy Broome, who described herself as "resident housekeeper", a cook and a couple of servants. Among the lodgers were Francis Kenway, Customs Officer. and Peter Vernon, Coast Guard.

"Do you think we need to look at 1901 as well?" I asked.

"Yes," replied Rosemary. "But I think we could do with some lunch first. My eyes are going round in circles looking at all that handwritten stuff."

"That'd be a sight worth seeing," I remarked. "I wonder whether there's anywhere to get lunch here?"

But Maurice confirmed there was nowhere in the building that served anything other than teas, coffees, soft drinks and cakes and biscuits. So, having warned him we'd like to see the 1901 census for Deal after lunch, we headed into the city to find somewhere that was ideally not a chain nor expensive. After a while, we found a vegetarian restaurant which did a palatable soup and a rather strange tasting salad accompanied by heavy spelt bread.

"This is probably doing better for me than it tastes," I remarked to Rosemary, thereby earning myself several disapproving glances from nearby customers.

The same sense of slight disappointment came with the tea. It was called "red berries" and came out a deep shade of red with an extremely enticing aroma. Unfortunately, this wasn't matched by the somewhat insipid taste. I was about to mention this, but Rosemary put her finger to her lips.

"There seemed to be a few veggie zealots in there," she explained once we'd got outside. "When you commented about the salad, I felt the temperature drop about ten degrees. I realise these vegans don't eat meat, but I got the distinct impression they wouldn't be averse to spilling the blood of a carnivore like you."

"It's a minority thing, I suppose. If I was sitting in a steak house and said I thought my steak was underdone or the peppercorn sauce was a bit too bland, nobody would turn a hair. I suppose I look too much like a meat-eater, so criticising their salad looked like an attack on vegetarianism in general."

"And not wholly fair. I reckon we only eat meat a couple of days a week – and you're as likely to have a cheese salad or sandwich as one with meat in."

"I guess there was metaphorical blood dripping down my chin… But thank you for stopping me commenting on the tea… It was a pity. It looked and smelled so good – and then tasted of nothing."

"You should've had the lemon and ginger. I don't know about the lemon, but the ginger was almost overpowering."

But having satisfied the inner man and woman, probably with better sustenance than we deserved, we returned to the archives and found the records for the 1901 census awaiting us on our table. Maurice might look like a spotty tadpole, but he seemed to be efficient.

In 1901, Number 1 Sandown Terrace was still occupied by Dr. Henry Morley, a slightly expanded family and a governess in addition to the previous servants. Some of these had changed. But there seemed no obvious reason why we should be interested in Number 1. So we copied down all the details in a notebook – or, to be accurate, Rosemary wrote it down, her handwriting being legible by comparison with my unintelligible scrawl – along with all the other details.

The Culpepers had left Number 2 Sandown Terrace and it seemed to have become a boarding house, run by Mr. and Mrs. Herbert Farmer, who described themselves as 'lodgings agents.' They had no offspring living on the premises, assuming they had any. Both were in their mid-forties, so it was possible that any children they'd had were off their hands. Their lodgers were Simeon Mew, a 25-year-old bookkeeper; Jeremiah Unwin, a thirty-three-year-old schoolmaster; Patrick O'Neill, a thirty-eight-year-old 'overseer'; Albert Johnson, a thirty-six year old librarian; Norman Worthington, a twenty-six year old commercial traveller; and a single servant – Mordecai Grimley, aged nineteen. I reckoned he was probably kept pretty busy.

Numbers 3 and 4 were still a school, but under a different name – Sandown Preparatory School – and Mr. and Mrs. Barfoot had left. The school was now run by Percival Dromgoole, promoted from 'Assistant Master' to 'Master'. He seemed to have acquired a wife – Eleanor – and a small child, Lancelot. There was but a single 'Assistant Master' on the premises at the time of the census – Archibald Reeves, a man of 22 years of age. Those were the only names mentioned, so presumably the school no longer took boarders. But there were a couple of servants – Iris Clarke, described as matron and cook, and John Partridge, described as 'servant'. Both were in their early forties.

Number 5 Sandown Terrace had changed little – other than all but one of the lodgers being different. However, I was pleased to see that among them was James Whitlock, Customs Officer, George Lewis, Excise Officer and Frederick House, Coast Guard. Perhaps Whitlock or Lewis were doing what I did at the very start of my C&E career – moving round the country every few months, as an "Unattached Officer"? Rosemary duly wrote down all their details in our notebook – even though it seemed unlikely they'd be relevant to our investigation.

By the end, we had a long list of names on different pages, so we decided to set them out in a table:

1871	1881	1891	1901
1 Philip Wemyss & family	1 Joshua & Mrs Doughty & servants	1 Dr Henry Morley & family	1 Dr Henry Morley & family
2 Capt & Mrs Toller & servants	2 Gerard Culpeper & family	2 Charles Culpeper & family	2 Boarding House – Mr & Mrs Farmer (lodgings agents) + lodgers
3 Samuel Rust & family	3 Samuel Rust & family	3 Sandown Academy (Barfoot, Dromgoole & Blunt)	3 Sandown Preparatory School (Dromgoole & family, Reeves)
4 Stowe, Dent & Fernyhough + servants	4 Unoccupied (no-one in residence for census)	4 Sandown Academy	4 Sandown Preparatory School
5 Hubert Horsfall & family	5 Hubert Horsfall & family	5 Boarding House – Mrs Dorothy Broome (landlady) + lodgers	5 Boarding House – Mrs Dorothy Broome (landlady) + lodgers

Our next step would be to try and find out more about the people who'd been living in Number

3 Sandown Terrace, while keeping an eye out for those in Numbers 2 and 4, in particular.

We asked Maurice where we might best search for such information.

"You'll get some information from the PRO... the Public Records Office... from birth, marriage and death certificates. You might be able to get copies of wills too," he explained, talking normally, as there was no-one else in this room containing the archives. "It depends what you're trying to find out. If they're very important... and most people rarely are – they might be in the DNB... the Dictionary of National Biography... But otherwise, you'll have to trawl through the local newspapers of the time. Though there are collections in various archives, they'll be microfilmed in date order, but no-one has done any cataloguing. So, if you want to know about Joe Bloggs, you'd just have to look at every edition and see whether the name turned up."

"If someone was setting up a school... even a private one, would there be any record of that anywhere?" I asked.

"In the nineteenth century? There'd've been a Kent County Board of Education from around 1870. Exactly what records they kept I've no idea. Their records aren't kept here. So they're probably in the archives in Maidstone… I can give you a phone number to ring if you want to follow that up."

"Do you know where we'd find records of local Deal newspapers in the nineteenth century?"

"The local paper there is the *East Kent Mercury*, but it'll be owned by a chain these days… I'm trying to think… You might do best to give them a ring… They'll probably know what it used to be called… It might even have kept its name over the years, but they should be able to tell you… and where the archives are kept."

"We'll get a copy when we are back in Deal… Thank you."

6. A TRIP DOWN MEMORY LANE – OLD NEWSPAPERS, OLD HISTORIAN

That completed our business in Canterbury for the day, so we decided to get back to Deal as soon as we could and try to lay our hands on a copy of the *East Kent Mercury*. Fortunately, we left before the rush hour and were able to reach Deal in good time to buy a copy of the local newspaper and search through it for a suitable phone number. Of course, typical local newspapers don't include phone numbers for contacting their archives, so we returned to the flat and after three phone calls and being passed on from one person to another, we were finally given a number where the female voice at the other end of the line explained that the archive for the *East Kent Mercury* and its predecessors was held in Deal. Specifically, the archive was kept in a house in Middle Street – the first part of it, on the south side of Broad Street. It was open Thursday to Saturday from 10AM until 2PM.

At least that meant we'd have a day to look through whatever material was there before returning to Beckenham at the weekend. There were things we needed to sort out at home – and we both felt that we needed a break from all this digging around in the past. And, for all my longstanding interest in sorting out the details of whatever I was engaged in, I didn't welcome a day spent poring through microfilmed records of old newspapers. Fortunately, these were weekly, so that meant only a thousand or so papers to look through. However, unless we were extremely lucky, this was going to be the work of several days.

We arrived on the dot at 10AM. The archives were kept in a pleasant eighteenth century house in the end of Middle Street which has been cut off by the car park next to the Deal library. A middle-aged woman who looked as though she wished she could be somewhere else let us in and asked what we wanted. After we'd explained what we were after, she led us to a couple of desks in a room overlooking the back yard, where there were half a dozen desks with microfilm readers. Telling us to wait for a few minutes, she disappeared, returning with the reels of microfilm. She showed us both how to use the readers. Then she left us to our own devices.

I started in January 1880, Rosemary in January 1890. We were the only people in the room.

"Oh heavens!" exclaimed Rosemary. "I'd forgotten that newspapers as old as this have no news on the front pages – only births, marriages, death, official announcements and adverts."

"I doubt whether there'll be anything much more interesting on the inside pages."

"And we're looking for any incident that might be relevant – especially involving the residents of

Sandown Terrace... or any suspicious disappearances...?"

"Yes... But anything about the inhabitants of Number 3 and, I suppose, 2 and 4 especially would be worth noting."

We started peering at the microfilms. The first thing I noticed was that often the paper was only four pages, which at least meant I'd get through issues faster than I'd expected.

We'd been going about half an hour, then Rosemary remarked, "How stupid! I've been looking at this on every front page and it's taken me this long to spot it! At the top of the front page there's an advert for 'Rust's Tonic' or 'Rust's Pastilles', both of which are described as 'a sovereign remedy against coughs, colds and influenza'. Wasn't the man in Number 3 called Rust? And didn't he describe himself as a chemist and apothecary? Perhaps he made this stuff?"

"It's certainly worth checking up... Actually I think I remember 'Rust's Pastilles' from my childhood. My mother always had some in the house and used to give me them at the first sign of a cough or cold. They tasted like a mixture of blackcurrant and coal tar, from what I recall... disgusting. I always thought there was actually rust in the pastilles... a bit like cod liver oil and balsamic compound – so disgusting to taste that it sent your natural antibodies into overdrive to kill off the cold, rather than having to keep having stuff like that."

"I though you liked that Riga balzams stuff?"

"As a digestif, it works well. But only after fairly large portions of rich food."

"Well, I'll note it down in my notebook. There must be other ways of finding out a bit more about them."

"Does the advert give the name of the firm that made the stuff?"

"No. But if it is the same Rust, perhaps the stuff was made round here..."

We continued to look through the newspapers. At first, it was interesting because of its quaintness, but that novelty soon palled.

"Ah! *Mr and Mrs Gerard Culpeper of 2 Sandown Terrace, Deal are pleased to announce the engagement of his daughter Jemima Anne to Mr Philip Salt, son of Mr and Mrs Eustace Salt of Stourhaven, Strand Street, Sandwich'*, etc, etc," I announced. "It's a pity they didn't go for a double-barrelled name – 'Culpeper-Salt would be a rather fine surname..."

"You're joking!"

"As it happens, I am. It was Philip Sale, not Salt… unfortunately…"

"So where have you got to?"

"May 1880. I assume the young couple must've been living somewhere else in newly-wed bliss, as Jemima Anne didn't appear in the 1881 census."

We plodded on.

"The wedding was in August," I remarked, when I got to that issue. "One of those old wedding photos where everyone looks as though they were at a funeral… They were married in St George's church in the High Street."

"Good for them… And it might explain why Gerard Culpeper and his wife had moved by the 1891 census. They must've been rattling around in that house like two dried peas in a large pod."

In December 1880, Samuel Rust first appeared.

"At last! *Mr Samuel Rust, proprietor of Rust Chemist & Apothecary, has announced that he will be opening another establishment in Albion Street, Broadstairs, an addition to those already in Deal, Sandwich and Ramsgate. It is understood that the Mayor of Broadstairs, Alderman John Froome, will attend the formal opening.'* Did he just own chemists' shops at this stage or was he supplying them with 'Rust's Pastilles' and 'Rust's Tonic' and perhaps other stuff at this time?" I wondered.

A couple of issues later, there was an article about the opening of Rust's new chemists' shop in Broadstairs along with another grainy, extremely stilted photograph, including the Mayor resplendent in his chain of office.

"I'm in May 1891," said Rosemary about ten minutes later. "It says that Samuel Rust and Co are closing their manufacturing premises in Deal… *'by West Street'* it says… Where's that?"

"Down by the station, from what I remember. Perhaps it's where one of the supermarkets is now? Does it say why they were closing down?"

"Moving to bigger premises in Ashford which are more convenient for the railways, apparently… Also Rust has plainly come up in the world, as he's now Mr Samuel Rust of Sholden Hall, Sholden, Deal… that's the village we drive through just before we get to Deal, isn't it?"

"I think so."

"I suppose his pastilles and tonic must've been making him a lot of money… Can you still buy them, I wonder?"

"I've not seen them. But then, I haven't been looking for them either. I guess they're a bit powerful for modern tastes. People like their medicine tasting sweet… or at least that's what the chemical companies seem to believe. And who knows, Rust's stuff may have had ingredients that are regarded as unsafe these days… When you think about what originally went into Coca Cola…"

"It's a pity they don't seem to have the estate agents' pages you get in modern papers like this. We could've seen when these various people moved in and out of Sandown Terrace. I don't even know how houses were sold then…"

"I guess we might be able to find out when ownership changed from the Land Registry records… I assume they keep that sort of information somewhere… And I think, though I'm not sure, houses may have been sold by auction or possibly private treaty… If I'd read Dickens more carefully I might remember that sort of thing…"

"Dickens was approved reading?"

"By my father? Yes. Dickens showed up lots of social injustices in Victorian England. So he had the seal of approval… But as light relief from Marx and Engels and some of the dreadful Soviet literature… Not that I ever thought Dickens was exactly light reading! But compared to rubbish like "The Quiet

Don", he created loads of really interesting and believable characters… and the stories weren't predictable…"

"I suppose we'd better get on, tedious though it is."

We continued to plough through the old newspapers, finding nothing. In 1885, Samuel Rust opened his shop in Sandwich with rather less formality than subsequently. In 1888, however, he got the Deputy Mayor of Ramsgate, Alderman Frederick Foster, to assist at the opening of his new establishment there. Compared to the present day, his business had hardly expanded at much more than a snail's pace, but, of course, it was possible he'd been building up the manufacturing side… Did he make anything other than the pastille and tonic, I wondered?

But in January 1889, I finally reached something of interest.

"How about this!" I exclaimed. " *'Mr Gerard Culpeper of 2 Sandown Terrace was formally declared bankrupt at Canterbury Assizes on 13 January 1889. Unable to meet the £947 13s 10d which he owed his creditors and unprepared to reach an arrangement, he pleaded for time for his investments to recover their previous value, which would enable him to meet his creditors demands in full. But Mr Archibald Newby, Solicitor for his main creditors, Mr Charles*

Culpeper (brother to Mr Gerard Culpeper) and Mr Samuel Rust noted that the interest accruing on his debts would require his investments to rise three tenths above their previous highest mark, to reach that level within six months and remain at that level while he liquidated his holdings. They proposed that this was extraordinarily unlikely as the investments were in certain French wines, whose producers were at risk themselves because of the botrytis which has been decimating their vines. The court agreed with Mr Newby and ordered that Mr Gerard Culpeper's assets should be sold and if he did not seek suitable employment so that would enable him to pay off the remainder of his debts, he would be detained at Her Majesty's pleasure. Mr Gerard Culpeper informed the court that he had undertaken employment in Wilberforce and Simpkins, Notaries in Maidstone and intended to pay off his creditors at the rate of 6d per week. More than that would reduce him and his family to penury and starvation, he claimed. The court set his weekly payment at 10d per week."

"I guess that's how Charles Culpeper got hold of No 2 Sandown Terrace… If my brother did that to me, it might well give me a motive for murder… We should probably check when Mr Charles Culpeper met his Maker."

"I haven't noticed him in my obituaries yet. Has he appeared in yours?"

"No. But I can't say I've looked hard at every obituary."

"No. I fear I haven't either. But I don't think I've noticed any familiar names. Captain Toller and his wife had moved on by 1881, so if one or other or both of them had died, the Culpepers could've moved in before 1880 anyway. And that Stowe, Dent and Fernyhough apparently were no longer in Number 4 by the time of the 1881 census. But as they seem to have been some kind of lodgers, it's not entirely surprising that they might've moved on... or were away on the night of the census. It's even possible that Barfoot had already bought Number 4 and was converting the house for his Sandown Academy at that time... But I've seen nothing about the Sandown Academy... And you'd expect to see something about it..."

But I didn't have too long to wait. In April 1889, there was a short announcement in the paper that Mr Jerome Barfoot had announced the opening of the Sandown Academy, a preparatory school for boys hoping to attend a public school, in Number 4 Sandown Terrace. There was no mention of any assistant masters, but Mrs Margaret Barfoot is described as undertaking the role of matron and Admissions Clerk. But six months later was an announcement that Sandown Academy had expanded and taken on two assistant masters - Percival Dromgoole and Lionel Blunt. Presumably the Rust family had moved out at some time during the previous year and Barfoot had been getting Number 3 converted for use as a preparatory school, with some boarders. But it perhaps suggested that there had been lodgers who weren't present during the 1881 census, otherwise the house would've remained empty for the best part of ten years.

"I wonder why he didn't wait until both buildings were ready?" asked Rosemary. "Did the school term start in the autumn as now? I wondered whether it mightn't've started in the new year. In which case, why not make a single announcement?"

"I suppose we could find out about when the school year started then... And, of course, my suggestion that the Rusts had moved out such a long time previously might well be wrong. Perhaps they moved out only a few months earlier and Barfoot – or perhaps Dromgoole or Blunt – only got the opportunity to expand the school later, perhaps unexpectedly?"

"It might be useful to know who actually owned those two houses. After all, didn't Dromgoole take over running the school by the time of the 1901 census? Perhaps that suggests he had a sizeable stake, at least in the school?"

"I wonder whether there are any prospectuses of the school anywhere? Did the boarders sleep in the attics right next to the dead body - always assuming it was there then – or was it the servants?"

"Well, at least the dead body was a man – not an unpopular swot bricked up by his envious schoolmates!"

"I'm sure a Victorian prep school didn't teach bricklaying. And I'll bet the little boys who were sent to somewhere like Sandown Academy wouldn't know anything about bricklaying. I guess they'd be the sons of reasonably prosperous shopkeepers or professionals like solicitors or the local bank managers who were hoping to get their sons into the sort of third-rate public school that we were looking at for our son, Timothy, when we were trying to find out about links between merchant bankers and Civil Servants all that time ago."

"Timothy… I'd forgotten all about him! He was a bit of a blind alley if I remember rightly."

"Yes. We were fortunate that we could do the middle-class thing and make sure we lived in a good catchment area. I doubt whether Emily or Sarah would've done any better at a public school…"

"And they'd've been a lot unhappier… and probably turned out a lot less nice than they are… All of Simone's children went to private schools and they might all be doing well, with plenty of money, but they're not very nice people."

"To be fair, we've only ever met them once… and it may be more their parents' influence than their schooling."

"We should get on…"

But about twenty minutes later, Rosemary announced she'd got further information about Sandown Academy.

"It's a report of a court case – before the local magistrate, I assume. It's quite complicated… Mr Jerome Barfoot and Mr Percival Dromgoole were claiming that the other was in breach of contract in regard to the proprietorship of Sandown Academy. Barfoot claims that he accepted Dromgoole as an assistant master solely because Dromgoole had purchased Number 3 Sandown Terrace, by way of an underhand move just as Mr Samuel Rust was due to sell to Barfoot. The agreement specified that Number 3 Sandown Terrace would be used for the Sandown Academy for a period of 21 years following their agreement. Dromgoole alleges that the agreement specified that he would have the option to purchase Number 4 Sandown Terrace after three years had elapsed from the time of their agreement and that at that stage, Barfoot would relinquish the title of master to him and he would become the sole proprietor, both of the school and of both buildings…"

"Presumably the agreement wasn't written in gibberish," I observed. "So it must've been possible to prove one or the other to be right?"

"Apparently it was either a verbal agreement – according to Barfoot – or a written one – according to Dromgoole. He claimed that Barfoot had inveigled him into getting hold of his copy of the agreement for safekeeping and that he'd subsequently destroyed it. Of course, that meant he could produce no evidence that there'd ever been an agreement."

"An interesting problem for the magistrate."

"He seems to have done the best in the circumstances. Rather than swimming in such murky waters, he dismissed both claims on the grounds that neither party could produce any evidence to back up their claims other than their own assertions. He told them that unless they could produce verifiable written evidence, no court of law would countenance a decision in favour of either party. They would either have to get along or follow their separate ways. That's all there is… I guess there must be more later."

"When was this? Did you say?"

"No, I don't think I did. September 1895… If Dromgoole had an agreement to buy Number 3 Sandown Terrace after 3 years, I wonder why he waited so long?"

"Perhaps he didn't have enough money? Presumably if he gazumped Barfoot in getting Number 3 in the first place, he might've had to take longer to get the readies together?"

"I wonder if I'll find out whether Dromgoole set up Sandown Preparatory School? Did he do it right away after the court hearing? Plainly he managed to get hold of Number 4 before 1901. I hope there may be some more details here… Have you got to the end of the eighties already?"

"Almost… I'll go back to 1870 when I'm done."

About forty minutes later, Rosemary brought me away from the limited interest of 1871 Deal.

"I've got to late '97… November… *'Mr Percival Dromgoole announces the re-opening of Sandown Preparatory School, closed since March for renovation and extension. Following the successful purchase of 4 Sandown Terrace, after the closure of the former Sandown Academy, Mr Dromgoole can now accept up to 24 boys, with facilities for up to 8 boarders. The Sandown Preparatory School will gladly take on those boys who previously attended the defunct Sandown Academy. Mr Dromgoole states that'…* Then there's a load of guff about how he can turn out model Christians and citizens of the Empire, etc, etc."

"No mention of the former master of Sandown Academy, the splendidly-named Jerome Barfoot?"

"Not a word."

"The body in the attic?"

"I'd've thought that was rather too risky for Dromgoole after their court case… and there'd be quite a lot of people who'd know Barfoot had suddenly vanished, including his wife presumably… and I guess Dromgoole would've been a prime suspect, especially as he seems to have come out of it on top."

"But it shows how the papers have changed. You could guarantee these days there'd've been a reporter sniffing round the dispute between Barfoot and Dromgoole and trying to find out how Dromgoole managed to buy Barfoot out, assuming that's what he did."

"Perhaps he was just a better teacher and got more pupils, stealing them from Barfoot, so Barfoot started to lose money and had to get out while he had the chance?"

"I suppose so… We need to see if we can find a local historian who might be able to enlighten us."

It was time for us to pack up our stuff and go. The archivist – or, more likely in my opinion, guard of the old records – had started to hover in our vicinity and taken to looking pointedly at her watch.

"We aim to come back next week and look at the remaining editions from 1872 to the end of 1879 and from 1895 to 1900," explained Rosemary. "Thank you for your patience."

"Not one of nature's friendliest people," she continued, when we were outside and out of earshot. "I realise it's a tedious job, but she doesn't have to do much for whatever she's being paid.

"I wonder how these boarding houses like Mrs. Broome's got known to people... and Number 4 when Stowe, Dent & Fernyhough were staying there? I never saw any advert, but then I didn't crawl through every item in the personal columns," I remarked, puzzling over something I'd just noticed in my notes as I shut the notebook up.

"Nor did I. You read stuff like that a lot faster than me. If I read every word I reckon we'll be stuck in the room for another month... But on the particular point, I guess they might put a board up... Or they had an arrangement with local employers... So the Customs and Coast Guard, for instance, would know to put people on to Mrs. Broome and people like her. I wonder what the arrangement was for Stowe, Dent & Fernyhough? They didn't seem to have a landlady. Did they rent from someone who owned the building, but didn't live there? Did they have to provide their own servants? There's no obvious link between those three to suggest that they ended up there other than by chance."

"It's a pity that Victorian social history wasn't one of the areas of history I ever took any interest in. After you've had Engels's *'The Condition of the Working Class in England'* rammed down your throat, both in English and German, you tend to find virtually any other area of history more enjoyable."

"I think I did essays on imperialism, Gladstone and Disraeli, the Irish Question and the lead up to the First World War. The rest of that period of history is unknown territory to me. We did do some local history – but only at the time of the Industrial Revolution and the Luddites…"

"Particular favourites of my father of course… But lacking a suitable ideology…"

We drove back to Beckenham that evening and spent the next couple of days thinking about the body in the Marine Buildings – more properly Sandown Terrace – not at all. There were plenty of things to do, people to see and the pleasure of sleeping – and getting up to other things that didn't seem quite right in our daughter's bed – in our own bed.

By Monday evening, we were beginning to think about returning to what Rosemary called our "olde worlde sleuthing", to which I'd countered by calling it "sleuthing on sea."

"Do you think we should go to the Public Records Office in Kew, while we're in London and see if we can find a bit about when some of these people appear to have passed on?" suggested Rosemary. "Or are we jumping ahead of ourselves?"

"It might be worth exhausting the *East Kent Mercury* first. We really need to pinpoint whose death we need to check up on... and I'd quite like to see if we couldn't find a local historian who could fill in some of the gaps in the newspapers."

"And, of course, the missing man presumably may not be recorded as dead. I wonder whether anyone checks whether there is a corresponding death certificate for every ancient birth certificate? But I suppose plenty of people just disappeared from time to time and there may have been no reason to declare them dead... so according to the records they haven't officially died... and could be a hundred and fifty years old."

"I wonder whether British officialdom leaves things as untidy as that?"

"That was the nineteenth century. If someone just disappeared and no-one reported them missing, presumably their deaths would never be recorded. If they had property, I guess at some point it could be disposed of. But doesn't the Government hold on to quite a lot of that sort of stuff?"

"I don't know... In fact, there are a lot of things I don't know about this sort of thing... If you want to know about being a receiver of wrecks, I know quite a lot about that, as a former Collector London Port..."

"You'd've been quite busy along this part of the coast, I imagine... There must've been hundreds of wrecks on the Goodwin Sands."

"And the good citizens of Deal made quite a living out of them... I think I noticed in one of those history books that there was quite a rivalry between the men of the north and south ends of Deal over the spoils from these wrecks... I suppose it made a welcome addition to the money they got from smuggling..."

"So it's back to Deal then?"

We drove down the following day and called in at the library to see whether anyone could recommend any local historians to us. Rowena Warnle suggested a couple of people – Frederick Challenor and Esmee Culpeper. Both had published small pamphlets and were supposed to be compiling 'the definitive history of Deal' – by way of considerable rivalry, she noted.

"If they don't ask whether you've spoken to the other one, I wouldn't volunteer it... Probably Miss

Culpeper is your best source for North Deal... Challenor is really more into the Marines," she explained.

As the *East Kent Mercury* archive didn't open for another couple of days, we went in pursuit of Miss Esmee Culpeper, whose name naturally intrigued us. We contacted her by phone and explained our reasons for getting in touch. She suggested we join her in her "abode" for afternoon tea.

The 'abode' was in a house on the sea front, not far from the pier. We were to ring the bell on a door next to the entrance to what she called a "sempstresses' establishment" and she would come down to meet us. We did as bidden and the door was opened by a woman a good ten years older than us, with white hair, tightly tied back into a bun, with a long, intelligent face and pince-nez. He skin was sallow, but seemed to indicate that she'd lived in warmer climes at some stage of her life. She was tall, taller than Rosemary, but bent with rheumatism, so appeared shorter.

We introduced ourselves and she led us along a short corridor, which evidently led to a yard at the back. But halfway along, she opened another door and we followed her up a wooden staircase, past a very old-fashioned kitchen, where all the woodwork and walls had been painted different shades of green, along a short landing into one of the most magnificent rooms I'd ever seen. It was at least twenty-five feet square with windows looking out to sea and back into the town. It was panelled in wood, in a style prevalent in the late seventeenth or early eighteen century. There was a fine large old brick fireplace with a handsome wooden mantelpiece, which perhaps had been a later, Georgian addition. It was a grand room, that smelled of centuries of history. Despite the unprepossessing external view, this was one of the oldest houses in Deal and must have seen sea battles, countless wrecks, smuggling, skirmishes between the Customs and Coast Guard and the local smugglers, the arrival of the Marines, as well as two world wars, when the sound of the great guns could probably be heard from here. There could hardly be a more appropriate place for a local historian to live.

On the walls, I noticed several nineteenth century engravings, as well as three maps of the town and the Goodwin Sands – from the late seventeenth, early eighteenth and late eighteenth centuries.

"It's a fine room, is it not!" remarked Esmee Culpeper. "I'd like to tell you it was mine, but it belongs to a lady even older than I, who, being half-French, half-English, spends half her time in France and half her time here. I live below in the flat which is directly below you. But Marie-Claude encourages me to use her rooms when she's not here… You may see a couple of drawings of hers on the walls over there... She was flown over into France during the last war to work with the Resistance. After over two years, she suffered from nervous prostration and was invalided out. She learnt to draw in the military hospital near Ashford and when she returned, drew most of the older parts of Deal which appealed to her. She's agreed to let me reproduce several of her drawings in my history of Deal."

"I've been in many old rooms and old buildings in my time," I replied. "But I can't think of any that can rival this for its sheer sense of history..."

"And it's so beautiful!" added Rosemary. "The wood panelling is marvellous. Not just the style, but the way the wood looks!"

"I'm here too often... I tend to forget... You said on the phone you were investigating a body that's been found... in North Deal somewhere? Do sit down... I've just made us some tea."

We sat on a chesterfield covered in dark green velvet, slightly the worse for wear. Esmee Culpeper sat in a winged arm chair, similarly covered, leant forward and poured us out tea – Earl Grey, without milk or sugar. Apparently, we had no choice in the matter, though it was possible she couldn't conceive of any other way of drinking tea. She peered over the top of her cup at me.

"Our daughter has recently bought a flat in the Marine Buildings, which we now know used to be called Sandown Terrace. Her flat is on the second floor of the middle building. The bloke in the flat above – which covers the third and top floors – has been renovating because of serious damp problems. While he was doing so, he came across a wall that seemed to be in the wrong place and when he tested whether it was a false wall, he opened up a small chamber where a dead body was lying. The pathologist has told us that the body was left there roughly between 1880 and 1900. Unless it was an extraordinary way to commit suicide, it'd seem that foul play was involved. But, of course, after such a long time, the police aren't interested. We've done a certain amount of investigation work during our careers and we thought we'd see how far we could get in finding out who this bloke was, why he might've been killed and who might've killed him."

"I used to work for the Metropolitan Police and Nick for Customs & Excise," Rosemary added, by way of explanation.

"Anything you can find out would necessarily add to the strange history of that part of the town," observed Esmee Culpeper, looking at me. "What have you discovered so far?"

"We don't know yet exactly when Sandown Terrace was built… But we know it was there in

1871, as we've seen an Ordnance Survey map of the town then," I replied. "We've managed to find out who was living in all the buildings in Sandown Terrace in the 1871, 1881, 1891 and 1901 censuses. And we've been looking in the old copies of the *East Kent Mercury* to see whether anything newsworthy occurred during that time. We're a little over halfway through looking at those. What we've found out so far is that Samuel Rust, the maker of "Rust's pastilles" and "Rust's tonic" lived in Number 3 Sandown Terrace for the 1870s and much of the 1880s. After he left, there seemed to be a dispute between Jerome Barfoot, who'd established a prep school in Number 4 and Percival Dromgoole, who seems to have bought Number 3 from Samuel Rust, as to which one of them had the right to own the whole school. It seems that Dromgoole won, but it doesn't seem to have been settled in public."

"The other main thing we've noted was the bankruptcy of Gerard Culpeper, whose main creditors were his brother Charles and Samuel Rust. The outcome seems to have been that Number 2 Sandown Terrace became the property of Charles Culpeper and Gerard Culpeper moved to Maidstone," added Rosemary, who struck me as being faintly irritated by Esmee Culpeper almost totally ignoring her. "Was one of these a relative?"

"Charles Culpeper was my grandfather… a hard man who died extremely wealthy and alone in a large house in Folkestone. Gerard Culpeper by all accounts was a charming spendthrift who borrowed money on his house from his brother and next-door neighbour for some stock venture or other and came a cropper. The dispute split the family. My second cousins Geoffrey and Reginald would sooner spit in my face than converse with me. My father was one of six children and for all the wealth which my grandfather grasped to himself, among six it was spread quite thin. So there was never enough for anyone to make any recompense. Geoffrey is an accountant, Reginald a solicitor. If they could find a way to ruin one, more or all of us, they'd do so with the utmost joy."

"But there's no reason to suppose that the body deposited in the attic of Number 3 Sandown Terrace would've had anything to do with this affair?" Rosemary continued. Esmee Culpeper continued to address her replies to me.

"No. Not at all. The whole affair was conducted with icy politeness, according to what my father recalled. He was extremely young at the time, of course. Besides, my family occupied Number 2 Sandown Terrace… and you say that the body was found in number 3? That was occupied by Samuel Rust and his family at that time. A great bear of a man, Samuel Rust, according to accounts of him. Tall and big with a zest for living to match. A greedy man. A glutton. He liked his money and he liked his food and drink... Not that he was a toper... and he liked chasing serving wenches, according to the tales in my family. If it wasn't for his discovery of the formula for the pastilles and the tonic, he'd just have been a successful local chemist... But the tonic and the pastilles seemed to work. People found they made them feel better. So, Samuel Rust became extremely wealthy, bought Sholden Hall and spent the remainder of his life chasing even more serving wenches, eating vast quantities of food and enjoying the finest French wines that the Deal smugglers could lay their hands on."

"Do they still make Rust's pastilles and tonic? Does the Rust family still own the business?"

"They were sharp... Not so much old Samuel, but his sons, Lionel and Edgar... They sold the business to Empire Pharmaceuticals in the 1920s... before the crash, but kept hold of about a third of the shares. Of course, these took a nose-dive after 1929, but they recovered... and eventually Empire Pharmaceuticals themselves were sold to GMR Inc of Cleveland, Ohio... GMR stands for "Grandmother's Recipe", by the way. But Norman and Godfrey Rust, who'd inherited the shares of Lionel and Edgar, made sure they retained around a fifth of the shares. The company itself is practically unknown, but many of its brands are household names… Interestingly, I'm told that Rust's pastilles and tonic do better in the United States than here, though there is still a factory producing them somewhere in South Lancashire, I believe. In the USA, they also sell them in a lozenge form, I'm reliably informed. So, the Rust family live well and do only what they feel they wish to do… Not that they own Sholden Hall any longer. They've got various properties spread around Kent, London and France. Nicholas Rust is the Conservative MP for the Weald, of course. Terence Rust – he's the one who keeps an eye on the family's wealth for his various relatives – naturally sits on the boards of several blue-chip companies in the City. Neither are conspicuous. They follow the long-standing family tradition of doing what is required to safeguard the family fortunes. Unlike old Samuel, they lack charm and joi de vivre. Indeed, in some ways, they're something of a Victorian morality tale: their efforts to maintain their fortune mean that none of them appear to enjoy it much… You understand, I've met some of them from time to time… Even interviewed Nicholas Rust a year or two ago about my history of Deal… Such a cautious, cold, unimaginative man… I'd rather have met old Samuel, he'd've tried to pinch my bottom a few times, but at least he'd've shown some spark of life!"

"It'd seem that the body was walled up in that attic room some time when either the Rust family occupied Number 3 Sandown Terrace or when it was Sandown Academy or Sandown Preparatory School."

"Doubtless you've seen something about the Sandown Terrace schools in the *East Kent Mercury*. It's always remained something of a mystery. There's no doubt that Jerome Barfoot established the Sandown Academy in Number 4 Sandown Terrace, which he owned... as far as I'm aware. It's also evident that Percival Dromgoole subsequently bought Number 3 Sandown Terrace from Samuel Rust, but it's never been entirely clear to me where he got his money from. My grandfather believed very little of it was his own money and he was being backed by someone who wished to remain anonymous... or possibly who he had some sort of hold over... The one thing you could say about Percy Dromgoole is that he was a deeply unpleasant man. My grandfather had no doubt that there was no written agreement between Dromgoole and Barfoot about Barfoot selling the school, including the premises, to him under any conditions. He doubted there was even much of a verbal agreement, much beyond Barfoot agreeing to offer Dromgoole first refusal if – underline if – he ever decided to sell..."

"Yet he did... and not so long after the court hearing."

"Yes. That's where there's more mystery. Where did Dromgoole get his funds from? In 1893 or 94, apparently he made my grandfather an offer for Number 2 Sandown Terrace. It was turned down, on the grounds that it was undervalued to a derisory extent. But Dromgoole seems to have had associates – accomplices might be a better word perhaps – who spent the next couple of years making my grandfather and his family's life uncomfortable, even unpleasant at times... poisoned cats, servants threatened, dead fish in the front garden, rats introduced into the basement, blocked drains... that sort of thing. But my grandfather was exactly the sort of man not to do something like that to. When eventually his family had had enough, he agreed to sell... but to Hubert Jessop, who offered him a fair price. Jessop was a local Solicitor who owned several properties which he rented out or put in the hands of one of his agents, who managed the tenants while living, usually in the basement. At the time of the 1901 census, it was a man called Herbert Farmer, as you probably know... But the question I've occasionally asked myself is: did Dromgoole intend to purchase both Numbers 2 and 4 Sandown Terrace? Or did he make an offer for Number 2 because his attempts to force Barfoot to sell him Number 4 were being thwarted? And, if the former, where on earth did the money come from?"

"Did your grandfather have any ideas about that?"

"Not really. Sometimes he wondered whether it might not be Samuel Rust or one of his sons. It seems likely he took a dislike to Barfoot. But whether that was an unfortunate antipathy or whether Barfoot had annoyed one of them, perhaps by making an offer on Number 3 Sandown Terrace, I couldn't say. From what I've ever heard about Barfoot, he was an enthusiastic pedagogue, but otherwise a very dull man, over-fond of his bible... He was a member of some noncomformist sect... one of their elders... now which one was it... the Baptists of the Tabernacle, if I remember rightly. They met in a house in Ark Lane... probably bought deliberately, as I believe they were millenniarists... But fortunate in that none expected to still be extant when the millennium occurred..."

"But you don't know how Dromgoole ended up with Number 4 Sandown Terrace and the whole school?"

"No. My Grandparents had moved by that time. It's possible that Dromgoole hounded Barfoot as he'd try to hound my grandfather. He certainly wouldn't've been above passing rumours around about Barfoot either... But the most likely possibility is that once he'd got enough money, he just set up his own school and competed effectively with Barfoot for pupils. I guess if Dromgoole had someone backing him with funds, he could probably offer cheaper rates and doubtless a swankier prospectus... I doubt he had any better qualifications than Barfoot. Both had been assistant masters at minor public schools – several in Barfoot's case, one in Dromgoole's. He was also almost certainly more personable… and, whatever he really believed, would've made sure he was assiduously C of E… So the most likely explanation was that Barfoot couldn't afford to keep going and had to sell up to Dromgoole… You might be able to discover what the building got sold for and that might tell you whether Barfoot got a fair price or whether he got whatever he was offered."

"Do you know what happened to him afterwards?"

"I've a feeling he may have moved to Margate and set up some sort of more modest establishment there… But he certainly left Deal… and my interest in him lapses at that point."

"Is there anything else you've come across about Sandown Terrace at that time which might be relevant?"

"I don't believe so. Though it was a strange piece of speculative building, being plonked down in the middle of nowhere between North Deal and Sandown Castle, it has no particular history to it. Virtually from the start, at least one of the buildings had tenants rather than the owners living there. Such people come and go. Many are honest, decent people with a good reason for wanting temporary accommodation... For instance, if you were a Coast Guard or a Customs Officer at that time, you might well prefer lodgings in Deal and living with your family some way distant – to avoid pressure being applied on you or risk suffering retribution. But among such transitory people, there'll always be the odd one who's fleeing from something or someone or other, or avoiding someone or something... and quite possibly using a false name. I believe Samuel Rust used to lodge some of his assistants in Sandown Terrace – the young men who helped him with his experiments as he worked out the formulae for his pastilles and tonic."

"He actually undertook his experiments in Sandown Terrace?"

"No. Of course not! He had a small building just off Alfred Square in what was then still called Middle Street - now Sandown Road. If you walk along Sandown Road, just before you reach Alfred Square, you can still see the large chimney of his little laboratory."

"How many assistants did he have, do you know?"

"As far as I'm aware, one or two at most. Samuel Rust concentrated on pastilles and tonic, specifically for winter coughs and colds, as he reckoned that was where the money was. You must understand that

Friar's Balsam and Balsamic Compound were still relative newcomers – and could only be taken in liquid form. Hence his search for the pastilles... and the tonic was aimed at warding off colds, fevers and chills and would be taken virtually all year round... especially if you lived off the sea as did most in these parts."

"I remember them from my childhood," I said. "But I don't recall any mention of Deal on the bottle or the tin. I realise they weren't being made there then, but often these things keep something very like their original labels."

"It never mentioned Deal. Samuel Rust was aiming at the nationwide market and he felt Deal would be seen as too parochial and possibly confusing, assuming anyone had ever heard of it... and might therefore be distrusted. So the original labels didn't mention any place of manufacture... but after he moved the factory to Ashford, he felt less constrained, though the place of manufacture is very much in the small print. If you visit the Deal Museum, you can see examples both of the tins and bottles manufactured here and those made in Ashford. You'll need a keen pair or eyes or a magnifying glass to read where the latter were made."

"You mentioned the oddity of the building of Sandown Terrace," continued Rosemary, still ignoring Esmee Culpeper's studied rudeness. "We could see from the 1871 Ordnance Survey map that it was very much on its own. Do you know anything about its history?"

"A speculative build by Jeremiah Shorne of Ramsgate. When talk started about demolishing Sandown castle, he believed that North Deal might become a salubrious place to live. The land was available at a low cost and it was conveniently set apart from the smugglers, wreckers and other troublesome sorts who lived in North Deal at the time... and, of course, honest but poor fisherfolk and so on. The houses were built for families with servants – even though at least one began life as lodgings. You should always bear in mind that in those times, access to a metalled road wasn't considered particularly necessary for many. Coaches could reach the front of Sandown Terrace along what would either have been called Beach Street or even just North Deal at that time..."

"What time are we talking about?"

"Late 1850s. You can probably get the exact date from the Land Registry... I can't remember off-hand." She continued to look straight at me, even when answering Rosemary's questions. Very odd! "But to continue: many people could ride and would take bridle-paths to Sandwich and elsewhere. North Deal was perhaps more accessible then than it may seem now. I reckon at a decent trot you could get to

Sandwich from Sandown Terrace faster by horse than you could today by motor car."

"Is there more you can tell us?" I said. I was getting the distinct feeling that Rosemary was about to say something that would cut off this source of information for good.

"I don't believe so. But please let me know the outcome of your investigations."

"Thank you for the tea… and your helpful information."

We departed… and walked a few yards to a little fish-and-chip-type café called "The Caterer", where a pleasant young man got us mugs of proper tea and toasted teacakes.

"If we have to see that woman again, you can go on your own," growled Rosemary. "I've rarely come across anyone as rude as that in my life… and the others I've met have generally had a good reason for it."

"I reckon there's a tradition of coldness and rudeness in the Culpeper family that she, as an aged member, feels obliged to uphold," I remarked. "And she was quite informative, though…"

"… whether it's taken us any further forward remains to be seen."

"Let's see what we get from our next visit to the *East Kent Mercury* archive and then take stock."

Before our next visit, we visited Ramsgate and Margate, noting mainly the rather sad decline of what had plainly been rather fine seaside towns in their heyday. Indeed, the only thing that seemed to be flourishing was a curious, remarkable phenomenon known as the Shell Grotto, a very curious series of underground caverns completely decorated with shells – along with its own mystery: who had created it? Was it as legend had it, the Romans or, more likely, a much more recent creation? But we felt we had a sufficient ancient mystery on our hands. And a slightly dispiriting week was completed when we spent half a day in the archive and picked up nothing which we didn't know already.

7. A VOICE FROM THE HERE AND NOW

We decided to head back home. We felt we'd take stock better if we were away from Deal... and in any case, we'd long planned to spend the next week at our flat in Budleigh Salterton. We needed time and space to re-read our notes and then think and discuss what, if anything, they told us. We drove there on Sunday and arrived in time for a late lunch in a local pub and then walked along the pebble beach. The sea and the pebbles were pretty much all there was in common with Deal. As we walked towards the west, looking at our flat in a former hotel, we could see the rich red of the cliffs and a couple of yachts out in the Channel, unlike Deal where, though we might see France on a clear day, we were too far round to see the white cliffs. And Deal itself was flat – with the sight of huge ferries and container ships on the horizon. Budleigh Salterton was pretty, but it was essentially an overgrown village. Deal was a town, built between historic castles, with a distinct air of history about it. Budleigh Salterton was comfortable, relaxing. Deal was intriguing – I felt there was more beneath the quirkily elegant surface than the town was letting on. I'm not sure quirky elegance were quite the words I was seeking, but I couldn't think of better...

We sat on our couch in our flat, looking out across the bay. The late afternoon sun was shining on the sea.

"Do you think we're going to get anywhere near finding out who that dead man was?" I asked Rosemary.

"Possibly not. But we should be able to narrow it down a bit. For instance, the body was walled up in the attic of Number 3 Sandown Terrace. So the most likely people to have killed or been killed are the residents of that building… But if you can build a wall, equally you can knock one down – or at least knock a hole in it sufficient to shove a dead body through. So we shouldn't rule out the residents of Number 2 Sandown Terrace in particular, as the cavity was that side… and logically you'd dig through the wall on your side, dump the body, build the wall just beyond the body and then repair your own wall."

"There's a flaw in that logic, Sherlock."

"Oh yes?"

"If you remember, the way the cavity wall was constructed, it was pretty clear from the mortar that the wall had been built from the other side – from Number 3 Sandown Terrace.….So if anyone from outside Number 3 was involved, it's more likely to have been Number 4… Perhaps we ought to see whether there's any evidence that either wall has ever been opened up in the way you suggest?"

"But when we come to the people, we're necessarily speculating a lot. But it seemed to me that if Samuel Rust was a man who liked the ladies, wasn't he the sort of bloke to go bonking the chambermaids? As they didn't have any contraception then, there must've been a fair chance he got one or more of them pregnant… Perhaps there was an angry father, brother or boyfriend who wouldn't be paid off and had to be removed permanently and silently?"

"It's a theory, certainly! But it might easily be something tied up with the dispute between Barfoot and Dromgoole… and though I've said it was less likely Number 2 might be involved, the dispute with the Culpeper's also seems a possibility…"

"Or even a dispute between the men lodging in Number 4, before Barfoot bought it for his school."

"That actually seems more likely than most of our other ideas. After all, nothing we've heard suggested that the Rust family, the Culpepers, and Barfoot and his wife weren't entirely respectable people… and it'd be quite difficult to kill anyone in houses as stuffed with people as theirs were without someone else being aware of it. Even if Samuel Rust had wanted to deal with an angry or blackmailing relative of one of his chambermaids, could he really have kept his murder from the other servants – some of whom presumably lived up in those attics? And if you're going to kill someone who's blackmailing you for getting a chambermaid pregnant, are you really going to risk letting yourself in for being blackmailed for committing murder?"

"In any case, wouldn't it be a lot easier to knock someone on the head in the street or get them drunk in a pub and take them out in a boat and drop them in the sea? Coroners were hardly very sophisticated in those days. All you'd have to do is claim you'd seen Mr. X going off fishing in a boat… and you knew he'd had a skinful, but he insisted on going… whereas you'd taken him out in one boat, tied up to yours. You shove him overboard, leave his boat where it is and come back in yours. Is anyone likely to see you? There wouldn't be any streetlights and if it was a cloudy night, it'd be pretty well pitch black…" I suggested.

"But that does help us a bit… In those circumstances, the body would turn up and be recognised. So why do you have to take a greater risk and wall it up in the attic? Because you don't want the body to be found for as long as possible. That suggests when the body was found, fingers would be pointed at you… and not just that you happened to live in the same house, but that there were others who knew you and Mr. X had the sort of dispute or hatred of each other that could turn to murder."

"But, of course, the only people we've seen who might be in that position are the Culpeper brother and Barfoot and Dromgoole… And as far as we know none of them actually vanished off the face of the earth… Though I suppose we should check with the Public Record Office. It should enable us to tell who died and when."

"And if there's no record of death? Do we treat that as suspicious? I guess we do and then we see whether there are any other ways of checking when and where they died… But if we find nothing, it gives a possible identity for the victim."

"If you include all the adult males in Numbers 2, 3 and 4 Sandown Terrace, that's a fair number to check… But it can't be any more boring than going through back issues of the *East Kent Mercury.*"

"You can say that again… But we may be able to narrow it down a bit. For instance, if you bumped me off and tried to hide my body, there'd be plenty of people who'd notice I'd disappeared – and they'd definitely start asking questions within a week or two. You might be able to fob them off for a while, but not indefinitely. Unless you'd got some really plausible forged evidence – like an air ticket booking to Paraguay – sooner or later, someone is likely to inform the police. Now I realise things were less tied down in the nineteenth century, but even so, it seems to me we should be looking for someone who was unlikely to be missed. After all, we saw nothing in any edition of the *East Kent Mercury* which mentioned that anyone living in Sandown Terrace was missing.

Though I reckon I came across a couple of dozen other notices… often possible 'missing at sea', of course."

"Yes. I came across a fair number too – and, of course, one of them could've been our body in the attic – but we have no way of finding any link between the missing man and the body… we don't have the luxury of dental records…"

We listed the names of the men who could fit the bill of the dead man – all male inhabitants of Numbers 2, 3 or 4 Sandown Terrace, with a ranking system for those that seemed more or less likely to be the victim.

Captain Francis Toller	1871	2 Sandown Terrace	2 (nothing known)
Michael Shaw (servant)	1871	ditto	2
Samuel Rust (chemist/ businessman)	1871/81	3 Sandown Terrace	3 (not missing)
John Horton (servant)	1871/81	ditto	2
George Blenkinsop (servant)	1871	ditto	2
Jacob Dunne (servant)	1881	ditto	2

Matthew Stowe (chemist)	1871	4 Sandown Terrace	1
Peter Dent (Maltster)	1871	ditto	1
William Fernyhough (Excise Officer)	1871	ditto	2 (probably checkable)
John Welshe (servant)	1871	ditto	1
Amos White (servant)	1871	ditto	1
Gerald Culpeper	1881	2 Sandown Terrace	2? 1
Peter Dellow	1881	ditto	2
Charles Culpeper (Marine Engineer)	1891	ditto	3
Horace Wells (servant)	1891	ditto	2
Jerome Barfoot (Master)	1891	3,4 Sandown Terrace	2
Percival Dromgoole (Assistant Master)	1891/1901	ditto	3, possibly 2
Lionel Blunt (Assistant Master)	1891	ditto	2

Leonard Strevens (servant)	1891		2
Peter Clement (servant)	1891	ditto	2
Ezekiel Barnes	1901	ditto	2
Herbert Farmer (Lodging Agent)	1901	2 Sandown Terrace	2
Simeon Mew (Bookkeeper	1901	ditto	2
Jeremiah Unwin (Schoolmaster	1901	ditto	2
Patrick O'Neill (Overseer)	1901	ditto	2, possibly 1
Albert Johnson (Librarian)	1901	ditto	2
Norman Worthington (Commercial Traveller)	1901	ditto	2, possibly 1
Mordecai Grimley (servant)	1901	ditto	2
Archibald Reeves (Assistant Master)	1901	3,4 Sandown Terrace	2

John Partridge (servant)	1901	ditto	2

The third category was for people who'd be quickly missed – and therefore seemed unlikely to be the victim. The first and second categories essentially represented our assessment of how unlikely it might be that the man would've been missed and his proximity to where the dead body was found. Of course, they might easily have had wives or sweethearts who weren't living with them at the time of the census, but we could only go on what we knew at this stage. And there was, of course, an awful lot we didn't know. But we didn't need to check everything about them. If we could find a death certificate which seemed satisfactory, we could safely assume they'd died where it said on the death certificate. So we agreed to pay a visit – probably the first of several – to the Public Records Office in Kew on our return from South Devon.

"But, of course, finding who the victim was is only a first step," observed Rosemary.

There wasn't a lot more we could do at that stage, so we endured a couple of days of virtually incessant rain before deciding to cut our losses and return to Beckenham.

There was a fair amount of post as usual when we returned. At least half was junk mail and there were a couple of bills, which were for information as we paid most utility and other bills through direct debit. But one made us sit up and take notice.

"'Dear Mr. and Mrs. Storey, I am led to understand that you are looking into the death of a man whose body was found in Number 3 Marine Buildings, Deal, recently,'" Rosemary read out from an ordinary sheet of letter paper. "'This death occurred a very long time ago. The police are not interested in discovering who the man was. So why are you? Will you not let this matter rest, please? There is nothing to be gained from it. In the first instance, you are most likely to spend a lot of time and discover nothing. Even if you do learn something, you will never have certainty, as evidence is necessarily lacking after the passage of so much time. But in the process, your investigations could cause distress and concern to those who bear no responsibility for actions undertaken over a century ago and could cause several people untold harm. I would therefore urge you to desist from your investigations. If not, actions will* (the word 'may' has been crossed out) have to be taken. I trust that I shall not be required to contact you further in this matter.'* No signature, of course."

"At least it's plain enough. You remember those notes we got sent when we were in the flat? No one could be confused about what this person wants."

"But it does raise loads of interesting questions. Not least, how did this person know what we've been up to? And how did they know our address here? Who told them? And, of course, more important, what do they know about the dead body? From the letter, you'd think there's at least one person out there who knows who the man was and probably why he was killed…"

"And it'd seem that knowing that would make life difficult for a number of people… But self-evidently not the murderer…"

"But presumably, either the murder enabled his family to do well, so their present prosperity is based on it… or perhaps they have a family reputation to consider… It wouldn't look all that good for an MP, for instance, to have a grandfather who was a murderer…"

"I wonder what the writer means by *'actions will have to be taken'*? I suppose he or she isn't intending to be helpful, but to get us to desist. But I wonder how they'll know we've stopped or whether we're continuing? I can't see much reason for us returning to any of the places where we've been looking for information…"

"Unless we've overlooked something… which, in view of this letter, I'm getting a feeling we have."

"But we're not going to stop, are we?"

"Not at this stage. The letter is quite courteous and I guess the next step is as likely to be a more definite warning, rather than a rocket-grenade through the front window, I hope. I suppose if whoever it is knows about such matters, they might guess we'll be heading for the Public Record Office at Kew sooner or later. But are they really going to hang about there every day just in case we turn up? And how would they recognise us?"

"That goes back to your original questions. How does this person know what we're up to? It must be connected somehow to one of the people we've met and told about what we were up to. That's the pathologist – Julia Radford. No obvious connection. But was that her married or single name? Then the two archivists – Rowena Warnle and Adrienne Bishop. The Warnle's are evidently rich and well-connected, but as far as I know have no connection with Deal. The woman at the *East Kent Mercury*' archive... Did we get her name?"

"Not that I can recall."

"And, of course, the egregious Esmee Culpeper, who has a very strong connection... Perhaps too strong to be thinking of writing a letter like that."

"There's little a woman of that sort could do that'd surprise me… But in any case, we haven't sworn anyone to silence… Indeed I didn't think we needed to… So any of them could've spoken to friends and colleagues – not least people they thought might be interested… So I think the field of suspects as the letter-writer is likely to be quite large."

"Now if I were Sherlock Holmes and you Miss Marple, we'd examine the letter and envelope and find no end of clues. Whereas all I can see is that it was posted here in Beckenham… presumably to disguise where the writer came from… and the paper and envelope are Basildon Bond, which is posher than the stuff you'd get in a supermarket, but is exactly the middle range, conservative stuff a middle-class person would buy. Which is not a great surprise. If you worked on a till in Sainsbury's, you're not likely to be all that bothered about your great-great grandfather being a murderer."

"The language used is that of a fairly well-educated person. There are no spelling or grammatical errors and they use words like 'desist', 'instance', 'untold' and 'distress', for example. This is someone who reads a fair amount, I'd say, and is either at least middle-aged or has lived in a rather old-fashioned environment for much of their lives."

"I doubt whether Miss Marple could've done a lot better."

"There's another thing. Assuming the person doesn't live in Beckenham, either they travelled here on purpose – which suggests they have plenty of spare time – or Beckenham is on their journey to work."

"But perhaps it was also done like that to remind us that whoever it is can get themselves to Beckenham easily enough, so that when they write about 'action', they intend something active and aimed at us here… Of course, I may be reading too much into it…"

"It doesn't entirely fit with the impression I get of the letter-writer. But the writer and the person who delivered it may well not be the same person… a kindly nephew doing an errand for his elderly aunt, perhaps?"

"Now we are getting into the realms of fantasy!"

"Possibly… But we need to be more observant than we have been lately. If anyone is watching us or following us, I doubt whether they're very professional at it."

"And I also think we need to consider what we're going to do next and how we might use it to help us find out who wrote the letter… I reckon that may well be an easier route to finding out who the body in the attic was and who killed him."

"More of your famous 'back-ullaging'?"

"Better than Okham's razor, surely?"

"Anything but that!"

We spent the next day at home, sorting out various things in our house and filling up the freezer. As we went about our business – not least lunches with former colleagues in central London – we kept our eyes open, to see if we were being watched or followed. But we couldn't see anything. I reckoned it was possible that whoever it was might know people in places like the Public Record Office – or especially those archives more obviously connected to Deal – and would learn what we were up to by that route, rather than by following us. Indeed, unless they were extremely confident in their ability to blend into the background or were extremely nippy, following us was potentially risky. If we identified who was following us, our chances of getting to the truth about the dead body in the attic of Number 3 Sandown Terrace would be greatly increased – as would the likelihood of "distress" and "concern" to the descendants of whoever had been responsible for the murder. Even sending the letter constituted a significant risk, it seemed to me. Inevitably it had provided us with some clues. But more important, it'd turned a sometimes-tedious academic exercise into something that was beginning to feel more like a real investigation. And as much as Rosemary and I claimed that we were long past that sort of excitement, we both knew that wasn't entirely true.

So our trip to the Public Record Office at Kew was potentially more interesting than we'd anticipated a few days earlier. We travelled by train, knowing it'd be a lot less tiring than the car journey round the South Circular. As we travelled, we could see no one apparently shadowing us. But once we'd got on to public transport, it wasn't easy to spot anyone anyway. And when we got to the Public Record Office, a fair amount of our attention was diverted by the need to register before we were allowed in. Fortunately, we'd read up in advance, so we had the necessary documents confirming that we were who we said we were and that we lived where we said we lived. As usual, Rosemary was better at dealing with this bureaucracy than I, standing quietly impatient.

"For someone who enjoys getting into the details, you should have more sympathy with them trying to make sure they get it right," observed Rosemary, who knew exactly what I was thinking.

"We're just going to look at some old death certificates, not the Domesday Book," I muttered.

"Have you spotted anyone who might be keeping a look-out for us?"

"Yes. There could be a dozen or more people who might be watching us, but I reckon they're either waiting to get their passes or waiting for someone else who's having to go through the same tiresome ritual that we have."

"You were never the greatest at that sort of thing anyway... Is there anyone who looks as though they don't fit in?"

"Not that I can tell. It's a fairly motley bunch. I guess there are middle-aged women checking on their ancestries, researchers for will-hunting companies, and academics. Any of them could equally be something else."

Finally we were allowed inside and, after a while realising that we had no idea where to go or what to do, we found someone who looked as though they might be able to help. As it happened, we'd got a secretary, but she found us someone who could help. The help turned out to be informative, if unwelcome.

"Basically, you've come to the wrong place," she said. "I don't know who suggested you should come here, but they misinformed you. There've been quite a few changes in the last few years, but if you want death certificates, you need to go to the Family Research Centre in Clerkenwell. It's part of the General Register Office, which gets a copy of every death certificate. The FRC is quite new. It just opened last year, but if you've got names you'll be able to track them down… But if you don't know when, it could take some time. They have been computerised – but unless you've got some very unusual names, you could find yourself ploughing through hundreds of names."

"If we have a name of someone and can't find a death certificate, would that suggest they went missing and their deaths were never recorded?" asked Rosemary.

"That's one possibility. The other one of, course, is that they emigrated… or changed their name or were using a false name when they died."

"You've been extremely helpful. We can now make our way back to Clerkenwell and find the Family Research Centre."

"It's Number 1 Myddelton Street, if that helps."

Feeling somewhat irritated by a wasted journey – with the accompanying bureaucracy – we made our way back to the station.

"I wonder why Rowena Warnle suggested we went to the Public Records Office at Kew?" remarked Rosemary. "She must've known it'd be a wasted journey. Was it plain ignorance? Or something more… to delay us?"

"I suppose at that stage we were talking mainly about the censuses. I imagine you could get them here in Kew – but then she suggested we looked at the records in Canterbury. Perhaps we weren't very clear at that stage about needing to look at death certificates?"

"It's possible, I suppose. I guess that letter put her well and truly on the list of suspects… as the writer, not the murderer…"

"And it might explain why we didn't think anyone was watching us here."

"Perhaps it might be possible to spot someone in darkest Clerkenwell."

As we sat on the train back to Waterloo, we looked on the A to Z to find Myddelton Street in Clerkenwell. Fortunately, it seemed quite easy to identify, as it was along Exmouth Market from the huge Mount Pleasant postal centre and right next to Finsbury town hall. We decided to go there and even if we couldn't get much done that day, at least we could get ourselves through the bureaucracy and discover how the system worked. But it was nowhere near a Tube station, so we got the Drain to Bank and managed to find a bus that took us up Farringdon Road on its way to King's Cross.

The Family Research Centre was right on the corner of Myddelton Street and Garnault Place, appearing unobtrusive mainly because of the excitable Restoration-Revival architecture of Finsbury town hall, which contrasted even more noticeably with the restrained, almost triangular buildings of the Georgian period between Exmouth Market and Tysoe Street. Within fifty yards, London's strange architectural heritage was neatly summed up.

Inevitably, there were bureaucratic requirements at the Family Research Centre – and it was busier than we'd expected. I hadn't realised how popular genealogy was. Most people there were middle aged, like us – but there was no one I recognised, nor anyone who gave the slightest impression that they were interested in us, let alone actually watching us. If somewhere like this wasn't being watched, I wondered how the writer of the letter would discover whether we'd stopped our researches or not.

Having received our passes and been given brief instruction how to look for death certificates, we decided to look for a relatively easy one – someone with an uncommon name, Samuel Rust. Within half an hour, we'd identified his death certificate and learnt that he'd died of pneumonia at his home in Tunbridge Wells in 1901. Other unusual names followed. By the end of the afternoon, we'd ruled out both Gerard and Charles Culpeper and Fernyhough, the Exciseman – as victims, at any rate. All appeared to have died in their beds in unsuspicious circumstances. By the time the office closed, we hadn't got through the Dromgooles or the Barfoots… I'd insisted Rosemary looked at the latter, as she kept calling them "Barfeet".

Travelling back in the rush hour - something we'd unwisely forgotten – we agreed we'd go back there the next day and see how far we could get.

But not long after we'd got home, we got a phone call from Emily.

"We've suddenly got a few days free. Would it interrupt your investigations if Greg and I had a long weekend in the flat in Deal?"

"No," I replied. "Our investigations are based in London at the moment anyway. We're currently looking through loads of old death certificates…"

"Whatever for? I wouldn't expect the dead man to have a death certificate if no one knew he was there."

"Quite so. But the only way of find out who hasn't got one is to identify all those that have. We've got a list of names from the censuses of people who were living in Sandown Terrace at the time of the censuses and basically we're going to have to check the death certificates for each of the men of similar age to that of the corpse in the attic."

"I suppose the fact that someone doesn't have a death certificate isn't complete proof the body was him?"

"No. And there may well have been people living there who moved in and out between censuses. But it's the closest we're likely to get... Your mother wants to have a word..."

I handed the phone over to Rosemary.

"We had a rather odd letter telling us to stop our investigations because it might cause problems for some people, presumably descendants of the murderer... or who benefitted from that man's death, at any rate. The letter included threats of unspecified action if we didn't desist. We haven't desisted so far... So it'd be worth your while to keep a look out, just in case. As the letter was sent to our address here, whoever wrote the letter must have a fair idea who we are... But they might think you and Greg were investigating too... So keep your eyes open, as I said."

I couldn't hear what Emily said – but guessed it was something along the lines of why didn't we let sleeping dogs lie.

"We could do. But when someone evidently knows what happened and goes to sufficient lengths not just to find our address but to travel to

Beckenham to post the letter, we find it difficult just to let it drop."

They both knew each other well enough for Emily not to pursue the point.

We spent the next couple of days at the Family Research Centre, at the end of which, and having apparently exhausted the information held there, we failed to account for the death of Jerome Barfoot, Percival Dromgoole, Mordecai Grimley, Matthew Stowe, Jacob Dunne, Horace Wells and Patrick O'Neill. It was more than we'd expected. The advice of one of the clerks at the Centre was that some of them might've been caught up in the Boer War or the First World War – and we should check military records – or, for instance in the case of a man with a name like Patrick O'Neill, it was possible he'd gone to live in the new Irish Republic and had died there.

We were getting ourselves round to the idea of a further visit to Kew, to see whether there were relevant military records there… or at least to find someone who could advise us, when we got another phone call from Emily.

"There's a letter addressed to you here at the flat. Do you want me to open it? It might be another one from the person who wrote the other letter."

"Yes, please," I replied. "But try not to damage the envelope too much…"

"I don't think it can be the same person… It's from a man who calls himself a local historian… called Frederick Challenor… He says… Let me read it out… *'Dear Mr. and Mrs. Storey, I'm led to believe that you have met Esmee Culpeper in connection with the corpus delicti which was recently discovered in an attic in the Marine Buildings. You should beware of what she has told you. Her methods are slapdash and based almost exclusively on public records, notably the archive of the "East Kent Mercury", and Culpeper family gossip. Whereas I have spent the last thirty years, undertaking painstaking research in local graveyards, church and other local records as well as interviewing almost every elderly person who has dwelt in Deal. I have spoken with several people who were alive at the time which interests you. I realise this may just seem like me blowing my own trumpet. However, I will give you something to test Esmee Culpeper and myself. She considers that the Marine Buildings, formerly Sandown Terrace, were built in the mid-nineteenth century, whereas in fact they were constructed towards the end of the eighteenth century. You may wish to check that fact in the Land Registry or in the Deal Museum, but it should explain why I have felt the need to write to you. Should you wish to pursue your enquiries with a more reliable local historian, I am at your disposal, at the above address and on Deal 7234466, Yours sincerely, Fredk Challenor.'* I don't think that could possibly be the same person, do you?"

"No. It doesn't sound like it. It sounds like it'd be worth us getting in touch with him."

I explained to Rosemary.

"At least he can scarcely be ruder to me than Esmee Culpeper was…"

"Perhaps he'll speak only to you and ignore me instead?"

8. A LOCAL HISTORIAN AND AN ANTIQUARIAN BOOKSELLER OF OLD DEAL

I phoned Frederick Challenor and agreed to meet him on the following Tuesday. Emily and Greg were returning to London that day, so we thought it'd be nice to have lunch with them by the sea. We ate in the cafe at the end of the pier, not least because it had a good range of plain English food and was cheap. I enjoyed the feeling of sitting in a place which felt remarkably like an old-fashioned transport café, but was actually well over a hundred feet out to sea. And the scampi, peas and chips with accompanying mug – not cup – of tea was worth every penny.

While we were eating, Rosemary and I explained to Emily and Greg what we'd learnt about the Marine Buildings and the people who'd been living in them during the period when the man in the attic had been killed.

"Of course, we've now got some names of men who haven't got death certificates," explained Rosemary. "But there'll undoubtedly be explanations for most, if not all of them... In fact, we suspect that the person who wrote the letter to us is more likely to lead us to who the victim was and who did the murder."

"It seems rather odd to be so concerned about someone who was murdered over a hundred years ago. Even if your grandfather or great-grandfather was a murderer, you'd have to be on a very high-profile position for it to be a problem," remarked Greg.

"The only thing we can think of is that somehow this murder contributed to a family becoming or remaining rich, and the family of the victim might have financial claims on them. But, as you say, it could just be a matter of public reputation."

"One of the descendants is an MP – but he's a back-bench Tory," I added. "I can't see that his position could really be affected by any revelation. We need to do a bit of research on him, but unless it'd make him out to be a complete hypocrite, I can't see it doing him any real harm."

After lunch, we went in search of Frederick Challenor. He lived in a rather fine old house, called Melbourne, in Middle Street, on the corner of Farrier Street. It was an odd asymmetrical shape, built in brick in the late eighteenth century, I would've said, on three storeys plus a basement. We walked up a couple of steps to the front door and rang an elegant brass bell.

We waited for a couple of minutes and then the door was opened by a short man of around our age, with thinning dark hair and a round face disguised heavily by a long forked beard streaked with grey. He was wearing a dark red velvet smoking jacket, with a yellow-ochre coloured corduroy waistcoat and matching trousers, with a large orange velvet bow-tie.

"Frederick Challenor," he announced in a refined, plummy voice. "Mr. and Mrs. Storey, I presume? Come ye inside."

We followed him inside, up a fine oak staircase, past walls decorated by old oil paintings of Deal, into a room on the first floor which looked out over Middle Street. The room was trapezoid in shape, with the walls comprising entirely bookcases, stuffed with books of all sorts – mostly old, many leather-bound. There were four large comfortable armchairs, a small coffee table and, in the corner, a large Georgian desk with griffin feet on a ball legs and a chair in similar style. Frederick Challenor ushered us to a couple of the armchairs, which were leather and not impossibly Victorian.

"Might I suggest a cup of tea to whet our whistles?" he suggested. "It's Darjeeling. I prefer it with a few drops of lemon, but I have milk and sugar, if you prefer?"

"Just as it is for me, please," I replied. It seemed to be the best way to find out what Darjeeling tea tasted like.

"A tiny drop of milk for me, please," added Rosemary. Whatever Frederick Challenor's epicurean tastes and bachelor appearance, at least he wasn't ignoring her.

"You are investigating the corpse that was found recently in the Marine Buildings, I believe?" Challenor began.

We confirmed that was so.

"The Marine Buildings, formerly Sandown Terrace, are a curious construction. Despite what some people here would have it, they aren't a mid-Victorian construction by Jeremiah Shorne of Ramsgate, but a late eighteenth century speculative build by Daniel Frith of Sandwich. There are Regency additions and that rather horrendous Victorian excrescence at the north end, but it's essentially five family dwellings with the usual arrangements for their servants. Why Frith decided to build there, close to the old gallows, with but a mill and Sandown castle for company, I've never really comprehended. I can only speculate that the land came cheap and somehow he persuaded himself that North Deal would suddenly become fashionable for the comfortably-off burghers of Deal or Sandwich. It was plainly not convenient for the salts at the other end of town. To the south, the nearest houses would've been well over a hundred yards away and a nest of smugglers, wreckers, scavengers and fishermen.

Certainly not an area to walk through in the dark; and with caution during the day. Though one could ride through, a family in a coach might well have been more reluctant, so I've long suspected in its first years it was more used by the military of Sandown Castle. Certainly, it would've made a pleasant and convenient residence of the officers."

"But…"

"But you're more interested in what might've happened a century or so later… I wish to demonstrate my credentials. Miss Culpeper pores through other people's histories of Deal. Old maps and every edition of the *East Kent Mercury*, but much of what has happened here appears in none of these. You need to talk to people who were alive at the time, those who were young, those who were already adults. I've been doing that for over forty years. Of course, not everyone's account or perception is accurate. Most aren't. But if you gather a lot, you see things from different sides, can correlate and sift. Let's take an example – the dispute between Headmaster Jerome Barfoot and Assistant Master Percival Dromgoole. If the account in the *East Kent Mercury* is to be believed, there was some sort of agreement between the pair of them when the school was originally founded, Barfoot claiming it was verbal and vague, whereas Dromgoole claimed it was written and specific as to his opportunity to purchase

Barfoot's share of the school, not just Number 4 Sandown Terrace, but also the title to the school. But immediately we have to ask ourselves, why Barfoot would've agreed to such a contract. He was an experienced teacher, whereas Dromgoole had barely left his crammers'. Barfoot had the name, reputation and, more to the point, his own money to purchase Number 4 Sandown Terrace. Dromgoole, on the other hand, had virtually no money of his own and no reputation, and singularly little experience. So, other than a throw-away remark – which might well have referred to ten or twenty years' hence – why would Barfoot sign a written contract, allowing Dromgoole to buy him out within a few years?"

"So Dromgoole was a liar?" observed Rosemary.

"Not necessarily. Some of the folk I've spoken to suggest there are several possibilities. The first is that Dromgoole may not have had much money of his own, but he had access to lots and it's not inconceivable that the conversation which may or may not have led to some sort of contract was related to a substantial price to be paid for Barfoot's share... a lot more than Barfoot ever expected Dromgoole to come up with. So when he did, he reneged on their agreement – mainly because it was completely unanticipated. Another possibility is that there was never anything other than a vague conversation, but that Dromgoole had something over Barfoot, which he was prepared to use against him if he didn't agree to sell. In the event, he didn't use it and he only gained what he wanted a few years after the court case. It was the supposition of many that Barfoot initiated the case to call Dromgoole's bluff… and to an extent he succeeded. At the very least, he put off the fateful day… The suppositions were mainly of a distasteful nature concerning Barfoot's unhealthy relationships with some of his pupils… In a way you could see where that might come from. It's said he used to take all the boys for a swim naked in the sea every day of the year, claiming it was extremely beneficial for their health. But the sight of master and boys naked was always likely to make tongues wag… And now, of course, there's the possibility that Barfoot had something to do with this body in the attic of Number 3 Sandown Terrace…"

"Though we should remember, Barfoot owned Number 4 Sandown Terrace and there's no evidence he had access to Number 3."

"If I were you, I'd get some tests done on the attic walls. You realise that in Middle Street you could travel virtually the whole length of the street through the attics or cellars to escape the Exciseman. But if you examined the attics, they'd appear to have solid brick walls between every house. It was mostly the same in the cellars."

"But suppose Barfoot was in some way connected to the body in the attic – why didn't Dromgoole pursue it in court when he had the opportunity? Why did Barfoot call his bluff? Isn't it more likely that Dromgoole threatened to claim he was a paedophile, but realised he'd got no evidence when it came to court and backed down?"

"It certainly seems likely he'd gotten no evidence – or not enough. But maybe he had witnesses who were dissuaded from testifying... something which has been mentioned to me by a couple of people... in relation to his misdeeds with his pupils – not the dead man – you understand."

"From what we've heard about him, I could see Dromgoole threatening witnesses, but that doesn't seem consistent with Barfoot's character."

"I was thinking more about the men who were backing Dromgoole. After all, if the name of the school was tainted by that sort of allegation, parents might prefer to send their young sons elsewhere. It's not as though there wasn't competition... both in Walmer and Sandwich."

"So who were these shadowy figures who were backing Dromgoole? Have your sources got any suggestions?"

"Plenty of suggestions, but nothing you could really call the sort of evidence you could use in a court of law. But obviously, one of those mentioned was Samuel Rust... and another Charles Culpeper..."

"Esmee Culpeper told us that Dromgoole made an offer for Number 2 Sandown Terrace and subsequently harassed him. Why would he do that if Culpeper was backing him?"

"As I said, these are what old men told me. There was nothing certain... Another name mentioned was a local solicitor called Hubert Jessop, who owned several properties, mostly in North Deal. Other names mentioned, like Wilfred Fellows and Reginald Davies, were in people's minds purely because they were well-known to be rich and interested in acquiring property in Deal. But, as the property at Numbers 3 and 4 Sandown Terrace continued to be used as a school until the first war, it seems to me that Dromgoole's backers were content for it to be used for such purposes, when undoubtedly they could've made more money converting it to lodgings."

"Do you know what happened to Barfoot and Dromgoole? We've found no record of the deaths," Rosemary continued.

"After he sold out to Dromgoole, Barfoot left the district. Part of the agreement was that he wouldn't open a school that'd be in competition with

Dromgoole. No one really knows where he went – and, of course, for historians of Deal, his departure means he's no longer of much interest to us. People said he'd gone to Margate, Rochester, then Ashford, possibly even to London… And Dromgoole seems to have got lost in the fog of war, as they put it. The school was closed in early 1915, when it became clear the war was going to last and the premises would be required for military purposes. As he almost certainly didn't own the premises, he probably got little compensation… and the real owners would've hung on to the title to the property… but you'll need to check with Land Registry records about all that sort of thing. It's not really an area of much interest to me… Of course, Dromgoole and Barfoot would've been too old to have been conscripted and Dromgoole evidently found somewhere else where he could feather his nest. By 1918, he was definitely away from Deal and never returned. The school never re-opened and my knowledge about him dissipates."

"But you have no more specific knowledge about what made Barfoot eventually agree to sell to Dromgoole even after the court case?"

"No one had any direct evidence of course. The gossip at the time was that Dromgoole finally got something on Barfoot that he couldn't deny… the same suggestions about untoward relationships with some of his pupils. Incontrovertible evidence would've compelled Barfoot to sell... But a few suggest that Dromgoole's backers were prepared to put forward yet more money and Barfoot knew a good deal when he saw one. Again, if you can track down the Land Registry material, you may be able to compare the price which appears to have been paid for Number 4 Sandown Terrace with the price paid for similar properties – not least what Hubert Jessop paid for Number 2... You'll understand I haven't delved into this in much depth. It's very much an aside to my main areas of interest, which are more to do with the centre of Deal, the Navy, and the Marines. The discovery of this body starts to make it more interesting, "

"From your knowledge of the town at that time, do you have any ideas as to who it might be?"

"No doubt you will've made the same deductions. The manner of hiding the body suggests it was intended that the body shouldn't be found, at least for quite a long time. This indicates to me that if the body was found, there would be an obvious link to the murderer. It also suggests that the individual wasn't someone who'd be missed... or not missed quickly. So – a man without family or close friends. You can always fob off acquaintances with a tale that someone has taken a job elsewhere in the country, but not family or close friends who would've expected to have been informed. Most servants to families like the

Rusts would've been local, but Jacob Dunne who was one of Rust's servants, was an orphan and Horace Wells, who was a servant in either Number 3 or Number 4, wasn't local. No one knew where he came from, but he was apparently an exceptionally capable handyman – could fix anything – but he disappeared as mysteriously as he'd arrived. One the other hand, no one ever said anything about him other than extremely favourable. Beyond them… Mordecai Grimley, Matthew Stowe, Peter Dent, William Fernyhough and Patrick O'Neill would all be possibilities. None had local ties… even the servant Grimley is supposed to have come from Dover…"

"I reckon Grimley would be too young," I observed. "He was only 19 in 1901 and the body in the attic is thought to be of an older man… and 1901 is at the very latest end of the range the pathologist gave us for the time of death."

"You may well be right. But none of the others had local roots… And whether they had friends or acquaintances in the area, I can't really say. None of them were really much known to the people I've been conversing with over the last forty years. If someone had gone missing, there was a custom for many years of friends to publish a short notice seeking the whereabouts – or more likely the body – of the one who'd disappeared. Naturally, in all cases I've ever heard about and the notices I've seen, the missing person was expected to have drowned at sea. Most of such notices perished long since... But a few remain, much cherished by those who collect such ephemera... So I wouldn't hold out much hope of anything in that direction. Many of these transient lodgers may have had no friends or family locally... And few would have many good words to say about Fernyhough – but then he was an Exciseman, so what would you expect? But I imagine the Commissioners of Excise might've noticed if he'd just gone missing."

"I'd expect so. At that time and much later, the Commissioners held strongly to full and accurate records... And in any case, we've found his death certificate. So unless someone started to impersonate him, we can safely say he wasn't the corpse."

"Of course... It was said to me by someone you had a background in Customs and Excise."

I wondered who that might've been, but I'd already worked out that it wouldn't be productive to ask.

"Are there any records we could get hold of that might tell us more?" asked Rosemary.

"Not really. You'll get some idea of who actually owned these places and what they paid for them from the Land Registry, if you're lucky. You can't count on everything being there, I fear. Otherwise, if you've perused the *East Kent Mercury* and been through the censuses and checked births, marriages and deaths, there's little else. If you look through the local antique shops, you might find the occasional document of old Deal, but the chances of it being relevant must be thousands to one, I imagine. There's an excellent little bookshop in Beach Street, almost opposite the Royal Hotel, which has lots of old books, engravings, maps and other antiquarian paraphernalia. That might be worth an hour or two's consideration. The owner is immensely helpful and knowledgeable... about his stock, rather than particularly about old Deal. He isn't a local, you understand. Other than that, I believe I've told you all that could possibly be relevant... and regrettably, many of those I've spoken to over the years have now passed away, so unless you believe in séances, follow-up questions aren't possible."

That was evidently all he wished to say to us. So we rose and thanked him and he ushered us out of the house.

"These people do live in rather fine houses, I must say," remarked Rosemary as we made our way to the seafront. "But I wasn't sure he told us a lot more than we'd already worked out for ourselves. It was all circumstantial and mostly completely uncheckable."

"At least he was prepared to speak to you... Do you think it's worth looking in the bookshop he mentioned? It can't be more than a hundred yards or so from here."

"Why not."

So walked along Beach Street as far as the Royal Hotel. Almost opposite was "The Golden Hind", a very old-fashioned looking bookseller, where I'd previously bought a print and Rosemary a book. In the window were several prints of Deal scenes, notably the castles, the pier and nautical scenes, along with a couple of old maps. We went down a couple of steps and into the shop. As we opened the door, a small bell tinkled at the back of the shop. The owner emerged from a back room and we explained that we were just browsing, but were particularly interested in any information about north Deal, especially Sandown Terrace in the last third of the nineteenth century.

"I stock mainly books, maps and prints, as you can see," the owner explained, in a pleasant, educated accent. "I have a few old boxes of postcards, which you're welcome to look through... The books of local interest are over in this corner."

At this point an elderly beagle wandered into the main part of the shop, gave us a good sniffing, and then waited to be stroked – which we did. The dog seemed remarkably calm... and had an unmistakeable aura of learning, as though he spent his time reading all the books which surrounded him.

I looked through the books, while Rosemary took on the boxes of postcards. The books were either rather general histories of the town or related to specific things – like the castles, the Marines, the Goodwin Sands, the Navy and that curious anchorage in the Downs. I'd rather hoped there might've been a history of smuggling, but though there were chapters in a couple of the general histories of Deal, there was no great detail. I suppose that because of my career, part of me wondered whether the body in the attic of Number 3 Marine Buildings might not have been a Customs officer or Exciseman who'd got a bit too nosey and whose body had to be disposed of, so that retribution wasn't meted out on the smugglers of north Deal.

And that, in a nutshell, was our problem. The victim could easily be someone whose name was still unknown to us. There was no particularly strong reason why it should've been a resident of Sandown Terrace. Supposing as well as being an avaricious and unpleasant schoolmaster, Percival Dromgoole was also the leader of a band of smugglers… Indeed, the money used to pay for Number 3 Sandown Terrace might've come from the smugglers, who could use the top floor as a look-out and signalling place – and presumably hide contraband in the cellars. Suppose a

Customs officer had spotted Dromgoole in one of his nocturnal smuggling excursions and Dromgoole had felt it necessary to kill him and dispose of the body so it couldn't be found? It plainly couldn't be William Fernyhough, as we'd found his death certificate – one of those who died in the great flu epidemic of 1919, at home in Lewes. But there would've been plenty of other Customs and Excise officers trying to catch the smugglers in those years. And though the Commissioners would undoubtedly have noticed when one of their officers went missing, if nobody could be found, there was only a limited amount that could be done… and perhaps the fact that a Customs officer was missing wasn't the sort of thing that would necessarily be reported in the *East Kent Mercury*. But I wasn't sure where I might learn about missing persons…

"For quite old buildings, it's slightly surprising that Sandown Terrace featured so little in engravings of Deal," observed the bookshop owner. "It's one reason why I suspect people don't realise quite how old they are. I've always suspected that whoever built them thought they could copy the fine buildings that were on what's now known as Prince of Wales Terrace… But North Deal was a lot rougher than that part of town and a long way from anywhere… And not the most favoured area… If you can see on this map of 1698, it's close to where the gallows used to be."

"That - and those other maps – are very fine," I replied. "If had a permanent base here, I think I'd be leaving your shops with them... and a couple of the engravings... You don't have any with any Customs vessels in them, do you?"

"I had one in a few months ago... a Customs cutter in the Downs around 1850, but it was snapped up pretty smartish... I guess there are plenty of Customs people who live hereabouts... Not that Deal sees much of them these days, other than a modern cutter coming past occasionally. Compared to a century or so ago, Deal is a respectable, law-abiding town these days."

"There aren't any books specifically about north Deal, are there?"

"Not that I know of. The centre of life in Deal was the Navy and then the Marines... Of course, smuggling was important for a long time, but by its nature, it's not the sort of thing where people keep records or talk too much about what they've been up to, so when you read about it, it tends to be gossip, tall tales and a certain amount of architectural discoveries."

"And presumably there are no archives of letters or private papers going back to the last century?"

"Not that I'm aware of. People tend to burn most of that sort of material or throw it away. Have you kept any of your parents' or grandparents' private papers? I know I haven't – and I'm an antiquarian as well as a bookseller."

"No. I can't say I have. I probably should've done. I now realise I know remarkably little about their lives before my memories start. All I've got are a couple of photo albums, including many pictures of people who are completely unknown to me... and my parents weren't ones for adding any descriptions of their photos."

"And, of course, people don't tend to say much on the back of postcards either," added Rosemary, looking up from one of the cardboard boxes. "Apart from 'wish you were here' or telling Auntie Ethel that they've arrived safely."

"It was rather a long shot... I assume you've not found anything?"

"There are a couple which might or might not be relevant. Unfortunately, the postage stamps have been smeared so I can't read the dates. One is addressed to Mrs. Eleanor Stowe of Bexley, Kent. It says that she's having a nice time, as per usual, but she tried to see Matthew, but only another lodger was there and he said Matthew was away... It's signed Doris Whittle, a name which means nothing to me... But I recall Matthew Stowe was one of the lodgers in Number 4 Sandown Terrace in the 1871 census, but not in 1881, when the place was empty… But, of course, he could've been away when the census was taken. I suppose it might've been him referred to in the postcard… It's a picture of Deal Castle on the front."

"It's a pity the date isn't clearer, but that's completely indecipherable," I said, peering at the postmark. "What about the other one?"

"It's from 'Rebecca' to Hannah Groth of an address in Clapton, London. '*Avram came down here on business with a man called Percy. Seems to have concluded it. I'll be glad to get home. A dull town with a grey sea and a bitter wind*'. The only reason for any interest is that Dromgoole seems to have been known as Percy and we know he had anonymous financial backers for his purchase, first of Number 3 Sandown Terrace from Samuel Rust and then Number 4 from Jerome Barfoot."

"That seems stretching it to snapping point, but we might as well buy both postcards… You never know… and at least it shows us what Sandown Castle used to look like…"

"Actually, I have a contemporary photograph of it with various military personnel shortly before they started to demolish it," observed the antiquarian bookseller. "It's not a brilliant photograph, even for those days… but it's pretty well unique so it's got quite a high price…"

"£50 is a bit more than we'd really want to spend… But do you have any engravings or maps of north Deal?"

"There is a late eighteenth century engraving over here somewhere… There is it… There… You can see the windmill and the top of Sandown Castle… You can tell it was a fairly rum part of the world. Central and South deal were considerably more salubrious… I could do this one for £20."

"It's quite interesting to see what it looked like before Sandown Terrace was built… It certainly looks as though it must've stuck out like a very sore thumb when it was originally built," remarked Rosemary. "We could get it as a present for Emily and Greg… She's interested in the history of the area, even if he's not."

"I like the men cooking – fish presumably – on the beach and that closed cart that looks like a bathing hut…" I said.

"Much too early for bathing huts, of course," said the antiquarian bookseller.

"I suppose it was to carry stuff which was ferried in by small ships from bigger ones at anchor in the Downs," I concluded. "It doesn't look very busy, but then I suppose the engraver wasn't trying to capture the day-to-day life of the place…"

There seemed to be nothing else there relevant to our enquiries, so we bought the engraving of North Deal and made our way back to the flat.

"He was a pleasant man," observed Rosemary. "And as helpful as he could be. I've never been wholly convinced that the two local historians told all that they knew... or thought they knew... It might be that it was just tittle tattle, but I felt both of them were holding something back."

"I suppose they might be concerned that we'd steal their thunder," I replied. "But, as you say, he was a pleasant man... I must say there's a bit of me that'd quite like to work in a shop like that. I know my father would've been horrified, but I love the sight and smell and feel of those old leather-bound books. There were a couple all about London and its suburbs just after the mid-nineteenth century that looked really interesting. But there were probably at least two dozen which I'd enjoy working my way through... and if I lived in Deal, I reckon I'd be after at least half a dozen of those engravings and three or four old maps too."

"In its way, Deal is a rather unassuming town, but it's closer to history in a way that Budleigh Salterton never was. I don't think I'd swap our flat for Emily's, not least because of the weather, but there's more to do here, while Budleigh Salterton really is for relaxing.

I hope Emily and Greg will try to get to know Deal really well. I think it'll repay the effort."

We made ourselves a mug of tea – with tea we'd brought with us. Emily and Greg tended to drink Earl Grey or fruit teas which weren't, to coin a phrase, our cup of tea at all.

"So what else can we do to narrow down the men whose deaths haven't been recorded?" I asked.

"I suppose we could try to track them through subsequent censuses. But ideally you need to know where they were living… It's a pity all this stuff hasn't been put onto a computer database somewhere like the Public Records Office, so you could just key in a name and perhaps date of birth and pull up all the information on a screen. Of course, you'd get a fair number of people with the same name, but you could eliminate them much faster than having to go the extremely long way round that looks like our only route."

"And if they changed their names, you couldn't track them down anyway… I don't know whether you can just change your name, or whether you have to do it officially so it gets recorded? Do you?"

"From what I recall, if you want to change your name, you can do it officially by deed poll and it'll be recorded, but you don't have to… and I guess in the nineteenth century people were less likely to go down the official route… Besides, the reasons why you might be wanting to change your name might well mean you wouldn't want the change to be done officially… and I doubt when you died back then anyone checked whether the name you were known by when you died was the same as you were born with."

"I suppose we could check the official records just to see if any of our men are in them… Anyone we can knock off our list could help…"

"Always assuming it wasn't someone who never lived in the building, but was concealed there – possibly even by someone who didn't live there either."

"I agree that's possible. But we know it wasn't done when the buildings were being constructed. So it'd have to be someone with access to the attic who wouldn't seem out of place or be challenged. And getting a dead body right up there from out of the street without someone noticing or asking questions would be quite an accomplishment, it strikes me."

"So, on your theory, the man was killed in the building… presumably in Number 3… and probably not far from where the body was hidden?"

"Or next door, if there's any evidence of the wall between the attic rooms having been rebuilt… And if we can, we ought to go up there again while we're here and just check that out. If there's no evidence that the walls between two and three and four and three haven't been rebuilt, I think that rules out the murder having taken place in either two or four. And would you really take the risk of carrying a body from the next door building all the way up to the attic in Number 3 and then bricking it up? After all, as far as we can tell, Number 3 has been lived in continuously…"

"Apart from when Dromgoole bought it – in a manner of speaking – from Samuel Rust. Didn't the *East Kent Mercury* suggest that there was a time when Number 3 was being prepared for use as a school after being a family home previously?"

"I think you're right… That was probably the only time in Number 3 when someone might've been able to get into the building with a body in sack, say, without being challenged… and could claim it was sand or cement for some building work upstairs… and bricks and mortar going in, even some rebuilding of walls, wouldn't've seemed odd and could've been unnoticed."

"So that might indicate when the body was hidden then. But we shouldn't rule out the possibility that it happened when Rust was still there… Your suggestion about a wronged maid or her revengeful fiancé could be right, and anything untoward might well have happened at the top of the house. Rust's family would hardly shop him to the police. And when it was used as a school, there could well have been times when only Dromgoole, and perhaps the odd servant or assistant master, were on the premises, so there could've been opportunities later... But I agree that would've been a time when the risks of concealing a body in that way were least... But it doesn't really help us to find out whether it was someone who lived in the buildings or not, of course."

"Unfortunately, I can't help feeling that the best way of finding out who was killed and who was responsible is to track down who sent us the threatening letter... and we may only get further with that when the person undertakes the threatened action, whatever it is."

"Not a very welcome thought!"

9. THREATENED ACTION IS TAKEN

We decided there wasn't much more we could do in Deal at present, so we'd travel back on the train the following morning, taking the opportunity to try out one of the restaurants that had taken our fancy. We'd walked past "Dunkerleys" a couple of times and decided we'd give it a try. When we got there, we discovered it was more of a fish restaurant than we'd bargained for – not being great fish-eaters – but we had an enjoyable meal anyway. We felt we'd eaten more than usual, so we walked along the promenade to Deal Castle and when we reached the pier, walked along it to get a bit more exercise and to let the strong breeze refresh us. Naturally, we looked towards the Marine Buildings, which we could just about make out in the twilight.

Oddly enough, it looked as though there was a fire in front of them. From where we were, it was impossible to tell whether the fire was in front of the buildings on the road or on the beach – where we'd seen families occasionally have a fry up, often with fish they'd just caught.

"That's quite a fire!" I said, succinctly stating the obvious.

"Odd place for one!" replied Rosemary. "That looks like a car on fire. I hope there hasn't been an accident along there… It looks pretty well right outside the Marine Buildings."

We plainly had the same thought, without needing to say anything, as we both suddenly speeded up our pace, as we almost jogged back to the Marine Buildings. As we reached the Coast Guard station, we realised that it was indeed a car on fire right outside the Marine Buildings. Of course, it couldn't be ours, as we'd travelled down to Deal by train, but the uncomfortable feeling surged up inside me that it was too much of a coincidence that this should occur at the same time we were staying in the flat there. The fire brigade was already at the scene and rapidly put the fire out.

"Yobbos, I reckon," opined the fireman we spoke to. "Deal has its share of 'em… Not had a burnt-out car on the sea-front in a while though."

"Nobody was hurt, presumably?" asked Rosemary.

"No. They probably stuck a lighted rag into the petrol filler and scarpered down one of the side streets."

We went upstairs to the flat.

"You realise that was an Escort, just like ours," said Rosemary. "And from what I could see, it seemed to be the same colour… and it wasn't there when we left to go to the restaurant… So someone drove it there and then set fire to it… That wasn't yobbos – that was someone carrying out their threat to take action if we continued with our investigations of the body in the attic."

"That was my thought too. I thought there might've been a note somewhere pointing that out to us."

"Let's just hope they've only set fire to an old Escort and we don't get home to find ours in a similar state."

That was an even more uncomfortable thought. But it seemed to me that without some sort of note explaining that if we continued to investigate the body in the attic, the next stage in the action would be more damaging to us personally in some way, it could just be a coincidence.

Needless to say, we caught an early train back to Beckenham the following morning and were initially relieved to find our car untouched. However, there was a similar letter to the previous one awaiting us. *"I fear that you have failed to take my previous communication sufficiently seriously. You are fortunate that I am reluctant to damage valuable property or hurt people. But if you do not desist, you should expect that reluctance to be overcome. I fail to see that this investigation serves any purpose, other than to fulfil your frustrations that you are no longer employed in your former professions or otherwise some morbid curiosity. But it may affect in a harmful manner others who have led blameless lives. I therefore regard it as entirely reasonable to demand that you desist your investigation forthwith or more direct action will be taken: have no doubts on that score."*

"Posted in Beckenham again, I see," I remarked.

"And dated yesterday… I suppose it would be possible to get from here to Deal and organise setting light to that car… But it must've been carefully prepared. After all, if we're right and that Escort was the same colour as ours, someone had to find it… and evidently quite an old model… and get it there and set light to it. But whether that means they know Deal well or whether they had picked out the car a while ago somewhere else and even drove it down there needs further thought."

"And how did they know we've been continuing with our investigations? I've had no impression that we've been followed. So, someone or perhaps more than just one person has been telling other people about what we've been getting up to. The question is who, of course?"

"It seems to me it must be someone with contacts in places like the Family Records Centre or who knows people like Frederick Challenor. They can't be just hanging around places like those on the off chance we might turn up…"

"Do you reckon we should contact the police?" I asked

"I don't think the police in Deal would be very pleased if we did. They really only agreed to us getting involved on the understanding that they wouldn't be involved at all. In any case, we ought to have a think about whether we want to keep on pursuing this or not. It seems to me that the writer of the letter is clear that next time, the action will affect us more directly... That might be just setting fire to our car, or something like that... But I can't say I particularly want anything like that to happen, even if it gave us a better clue about who was behind it."

"So you want to call a halt?"

"I didn't say that. You should know me better than that. But before we decide, we need to think about the position. Do we seriously think we're going to find out who the corpse in the attic was and who killed him? If not, is it worth running the risk of having our property or possibly one or both of us injured or worse? Or is it likely that the only way we're going to find out is to encourage this person... or these people... to come after us, in the hope that we'll be able to identify them from that? Can we work out from what we know already who it might be? Or, at least, narrow down the possibilities? Are there things we could do to reduce the risk to us or to our property? For instance – are there things we could do to prevent someone breaking into the garage and setting fire to our car?"

"Always assuming they haven't planted something already. After all, the writer of the letter was evidently aware that we were in Deal and not here. So he or she knew we weren't here... Perhaps we should do a bit of checking...?"

"And also for bugs," added Rosemary. "If they were using a private detective, there are plenty of those who'd think that bugging us would be a good way of finding out what we were up to."

We had a thorough search of our house and found nothing resembling any eavesdropping equipment. But then our house was pretty secure – I had the policewoman in Rosemary to thank for that. Then we went out to the garage to have a look at the car.

"I think someone has been in here," observed Rosemary. "Can you see those marks on the top of the garage door... There, in the middle?"

"Yes."

"Though these up-and-over doors are fairly secure, you can open them from the inside without unlocking them, as you know. Well, I reckon someone has lowered some sort of hook on a wire and hooked the mechanism inside and opened the door. I think it's the wire that's scraped away the paint just there."

"You don't think there's some sort of exploding device attached to the door?"

"No. But we can have a peep through the side window and see what we can see. It'd be rather a jump from setting light to an old wrecked car to blowing us up, it seems to me."

We made our way to the side window and could see nothing suspicious. So I opened the garage door – extremely gingerly. But nothing untoward happened. We went inside and examined the car. We opened the doors, boot and bonnet.

"If anyone has done anything to the engine, I really couldn't tell," I remarked. "I just put in oil, water and keep the tyres at the right pressure."

"From what I can see of the cables, nothing has been cut…"

"I'll look on the ground. Presumably if anyone had cut the brake cables some fluid would leak out… There doesn't look like anything… But I'll squeeze under the car, just to be sure…"

I wriggled underneath the car, realising that I was getting the top of my head, forehead and parts of my clothes filthy with oil, grease and dust. But I couldn't see anything.

"I couldn't see anything odd there," I said, getting back to my feet.

"Let's think about this," continued Rosemary, wiping oil off my forehead with a rag. "Let's assume we're right and someone had broken into the garage. You can't get into the house from here. The last incident was setting fire to a car. Is it reasonable to expect the person would do something similar? Since this garage is so small, all we can put in it is the car, the toolbox and a few cans of paint and brushes. I've looked at them. None of them have anything suspicious about them. In any case, if you want to set a car on fire reliably, you really need to ignite the petrol. So you have to put an incendiary device somewhere between the engine and where the petrol goes in... Did you check under the petrol tank?"

"Assuming I know what it is – and I'm pretty sure I am – there was nothing suspicious there."

"Of course, they might just have been having a trial run to see if they could get in. But doing it once is a bit risky. Doing it twice would be twice as risky... and they can't be sure when we might next be away... What's that little bit of wire poking out by the petrol cap? It's only about a quarter of an inch long, but why do you need any wire there?"

"I've never noticed any wire then when I've filled up."

"Nor me… Careful!"

I looked at the wire and realised that it seemed to be wound round the petrol cap. Extremely carefully, I unwound it.

"Do you think it might be some sort of booby trap?" I asked.

"That seems unlikely," Rosemary replied. "After all, I doubt whoever has gone to all this trouble wants some explosive device to go off when we're filling up at a petrol station – the only time logically when we'd be removing the petrol cap. I suspect it's a radio-controlled incendiary device and the wire is its aerial."

With great care, I opened the petrol cap and gently drew out a small electrical device which had been attached to the top of the petrol tank with blu-tak.

"A neat little thing," observed Rosemary. "I guess when it gets the radio signal from the transmitter it sparks and that in the petrol vapour in the tank, that'd set off an explosion."

"So they could blow up the car with us in it at any time?"

"I guess so. But from what we've seen so far, I doubt that was the intention. But let's get this thing well away from the petrol and think what this tells us."

I closed the petrol cap as Rosemary took the device into the back garden.

"I think I've neutralised it," she said. "But otherwise, we should keep it as potential evidence... If you look at it, it's plainly not home-made. This is a commercial device. So whoever is doing this either has some quite detailed knowledge of this sort of thing or is employing someone else who does."

"And I imagine you can't just walk up someone's drive and fish an up-and-over door open in a matter of seconds. So I reckon whoever did it must've had some cover – a van perhaps? And parked it in our drive, in front of the garage. And could we assume that they did it when they were here yesterday?"

"We could ask the neighbours... But I doubt the people in the corner house could see anything... And I think they both work anyway."

"OK. I'll see if Mr. and Mrs. Fox are in next door..."

"And I'll see whether I can find out where I might find out more about this device... like its range, for instance... And I reckon I know who to ask. There was a DS called Jim Ball who was seconded to us eight or nine years ago when we needed to eavesdrop on some particularly fly fraudsters… He was one of the Met's experts on electronics and that sort of thing. I know he retired a year or so after me, but the Met personnel people should be able to track him down for me… He could tell us not just about this device, but probably where it was bought."

"So we're pressing ahead?"

"If someone decides they're going to employ criminals to break into my house and try to blow up my car, yes, I bloody well am!"

"Criminals?"

"Planting this device was plainly done by a professional. Assuming it was some sort of private detective or something of the sort, most of them are ex-police. I believe they'd draw the line at getting involved in blowing up someone's car… especially a former colleague. They might bug you, but not do something that might risk you getting killed. So this has been done by some rogue or other – and if whoever is behind this wishes to do that sort of thing, they deserve to be pursued. They've already committed crimes, even if they were entirely innocent of the murder of the man in the attic."

Reflecting that perhaps this was the point at which we should inform the local police, but recognising that this wasn't the right moment, I made my way round to our next-door neighbours – Mr. and Mrs. Fox. Ever since we'd moved next door, they'd been friendly enough, but polite and formal. Evidently, they didn't expect to invite us in – and we felt it would be uncomfortable if we didn't reciprocate. In any case, our conversation was short. They'd seen a crimson van – probably a Ford Transit – parked in our drive late morning yesterday. Mrs. Fox thought they must be fixing a problem with our garage door. They were there for about twenty minutes or so and then drove away.

Rosemary was on the phone when I got back. After she'd finished her conversation, she explained that she'd managed to contact Jim Ball, who lived in Upper Norwood and said he'd call in the afternoon. Rosemary wasn't in the right frame of mind to discuss taking the matter to the police. I thought I'd wait – not least because Jim Ball might well make the same suggestion.

"It's all very well placing something like that so that you can set a car alight remotely without intending to hurt anyone," she muttered. "But who knows whether it couldn't've been set off by an electronic signal when we were driving along somewhere?"

While we were waiting for Jim Ball to arrive, we got a phone call.

"If this is some anonymous warning, they're going to get a piece of my mind," declared Rosemary, picking up the receiver.

Evidently it wasn't. Rosemary said little during the phone call and put the receiver down.

It was the pathologist, Julia Radford. "They've been looking through the stuff we left with them, as well as doing further studies on the corpse," she explained. "They can't really narrow down the time of death more than they have already... The bricks and mortar are contemporary with the time of death – not the building itself. So the man was definitely bricked up there between 1880 and 1900. They think that the scraps of paper we found were some official document referring to the Excise – but there's no reason to indicate that they had anything to do with the dead man. Indeed, the paper and ink were from some fifty years earlier. So she thinks it was just some scrap paper that'd been left around in that part of the attic... But she also now feels she made too much of the bones on the man's right side... Some of the wear and tear was from the way the body had been lying, she now thinks. Though he had engaged in some manual labour, she doesn't think the damage to his muscles and bones was such to have made him walk with a limp or anything like that. But other than that, the stuff we left doesn't add anything – not even those nails and the pen nib… and, of course, provided they weren't made after the time the body is supposed to have been put there, they aren't really relevant and might've just been lying around there anyway."

"Well, I suppose it's not a step backwards, at any rate. If she'd found that the pen nib was from the 1920s at the earliest, we'd be having to look at some completely different evidence."

"I guess they've got something useful from all that extra work. I'm not sure we have… I'm sorry. I'm still annoyed about someone being so irresponsible as to put a device like that in our petrol tank… The writer of those letters comes across as quite genteel and reasonable. Yet he or she is prepared to hire criminals to do something that is thoroughly dangerous – not just to us, but to anyone near our car if the device got triggered accidentally…"

"I guess whoever it is didn't envisage something like that…"

"If you employ crooks, you're responsible for whatever crimes they commit or stupid actions they carry out."

"And we need to remember that. Assuming we're going on with this without telling the police, we're going to have to be a hell of a lot more careful than we have been."

"Quite so."

Jim Ball arrived at about 4pm. He was tall and quite thin, with the look of a scrawny tortoise who had somehow managed to shed his shell. After the normal pleasantries had been exchanged and Rosemary had explained a bit of the background, he took the device into the back garden and examined it carefully.

"You never quite know what these things are going to do, so it's always best to check them out in the open air," he explained. "With a gas boiler and gas fires, you don't want anything going off indoors."

He continued peering at it and fiddling with bits of it, with a pair of tweezers and a couple of tiny screwdrivers.

"It's the sort of thing you'd use for a big firework display, when you don't want to get too close… especially when you can't be sure whether everything around you has gone off or not…" He continued. "The range is no more than fifty to sixty feet… You say it was in your car in the garage? I guess you could be parked around the corner or in the park the other side of the road to detonate it. You'd certainly be able to tell whether there was anyone around or not before you detonated it."

"Could it go off accidentally while someone was driving the car?" asked Rosemary.

"Theoretically – but it'd be extraordinarily unlikely. About one in fifty thousand chance, I'd say."

"Where would you lay your hands on something like this?"

"Specialist shops. As I said, these are used legally for firework displays. So the makers of large firework packs will stock these. Illegally, there will be several suppliers in London alone, but you'd need to know where to look… and you couldn't just walk in to one of these places and ask for something like this. They'd have to know you… or you'd need a good introduction from the right person. In the circumstances you've told me about, I'd say it's most likely these people are using a private detective to keep tabs on you… and he has connections who can get him stuff like this… for a price, naturally."

"And, of course, they aren't the type of place where you could walk in and see anything… And you certainly couldn't go in and ask who'd been buying stuff like this recently."

"Not unless you're the police… and even then, unless you've got something on them to put some pressure on, they'd be unlikely to tell you anything… And why haven't you put this in the hands of the local police? From what you've said, whoever is behind this may be reluctant to use violence, but once you start using people with fewer moral scruples, you lose control and anything can happen."

"I can't see what the local police could do – other than advise us to stop what we've been doing. And we can do that without their involvement."

"Hmmm… From what I heard about you, you weren't very keen on letting anything go unless the Commissioner himself ordered you to… and probably not even then."

"That's a bit of an exaggeration, but I recognise what you say… I don't like being threatened, and before we need to decide whether we just desist, as the person who's been writing to us has told us to do, there's some thinking we can do, without appearing to do anything more. At the end of that process, we'll have to decide."

"Well, just remember, you're dealing with at least one professional criminal here… one who's sufficiently well-connected to be able lay his hands on a device like this… If I were you, I'd also assume that if there's a private detective involved, he'll be trying to eavesdrop… But if you give me a day or so, I'll drop off a little gizmo that should help you spot whether anyone has put something in your house or car… It won't pick up the most sophisticated stuff, but I doubt anyone using a device like this is going that much upmarket."

We gave him a mug of tea and our thanks.

"I think we need to consider who we've been talking to between the first and second letters and whether that gives us a better idea of who might be behind this," suggested Rosemary, shortly after he'd driven away.

"Can we rule out Julia Radford? She rang us – and though we didn't tell her that we weren't interested any longer, we didn't tell her whether we were proceeding or not. Besides, in view of what little she told us, if she had been the person behind this, why would she have needed to call at all? I know you might say it was to cover her tracks. But not calling us would hardly expose herself… and ringing might just keep our appetites whetted. So do you reckon we could rule her out?"

"I think so. She might be in touch with others – but she didn't ring us until after the car was burnt in Deal. So I'd rule her out on those grounds too."

"A bit of Ockham's razor there, I think."

"Please be serious."

"OK. Can we also rule out Frederick Challenor on the grounds that he approached us, when he didn't need to…? And gave us a fair amount of information. He could hardly tell how much of it might be useful to us or not. If he didn't want us to proceed, he had no need to get in touch at all. Indeed, if he'd had any sense, he'd've waited to see whether we tried to contact him."

"I agree. I realise that he might've been trying to feed us some false information, but there'd be a risk we'd find out it was false – and then we'd start asking rather more pointed questions. And the person behind this wants us to stop – and the idea that he or she would offer us a tasty morsel to see whether we'd bite or not does seem very unlikely."

"But then you're looking at Rowena Warnle, Esmee Culpeper, the man in the antiquarian bookshop and someone in the Family Records Centre or one of the other places we've been to… or I suppose the unfriendly woman in the *East Kent Mercury* archives… Or perhaps someone who they know – and like to chat to about this sort of thing?"

"Can we narrow it down a bit? Where did we go, who did we see between the arrival of the first and second letters?"

"We had that abortive journey to the Public Record Office in Kew and then a couple of days at the Family Research Centre. Then we got the letter from Frederick Challenor and took the train to Deal and immediately after that we went to the antiquarian booksellers," I said, checking my notebook.

"It seems to me the possibilities are that we were seen in one of these places – either by someone watching out for us or because someone tipped off whoever is behind this that we'd been there. Or someone passed on the information that we'd been there, perhaps innocently…"

"Uh?"

"Well – suppose I know enough to realise that if we're continuing with our investigations, we'd probably go to the Family Research Centre. I might ring up and say that my friends Nick and Rosemary Storey are doing some genealogical research. I'd picked up some useful information for them, but if they'd already been to the Family Research Centre, there'd be no point in me contacting them. Would it be possibly to tell me if they'd been there? I can't see there'd be any reason why someone would refuse a request like that… It's the sort of thing you used to do, after all!"

"And the other possibilities are that one or other of the people we met – presumably excluding anyone in the Public Record Office and the Family Research Centre – is the person behind this. Or we're being bugged – either here or in Deal…"

"Or possibly in the car… I think we should get some fresh air…" Rosemary got up suddenly and led me into our back garden.

"If someone had access to garage to put that device under the filler cap, they could also have fitted a bug somewhere in the car. But if there's a bug inside the house, we don't want to let them know what we're thinking, do we!"

"No. But perhaps we should go and have a look and see whether they have been trying to bug us?"

"Let's just think about that for a moment or two… I suppose it won't be a top of the range device, if Jim Ball is right. So it wouldn't tell anyone whether we'd found it. But if we do find it and the noise activates it, we'd need to behave as though we hadn't seen it…"

"What sort of range would something like that have? Would someone have to be in a car or van somewhere reasonably near to listen in? Or might they just leave some sort of recording device somewhere and listen to whatever we'd been saying later?"

"I guess it could be either. But you'd think it'd get rather expensive to pay someone to sit around all day listening to what we might be saying…"

"I wonder what they'd do if we set off in the car? If there was no-one reasonably handy, if we suddenly decided to drive to Deal, say, we'd presumably be quickly out of range and they'd have the devil of a job trying to catch up with us – and might reveal themselves in the process."

"But presumably, they don't need to hear every word we say. If we mention in the house that we'll go down to Deal, they don't really need to hear what we have to say in the car, because if they've got the Deal flat bugged, they'd be confident they could listen to us when we got there… Anyway, it seems to me they don't need to react instantly to everything we're doing or saying. At the moment, they just need to know whether we're continuing or not. After all, we're hardly close to the name of the man who was killed or whoever killed him… And if we do find a bug in the car, we should assume there's one in the house and in Deal… and we should tailor our conversations accordingly… I feel we've already revealed more than was sensible before we started thinking about being bugged…"

So we went into the garage and examined the car. Sure enough, in a space below the never-used ashtray in between the front seats, we found an electronic device which had no obvious purpose. So we had to assume it was some kind of bug. We didn't talk while we were searching and Rosemary used a small brush to make it seem as though she was cleaning the inside of the car.

"But does that mean they've managed to bug our house?" I wondered. "We know when they got into the garage – and presumably planted both devices at the same time. But we've not seen anything that suggests anyone has managed to get into the house... and you spotted those marks on top of the garage door. So whoever did it isn't tremendously professional."

"We haven't really looked round the house. You'd think they would've done it at the same time. But Mr. and Mrs. Fox told you they were only here about half an hour. Could they have got into the garage, planted those devices, got into the house and planted at least one device there in that time? I doubt it. I suppose we could have a look to see if there's any evidence of someone trying to get inside? Otherwise, we'll just have to wait for Jim's gizmo."

We had a careful look round at the windows and doors on the ground floor and whether there was any evidence of a ladder having been used to get at the upstairs windows at the back. But we couldn't see anything. And we couldn't see how someone could've used a ladder at the front without risking being noticed by a neighbour. Though passers-by might just assume the windows were being cleaned or we were having some work done on the house, a neighbour

was more likely to remember a ladder at the front –
and though they probably wouldn't be able to
describe who was on it, it would inevitably alert our
suspicions. Presumably the writer of the letters
expected us to be alert, but also start asking questions
about how they knew what we were up to.

"I still think it'd be sensible to talk about the Deal
stuff in the garden, rather than in the house,"
suggested Rosemary. "And I think we need to talk
about what our tactics should be. We don't have
enough evidence to tell us who might be behind this
– and we shouldn't just start making assumptions at
this stage. We need to work out what we could do to
narrow down the field of suspects."

"OK. I suppose if we find a bugging device, Jim
Ball could tell us what its range would be… and
whether you could record what we said and listen to it
later or whether you'd have to stay within range of the
device?"

"We could ask. But I'm sure it must be able to
record, so someone doesn't have to hang around here
or Deal all the time. But the recording device must
have to be within range all the time. So somewhere
within the surrounding half mile or so – probably
nearer – there must be a listening and recording
device… I think I need to check with Jim whether the
gizmo he's going to bring over could detect that,
but…"

"…You'd better ring him from a call box not from the house phone…"

"I'll certainly do that… But I'm beginning to fear that when he comes with his gizmo it might be too late. If someone has managed to bug our house, our conversation with Jim will've been recorded. So they'll know he's coming back. I guess they'll assume we'll find the listening device – always assuming there is one – and our conversation will already have told them that Jim is an expert, so they'll realise we may be able to track down their listening device."

"Even if there isn't a device in the house, we know there's one in the car. So it seems likely there's a listening device somewhere in the neighbourhood…"

"So we need to try and see if we can spot where the listening device is, without alerting anyone who might be lurking in a car or van with it."

"I wonder if they're likely to try and remove the devices before Jim brings his gizmo? Assuming they don't realise we've already found a device, they might want us to come up with a blank. Then they might be able to put the bug back later. Otherwise, how are they going to find out what we're up to?"

"Well, we're assuming that they know what we've been up to because they've been listening to what we've been saying. But the bug was planted in the car while we were in Deal, so they can't have known we were going to Deal to speak to Challenor or that we spoke with him by that means… So it's still possible that they're getting their information another way… and the bug in the car was put there to make sure we were either in the car or not in the car when the explosive device was triggered."

"But in view of what the flats are like in Deal, they could probably have placed a bug there at almost any time."

"That's true… and they could remove it, of course, if they believe we'll take Jim's gizmo there to investigate."

"But I think the next thing to do is for the two of us to go for a walk… Perhaps do a little light shopping. I'll phone Jim from a callbox. Then we might go for an innocent walk around a few of the nearby streets to see if we can identify any vehicles that might be being used as a listening post…"

"And perhaps do it again later – but not too late – after the commuter cars have gone."

10. TRACKING A TRACKER

"I think we should assume, if there is someone sitting in a car listening to a bugging device, he or she will know what we look like," said Rosemary. "So, we really are going to have to look convincingly like we are going shopping or taking a walk."

"It's a pity we haven't got a dog."

"I might need to buy a collar and leash for you if you don't take this seriously!"

"OK. We need to plan a route that looks sensible. We could hardly come down Court Downs Road with bags of shopping from Sainsbury's, for instance."

"And there must be some roads round here where you probably wouldn't or couldn't park. Nearer the High Street, there are parking restrictions… and I reckon that roads like Stanmore Terrace and Burnhill Road, where the houses don't have any garages and people park out in the street, would be difficult to find a space…"

"And you probably wouldn't want to park opposite our house or too close along Manor Way…"

"So Court Downs Road looks a good bet. There are so many blocks of flats up there that a strange car or van wouldn't be noticed – provided you didn't park in one of the residents' car parks…

Unfortunately, it's not on our route coming back from the shops… Nor are Greenways or Uplands, which seem good places to park without being too obvious. From the High Street shops, the only obvious ways back are Burnhill Road or Kelsey Park and I don't think someone listening in to a bug in house will be parked in either of them."

"So we need a plausible reason for going up Court Downs Road… and not just going for a walk. Anyone who's been watching us will know we virtually never go for a walk without a reason. When we're here, it's usually shopping or going to the squash club… and staggering back afterwards."

"From what I remember, there's nothing but posh flats and a few houses in Court Downs Road. Then you come to Wickham Road, which has a garage at the Beckenham end and not much else. And though there are shops along the Bromley Road, why would we go there, rather than the High Street, which is closer and has a much better range?"

"I suppose there are no specialist shops there that we could suddenly find a need to visit?"

"I've no idea. I suppose we could go and see… To Bromley South by train and then get the bus back through Shortlands. We could always cut through along Westgate into Albemarle Road and then we'd look as though we were coming back from Beckenham Junction."

"But not today."

"No. I think we now go back into the house and talk about completely different things."

The following morning, we did what we'd proposed. We walked up the High Street and bought a couple of things in Allders before catching a bus back towards Beckenham, getting off at Oakwood Avenue and walking the rest of the way to the Bromley Road shops. It wasn't immediately apparent that there was a suitable shop for our purposes. There was a funeral directors', two take-aways, a betting shop, a newsagents-cum-general stores, a drycleaners, a video shop, a ladies' hairdressers and beauty salon, an estate agents, an off-licence, a chemists, the Oakhill Tavern, a florist and a new delicatessen – called "Quality – Naturally". Only the last seemed to have any possibilities.

We went inside. Immediately to our left was a rack with containers of every conceivable herb and spice combinations – including such exotic things as garam marsala, piri-piri spice, Chinese five spice powder, "smokey" barbecue seasoning, and so on.

"I quite like the sound of that," remarked Rosemary, pointing out a greyish-green container called "baked apple seasoning". "I really used to like baked apples when I was a child – and I don't think we've had them since then. When we get apples, we always make a crumble or a pie… mainly as an accompaniment to custard…"

"Yes – we used to have them with the core replaced by raisins and brown sugar."

"We could do that, but add this seasoning too… It's got all the spices I like in it."

"There's some mulled wine spice here… I guess it's not very different. It'd be nice to mull some red wine at Christmas. We haven't done it for years… Mainly because we couldn't get the spice… and when we tried to make up the recipe ourselves, it didn't taste very nice, if you remember."

"It looked rather strange too, as I recall."

"I think we need to look around a bit more. Neither the apple seasoning nor the mulled wine spices are the sort of thing we'd be dashing off to buy at this time of year."

We continued looking round the shop. I came across a whole lot of things I hadn't seen in years – notably a large selection of dried fruits – everything from mangoes through figs to apples and banana – and things I'd never heard of, like manuka honey, redbush tea, quinoa, tofu, spirulina powder, and so on. There were also several shelves of vitamins and assorted pills including garlic, echinacea, gingko biloba, cranberry, Korean ginseng, omega 3 fish oils, aloe vera, etc. Rosemary was looking at a selection of about thirty different sorts of flour and two dozen sorts of "healthy" breakfast cereals – none of which I recognised from any supermarket. Next to them were various healthy and/or foreign cakes and biscuits' and then a chilled counter with varieties of cooked meats including bacon and salami, at least thirty different cheeses and tiny buckets containing a dozen or more varieties of olive with various stuffings and seasonings.

"To be honest," I murmured to Rosemary. "Apart from the apple seasoning and the mulled wine spice, there's nothing I'd rush here to buy. At least, nothing I couldn't get in a supermarket."

"Not even the cheeses?"

"The only ones I couldn't get in Sainsbury's are those ones I detest – Wensleydale with added cranberries or that disgusting garlic-flavoured Boursin."

"It probably doesn't matter. I couldn't see anything that I could plausibly pretend to need. But I think I've worked out how we can get ourselves here without having to claim a sudden passion for dried apricots or quince chutney… But I think we should leave before we raise the shopkeeper's hopes any higher than they are already…"

We explained to the plump, fake-blonde young woman behind the counter that we'd be back later and made our way by a circuitous route back to our house, so that it appeared that we'd just come from the station.

"Of course," said Rosemary, "as we don't know whether the house is bugged. So somehow we need to be in the car and talk about the delicatessen… Perhaps you can turn your mind to a suitable reason for us to be in the garage…"

However, first we went back into the house and had lunch – a plain Cheshire cheese with sliced tomatoes on ordinary wholemeal bread, an apple and a mug of tea. We avoided talking about Deal, except for Rosemary to remark – in case we were being "overheard" – that it was the right decision not to risk damage to our property or ourselves by continuing with our investigations.

"Then we should probably give Emily back the keys to the flat in Deal," I replied. "I'll get them out of my pocket and put them by the phone so I don't forget to give them to her when we see her next… Oh damn! They aren't in my trouser pocket… and I was definitely wearing these jeans the last time we were in Deal…"

"Have you checked your jacket?"

I searched through the pockets of my jacket.

"No. It's not there... The only place I can think of is they fell out when I put the maps of Deal back into the car... I'll go and have a look."

I went outside and into the garage and started to look for the keys.

"Do you still use these?" I called out to Rosemary, holding up a rather mangled pair of sunglasses.

"Not anymore," she replied, coming into the garage. "I wondered where they'd gone. Where were they?"

"Down the side of the front passenger seat and almost wedged under it."

"It's a pity. If I'd known that when we were in Bromley, I could've got a new pair."

"You'd probably have forgotten anyway. You spent so much time chatting to Ursula Bolt..."

"We've known Ursula and Ken a long time. She's usually good value... It's not just idle gossip. She said there's a very good deli quite close to us on Bromley Road... I can't say I've ever noticed it when we've been driving along there... It must be quite new."

"You wouldn't notice because it's a bog-standard lot of shops - a bookies, a post office, and couple of take-aways – that sort of thing. I can't say I've noticed any delicatessen there…"

"If Ursula says it's good, it must be. Germans like her tend to be particular about their food… We ought to try it sometime."

"Is there anything we actually need from a delicatessen?"

"I don't know. Perhaps we should walk up there and see what they've got?"

"I suppose so. We can always look at the flats in Court Downs Road and decide whether we ever want to end up in one of them in our dotage."

I thought we managed that rather well," murmured Rosemary, as we left the house a few minutes later.

"Years of practice," I replied. "I assume you really do have a German friend called Ursula Bolt?"

"Yes. I met her at that evening class about genealogy. If we'd been dealing with a larger organisation I'd've been more careful, but I don't believe these people are putting in enough resources to check up on what I said."

We walked up Court Downs Road, trying to examine the various cars parked by the side of the road as we went past, paying particular attention to any vans, especially those which had no windows at the back.

"I'm sure this is the most likely place to park if someone is listening in on our conversations," remarked Rosemary. "Roads like Greenways and Uplands are too quiet and there are too many families who are likely to notice a strange car or van parked outside their front garden… But with all the flats along here, yet another parked car or van amongst those that have been left here for the day by commuters isn't really going to be noticed."

"Have you seen anything suspicious?"

"There was a grey Peugeot with someone in the front, who avoided looking at us… and a couple of closed vans where you couldn't see anyone… A white one and a light blue one."

"There was a darker blue one on the other side of the road and a Transit a couple of cars behind it."

We reached the end of the road, with our suspicions alerted to half a dozen cars and, mainly, vans. We continued on to "Quality – Naturally". And went inside to buy, if nothing else, the mulled wine spices and the seasoning for baked apples.

"And if we actually see someone with some suspicious-looking kit, what do you propose to do?" I asked.

"Nothing," replied Rosemary. "We'll get the car number and proceed from there."

"And otherwise? Do we just collect all the numbers of cars or vans we think look possible?"

"Hmmmm… I can probably call in old favours for a couple of registration numbers, but not half a dozen. I think we'd have to narrow it down."

"Easier said than done."

We bought the spices, a large slice of orange Cheshire cheese with proper rind, some green tea and a honeycomb – something I hadn't seen (and therefore not eaten) since my childhood.

"Without making it obvious that we're looking out for someone in one of these vehicles," said Rosemary just after we'd left the shop, "there's no way we can actually narrow it down. I think we just have to try and memorise the numbers of the ones we suspect… But I think we can get further. I'm assuming that if there is someone listening into our conversations, they aren't going to do it 24 hours a day. But equally, they aren't going to stop at 6 pm. So if we can somehow see which vehicles are left at, say,

8 o'clock. It could be a very late commuter, but it should narrow down the list, I hope."

"I could go for an evening jog along there… It's not my normal route, but I've run right round Kelsey Park a couple of times and I can't think we were being watched the last time I did that particular route."

We made our way back. Car numbers aren't particularly easy to remember after the first couple, especially when you aren't able to write them down. So we decided to remember three each. I would do the right-hand side of the road, Rosemary the left. All we could do was choose those vehicles that looked most suspicious – largely because they were closed vans and we couldn't see into the back. As it happened, the Peugeot had driven off, so we ended up solely remembering vans. Immediately we got home, we wrote down the registration numbers and the van colour.

"That's all we can do for now," Rosemary said. "Let's have a mug of tea in the garden."

"I assume you wanted to talk about this Deal stuff?" I asked once we were outside.

"Yes. I wanted us to think a bit more about who might be involved in this stuff messing us about. But we also need to think what we could do next to take the investigation of the body in the attic further. I was wondering about doing some searches in the Land Registry to see if we could find out who actually owned Numbers 2, 3 and 4 Sandown Terrace between about 1875 and 1900. It might tell us who Dromgoole's backers were, at least… and I'm not convinced that it mightn't be one of them whose descendant is behind these letters…"

"It should also tell us whether Barfoot sold up under some sort of duress or whether he got a fair – or even a generous – price for Number 4."

"But what else?"

"We said we'd check on any changes of name that'd been registered – though I reckon that probably won't knock too many names off our list… But if we continue to try and work out the connection between then and now, perhaps we need to check the wills of some of these people. Plainly we could search every telephone book in the country for anyone called Barfoot, for instance, and try to check them all out. But it'd be easier to look at his will and follow it through his descendants. It'd narrow down the possibilities quite a lot… and might well pick up changes of name."

"That could still leave a lot of names."

"But the wills should tell us how much people got left. It seems to me that the most likely reason someone doesn't want us to find out who was killed and who the murderer was is because it'd affect their present circumstances – which in most cases means their wealth. I realise it's possible they could be concerned about their reputation - and that'd be harder to spot, but not impossible. But if only one of the people lived there – let's say the Rust family – has passed on a fortune to his descendants, it strikes me they have the most to lose. But plainly, whoever was killed would need to have some sort of claim on that fortune. From what we currently know, that strikes me as cutting Samuel Rust out. He probably went round bonking the female servants, but unless there's the descendant of a bastard child of his, I can't see there'd be a great effect on the family wealth."

"If he had half a dozen bastards and they've been equally fertile?"

"It's a possibility. But only one bloke was killed – and he was the wrong age to be one of Samuel Rust's bastards. Otherwise, I can't see why we'd be a problem. Any of the bastards' descendants could do the genealogy and start making a claim against the family. These letters are tied to our investigation of the murder – which is why, for all his proclivities for female servants, I can't see how Samuel Rust fits the bill... Even if he bumped off a servant's boyfriend, brother or father, he's been dead the best part of a century – and I don't think a descendant of the dead man could claim compensation from Rust's descendants."

"So you think it's more likely to be the Barfoot-Dromgoole rivalry or possibly the Culpepers?"

"At this stage, yes. None of the names of anyone else suggest someone who made a fortune for themselves as the result of some murky deed while they were in Sandown Terrace… Why? What do you think?"

"The one thing I wish we could learn more about is Dromgoole's mysterious backers. Why did they back him? Barfoot seems to have been a strange man, but no-one has ever suggested he was personally unpleasant or unreasonable… and from his religious background, you'd expect him to be fairly honest. But few people have much to say in Dromgoole's favour. Yes, he could be charming, but he seems to have been a bully and untrustworthy. So why would you put your money behind him? Is it because he had something on someone and knew when to work on it to get what he wanted? And was that anything connected with the body in the attic? Other than that, I agree with you."

"If we're looking at stuff in the Land Registry or at various people's wills… Is that Somerset House, I wonder? I suppose it'll be evident to anyone who might be following us what we were up to… and if we do any obvious manoeuvrings to avoid being followed, that'd be equally suspicious."

"If we're being followed... I'm not wholly convinced that we have been... If they're using bugs, it seems to me they've just been listening to our conversations. Then, if we say we're going to meet Frederick Challenor, they could already be keeping an eye on his house... Or if the only important thing to them is whether we've stopped investigating or not, they probably don't even need to have us followed... A lot depends on whether we find a bug here and in Deal. If we don't find anything, then I'll have to revise that view. But if I was them, I wouldn't want to take the risk that we'd work out we were being followed and catch the man who's doing it. After all, he'd be nicely in the frame for stealing that car and setting light to it in Deal and also for putting the device in our petrol tank... and is he being paid enough to keep quiet about who's employing him if any pressure is applied?"

We finished our tea and went inside the house, talking about other things, including various made-up lunches and coffee-meetings with former colleagues in the centre of London. At this stage, we left dates and times unspecific, but we felt we needed to have established reasons for going to London that weren't linked to checking up the records of sales of the flats in Sandown Terrace or examining the wills of some of their residents. Of course, if there was no bug in the house, it was wasted breath.

At about 7:30PM, I set off on my jog, up Manor Way to Stone Park Avenue (off which road both Emily and Sarah had been born in a maternity hospital now demolished and replaced by flats) and along Eden Park Road, cutting through to Wickham Way by the schools, then along Wickham Way, across the Chinese Garage roundabout into Wickham Road and thence along Court Downs Road and home. I jogged in the mornings more often than not, especially since I'd retired, and always found an evening run more tiring. So I slowed up a bit coming along Wickham Way in order to be sufficiently alert to see which of our suspect cars were still parked in Court Downs Road. To my pleasure, there were two – a dark blue van and a white van, both plain, and neither with anyone visible.

But when I arrived home, I didn't mention anything about them, had a shower and changed. Then we ate, during which I marked the two cars on our list with a biro. Unsure where any bug might be, we didn't speak about it until the following morning.

"I'd quite like to see if either of those two vans are still there today," said Rosemary, as we drank some coffee, sitting on the wooden bench we'd quite recently installed in the back garden. "But at the moment, the most important thing is not to frighten them off, I think. We might do a little shopping later and I'll use the opportunity to ring a contact from a callbox… We might as well see whether either of those two numbers mean anything."

We were just about to set off when Emily called from her work, checking whether we were going to be in Deal the following weekend. Rosemary said we weren't – and it looked as though our investigations had run into a brick wall, so it was possible that we might go to the flat to pick up a few things we'd left there, but otherwise, we didn't envisage being there much, for a while at least. With any luck, that might put anyone listening off the scent… But, of course it depended on how much research they'd done on us – and therefore whether they believed we could be deterred in the way we appeared to have been.

While we were shopping at the butchers, the splendid cheesemongers and the greengrocer's stall (for some cooking apples) in Beckenham High Street, Rosemary used a callbox, presumably to phone a former colleague at New Scotland Yard. Meanwhile, I stood pretending to look in a shop window, while trying to see whether there was anyone following us. Because Beckenham High Street wasn't particularly busy at that time of day, we'd reckoned it'd be possible to spot someone trying to tail us – and so far we were fairly sure there was no one.

"Geoff got rather sniffy," Rosemary said, after she'd finished and we were walking back home. "He owes me several favours over the years, but he was muttering about data protection, as if I didn't know anything about it. He said that the exemptions to the data protection legislation didn't cover former police officers... But eventually I reminded him of some of the things I'd helped him out on... He certainly wouldn't be a DI if it wasn't for me! So he agreed to let me know whether either of the vans was stolen or registered to anyone who appeared to be a private detective... But he said he couldn't give me any names or addresses... But we'll see about that when I ring him in a couple of hours' time."

It seemed to me it was a rather pernickety law that allowed anonymity to someone who'd broken into our garage, at least – possibly our house – and planted a device to blow up our car and an illegal listening device. But I suppose if we'd made an official claim to the police, they could easily have done the work for us, without there being a problem. I was beginning to wonder whether we weren't at that familiar stage where we had to decide whether to press ahead on our own, or whether we shouldn't be bringing in the proper authorities.

We couldn't really hang about the High Street indefinitely, so we walked home. Shortly after we returned, Jim Ball phoned to let us know he'd got hold of the gizmo he'd promised us and could deliver it round later that afternoon. Rosemary agreed.

"We need to make sure we speak to Jim in the garden again," she said, as we went outside, ostensibly to do some weeding. "It was lucky he felt it necessary to look at the device from our petrol tank in the garden. Otherwise whoever was listening would've known we'd found it."

"Assuming there is a bug somewhere," I replied. "At least we know there isn't one in the phone... and I'm still not convinced that anyone got inside. You did a pretty thorough job on our security when we moved in."

"Well, between us, we've made a few enemies in our time... and Jim's gizmo should tell us one way or another... In some respects it'd be a pity. If you know you're being bugged, you can make sure people hear what you want them to hear... and we can't just pop into the car and have the sort of conversation we might need to have if we're going to smoke these people out."

"So, you have a plan?"

"Not really. Assuming I learn that we are being watched by some private detective, I can't make up my mind whether we should nab him and use the device he placed in the petrol tanks to squeeze some information out of him – like who's employing him – or whether he'd be smart enough not to tell us anything, or just to lie to us... and then whoever is employing him will find out that we're on to him... and use someone else, so we'd be starting from scratch."

"Or you'd try to observe him and find out who was employing him without him noticing? It seems to me that could easily go wrong – and if he spotted we were following him, he could do a bunk and we'd never get a chance to try and squeeze some info out of him."

"So?"

"If we decide to nab him... and we could, of course, just keep giving him the impression we'd stopped doing anything to do with the body in the attic... I think we have to get him in a situation where he's got little alternative other than to come clean... But, before you ask, I haven't worked out how we could do that."

A bit later Rosemary went out to phone her former colleague and I went to the top of our small garden, mainly to see whether if I had a bonfire with the weeds and twigs once they'd dried I'd be annoying my neighbours. I decided that I probably would. So, I'd need to bag them up and take them to the local refuse disposal site sometime. I peered across towards

Kelsey Park, but I realised I couldn't see into Court Downs Road. But I reckoned there was somewhere on the edge of Kelsey Park where I could watch our house without being seen by anyone coming from Court Downs Road. That gave me an idea.

Rosemary returned, looking reasonably pleased.

"Have you finished in the garden?" she asked.

"There's still stuff to be bagged up for the dump," I replied.

"Can I help?"

"Of course. I've done a lot of bending this afternoon."

We went outside.

"Well?" I asked.

"The white van is nicked, apparently. So, Geoff was able to claim that the information he gave me was in relation to a possible stolen and dumped car. That makes it all right in data protection terms apparently. The dark blue van belongs to Carlyle Security, who have offices in Clapham High Street. To save me looking them up, Geoff told me it's a small security business – mainly doing burglar alarms and expensive locks, owned by Simon Carlyle, a former Captain in the Royal Signals. Nothing on file about them."

"Not the sort of bloke to be intimidated easily, I guess. Even if we'd checked initially, he doesn't seem the sort of bloke to leave fingerprints anywhere. So if we want to get anything out of him, we'll need to catch him red-handed."

"I assume you've thought up some kind of plan? But let's see what Jim Ball's gizmo turns up before we do anything. If this Simon Carlyle can get into our house and leave a bug or two there, it strikes me as he's a more sophisticated operator than someone who can unhook our garage and put the explosive device and the bug in our car."

"OK. We'd better keep an eye out for Jim Ball."

Jim arrived not long after and fortunately appeared to be in something of a hurry. He explained how to use the gadget he gave us and indicated he'd like it back in a week or so.

After he'd gone, we made a very thorough check of everywhere we could think of in our house – and found absolutely nothing. To some extent, it was a relief. But it also meant there was that lingering suspicion that there was a device there, but it was too sophisticated for our gizmo to find.

Rosemary and I went outside to voice those thoughts.

"But we can't live like this for the next few weeks," Rosemary said. "Either we genuinely stop doing this investigation or we do something to make sure we're not under surveillance... So, what was the plan you'd been thinking up, Nick?"

"We aim to catch Simon Carlyle red-handed."

I explained my plan... and we decided to put it into action straight away.

"I'm sure I left my swimming bath season ticket in the car," Rosemary said, as we opened the garage door. "It's not in my sports bag or my handbag, so the only place it can be is in the car. It must've dropped out of my sports bag the last time I went there... You remember I drove because I was going out to the supermarket afterwards."

"Was your sports bag in the car or the boot?"

"I think I put it in the boot and then I took it out to fit the stuff from the supermarket in. There was a lot of stuff for the freezer, so I wanted to put it in the boot."

"OK. You look in the car. I'll check the boot."

Rosemary opened the front door of the car, so that what was said outside the car could be picked up by the bug in the car. Meanwhile I made my way round the side of the car.

"That's a bit odd!" I exclaimed. "There's a little bit of wire poking out by the petrol cap. Do you think someone has been trying to syphon petrol out of the tank?"

"While it was in the garage? Be careful... It might be connected to that Deal stuff. You know that letter we got... We both know that we thought that the car that was set on fire outside the Marine Buildings was a message to us... I reckon this could be some sort of device placed in our petrol tank..."

"So, what are we going to do about it?"

"I think we should go straight to the police. The police station is just by St George's church. We can tell them and they can decide how to proceed. I don't think we should try to do anything in case it's booby-trapped... It could go off if you just twisted the petrol cap a tiny bit."

"So let's get round there. You realise we're going to have to explain why we think we're at risk?"

"Better that than being burnt to a crisp!"

We locked the garage and went back into the house, then left through the front door, locking up carefully. We walked into Kelsey Park Road. But the moment we reached Burnhill Road, we both turned left and I started running up Burnhill Road, into Greenways and from there into Kelsey Lane and

Kelsey Way. I entered Kelsey Park in the middle of Manor Way and made my way through the park towards the lodge at the entrance to the park on the corner of Manor Way and Court Downs Road. There I stood, peering through the gap between a tree and a high hedge. Out of breath from running twice as fast as I usually did, I just had to hope that no one walking through the park would draw attention to my presence. Similarly, we had to hope that Rosemary, waiting out of sight somewhere in the part of Greenways that leads down to Manor Way, wasn't attracting unwelcome notice.

I'd only been there a couple of minutes, when a crimson van, larger than the dark blue one – almost the size of a Ford Transit – drove into our drive. A man in overalls got out and went over to the garage door. A minute or two later, I could see the door being opened. I raced over to the entrance to Kelsey Park on the corner of Court Downs Road and Manor Way, sped around the corner and more cautiously up towards our house. Then I threw a yellow tennis ball up Manor Way as far as I could, as the signal for Rosemary to come and join me.

The moment I could see her jogging out of Greenways, I started to move up towards the garage, as quietly as I could. I'd just reached the front when Rosemary got to the front of our drive. I waited until she joined me. Then I stepped into the garage and switched on the light. Simon Carlyle (or possibly an employee) was bent over the petrol cap, but immediately straightened up as he realised the light had come on.

"I hope you're not going to try and make this hard for yourself," I said. "Otherwise, we'll lock you in here and send for the police."

"After all, you've just added breaking and entering to attempted murder, as well as other crimes," added Rosemary.

"You knew! You set me up!" replied the man, in the accent of a grammar schoolboy from the South East. He was a couple of inches shorter than me, with very short, light-brown hair, a narrow face with eyes that were slightly too far apart. He was definitely wiry, rather than powerful. He stepped forward.

"I suggest you stay where you are, or we'll lock you in and get the police," I reminded him.

"Is that what you want?" demanded Rosemary.

"No," replied the man, staying where he was, but eyeing us like a wary boxer seeking to choose the right moment to strike a knockout blow.

"What's your name?"

"Gordon Blair…"

"Please don't lie to us. It doesn't matter to us either way if this gets handled by the police… I suggest you shut the door, Nick," replied Rosemary.

"If you already know my name, why did you bother to ask?"

"To see whether you'd tell the truth or not. Now – Your final chance. What's your real name?"

"Simon Carlyle."

"That's better."

"I'm right in thinking that you overheard what we said about the device in the petrol tank and were trying to remove it before we brought the police round to look at it?"

"Yes… Evidently you knew about the listening device in the car."

"Are there any in the house? And please remain where you are!"

"No. This place is like Fort Knox."

"Regrettably you haven't enough to earn any trust from us. So we'll probably have to ask the police to sweep the whole place… and our daughter's flat in Deal too, of course."

"I didn't say I didn't put something in Deal. There are a couple in the light fittings in the lounge and bedroom... and something in the phone."

"Let's hope that's all. But we'll need some more concrete reassurance about your truthfulness before we decide whether to summon the police or not. I think we might get you out of there to somewhere where you're less likely to try and make a run for it... Will you remove your belt and drop your trousers right to your ankles please."

"Why don't you just send for the police?"

"OK... Nick, will you pull the garage door down please?"

I began to tug at the door.

"I don't know what you want... But I don't want the police round," said Carlyle, undoing his belt.

"OK. You know what you have to do."

He untied his belt and dropped it to the ground, then undid his zip and pushed his trousers down to his ankles.

"Now come forward towards us... slowly!" ordered Rosemary.

"I can't go any other way," he muttered.

As he got within six feet of us, Rosemary and I backed away, so that when he finally emerged at the front of the garage, we were still over six feet away from him.

"Now sit down in front of your van and stay there," Rosemary continued. "Nick, will you keep an eye on him while I go and get a couple of things."

Carlyle sat down, eyeing me to see whether he might have a chance to overpower me and get away. But he quickly realised I was too far away. Within a couple of minutes, Rosemary reappeared, with a pair of handcuffs and a small dictaphone.

"Turn right round, so you're looking away from us and put your arms out straight behind your back!" she commanded.

Carlyle shuffled his way round until his back was to us.

"Just a second," I added, "I'll get a spade in case he tries anything."

"OK," said Rosemary, as I returned from the garage. "Hands out behind you!"

Carlyle stuck his hands out and Rosemary expertly slipped the handcuffs over his wrists.

"That's one skill I don't think I'll ever forget," she remarked. "Now, we'll help you to your feet and we'll go somewhere a little more private."

I helped Carlyle up. He made no attempt to resist me and she led him along the path between the house and the garage and pushed him into one of our old wooden garden chairs.

"Right," began Rosemary. "You will answer our questions fully and truthfully. I'm going to record what you say and after we've finished, we'll write down a short statement which you will sign. Otherwise – and if you prefer it we can do it straight away - we'll hand you over to the police. I guess placing an explosive device in a car and putting a listening device in it are enough to get you put away for a while. You certainly won't be able to continue in the security business… apart from the crooked end of it… Or is that where you are already Captain Carlyle?"

"No, I'm not. My business is entirely respectable… But I was asked to repay a favour by a fellow officer, a former officer. I'd no intention of hurting anyone. That's why I put that particular device in. I could easily have put something in that'd go off when you were driving. But this one can only be detonated by a signal from my transmitter."

"But you were happy to destroy our car and garage, presumably?"

"I'm sure you have them well insured."

"That's not quite the point is it? But let's leave that to one side for one moment. Who is the officer who asked you to do this… and set fire to the car in Deal? And bug the flat in Deal?"

"It was done in confidence…"

"If your former colleague is happy for you to go to jail and lose your licence for helping him out, that's a matter for the two of you. But if you don't want the police involved, you'll have to give us his name and address… and the reason for taping this and having your statement is so that if you lie to us, we've got evidence we can hand over to the police – and give to the local papers, if necessary – along with the photos we'll take of you and your van."

"I'll tell you his name. He knows perfectly well that the favour I owed him wasn't such that requires me to go to jail or lose my licence and my business. But it won't do you much good. He expressly told me that he was acting as an agent for a third party… and I doubt you've got enough to put the same kind of pressure on him as you have on me… He'd just deny our conversation, and where are you then?"

"That's our concern, not yours. His name, please."

"Henry Bent, former Major, Royal Corps of Engineers. He is a Director for a firm that builds oak-frame houses. I don't know his home address. The firm's name and address are Oak Heritage Ltd, in the Pantiles, Tunbridge Wells. We met for lunch in a restaurant nearby."

"And what were you told?"

"You were being a nuisance to friends of his, carrying out investigations which might destroy the family name and reduce them to penury. You needed to be deterred. A polite warning had evidently failed. So action that'd make you sit up and take notice was required... However, it was stipulated that you shouldn't be harmed in any way."

"So, did you decide to set the car alight in Deal, and then set fire to our car and garage if we took no notice of the warning of the burning car in Deal? Or did you have to check back with Bent?"

"I agreed with Harry that I'd give you a warning in Deal that didn't affect your property and if you didn't stop with your investigations, I'd do something that affected you directly either here or in Deal."

"So why haven't you done anything?"

"It was unclear whether you were continuing your investigations or not. I wanted to get a device into your house, but that proved impossible. So I needed you to go to Deal or talk about what you were doing in your car. But I was told there were certain places you'd need to visit, if you were going on with your investigations. You either go by car or, more probably, by train. So far you haven't been on any journey to any of those places. So I've had to hang around – or at least, leave one of the vans here – to keep tabs on what you were up to."

"And if we appeared not to be up to anything, how long were you expected to hang around?"

"Another week or so. Then more funds would have to be forthcoming. This wasn't just a favour repaid, but a job of work. I've been paid my usual rates. Whoever got Harry into this will have to decide how much more they're prepared to shell out."

"Your address?"

"Business or home?"

"Both."

"My business is Carlyle Security, in 104 Clapham High Street. I live in Putney, Werter Road, number 42."

"Phone numbers? We'll be checking them, of course."

He gave two phone numbers. I rang both. Both seemed to tally with what he'd told us. He seemed to be cooperating. Was it because this was a rather unimportant piece of business for him and it was more important to keep his activities away from the police? Or he did have some clever escape route planned which we hadn't fathomed out?

"Mr. Carlyle has been telling me about the favour he owed Mr. Bent," explained Rosemary as I returned. "I don't believe it adds much and we won't be able to check it, but it's on the tape, if you want to listen to it later."

"I'll see," I replied.

"I think it's worth me pointing out that the favour I owe Harry Bent might require me to undertake activities which put me on the wrong side of the law," said Carlyle. "But it doesn't extend to physical harm to anyone."

"Is Bent the sort of person who'd know people who have less well-defined boundaries than you?" asked Rosemary. "Indeed, where do his boundaries lie in this sort of thing?"

"I guess he might know where to look. There are always a few ex-squaddies around who don't mind a bit of rough stuff and could do with a supplement to the dole. Whether he'd want to venture down that path, I can't say I could give you a definitive answer. I didn't know him well enough. It might depend on his relationship with the people who want to halt your investigations… or how much they're prepared to pay him… and how far they're prepared to go, too, of course…"

"Who else knows you're doing this job?"

"No one. The main part of my business is fitting security alarms and locks. I've got a couple of chaps who do most of that side, along with a lad in the office to deal with phone calls and customers who want to buy locks or bolts. For the bigger jobs – say an office block – I spec out the job myself. And I've done a few of these surveillance jobs from time to time. Some of them have involved listening devices. So, as you might imagine, I don't want any of the troops knowing anything about that sort of thing."

"Your family?"

"We have a clear division of responsibilities in my household. I bring in the money and the wife spends it – on condition she doesn't ask questions."

"Your arrangements for reporting back to Bent?"

"Once a week phone call to confirm nothing has happened. I've got a cell phone which he can ring if he needs to. But he hasn't used it so far. If I'd seen you were continuing with your investigations, I'd phone him from a callbox, to let him know I was going to incinerate your car... He'll be expecting a call in the next day or so – not least because he knows the time he's paid for expires in a week."

"And if you tell him it doesn't sound as though we're continuing with our investigations?"

"I couldn't say. I've no idea who his clients are or how much they're prepared to spend. I guess if I was them I might go on for another fortnight or so."

"But if they decided to stop at the end of the week, would you just leave the devices here and in Deal?"

"No. I'd take them out. That's what I was trying to do here when you caught me. Unless you have a ground-level barrier, these up-and-over garage doors are reasonably easy to open... and I reckon I could get into the flat in Deal any time. The front door lock doesn't work well and it's often open... and the lock to the flat is a bog-standard yale that any self-respecting locksmith could open."

"I think we can spare you that trouble... As you'll understand, we don't want you blabbing to Bent about what's happened here... and along with this tape, your statement and these various devices are more likely to encourage you not to blab… But I'm sure you can understand our dilemma…"

"You won't know whether I've informed Bent or not."

"Exactly. Of course, if something untoward happens, you could be pretty sure that we'd pass all this evidence to the police immediately… and please don't think you could somehow get your hands on it. There've been several occasions in the past when we've had evidence or incriminating statements in similar circumstances and we've developed a number of ways of making sure that it can neither be retrieved nor vanish, even if we were both to be killed… Indeed, that would trigger events that would lead to you and Bent being first in line as the murder suspects."

"I can assure you I'm not getting myself involved in anything like that. I may bend the law on occasions, but I couldn't live with myself if I was responsible for injuring anyone. That's why I've been here a fair amount of the time. If I had to set fire to your car, I'd make completely certain you were away from home at the time."

"That's as maybe – but you've got to tell Bent something. I'd suggest you kitted us out with additional listening devices and we listened in on your conversation with him. But there'd be nothing to stop you phoning him or meeting him separately."

"I can assure you that you've got enough on me to ensure I keep my mouth shut. After all, you haven't pursued your investigations since the car was burnt in Deal. If you re-start after I've finished my surveillance, that's nothing to do with me… and I don't really want to admit to Bent that you caught me and that I gave you his name."

"Hmmm… What do you think about that, Nick?"

"I think you've said what you believe we want to hear, Mr. Carlyle. But please be under no illusion. If anything untoward occurs – even if it's nothing to do with you – this material will be rapidly in the hands of the police… and, as you know that Rosemary worked at New Scotland Yard, you shouldn't assume it'd be the local police either… And the other thing I should add is that we're not above bending the law either. Now we know where you live, don't forget we can play tit for tat… and you'd find it rather more awkward to go to the police if your car was set alight than we would, especially if you were planning to blame us for it."

"Bent told me a bit about you… I can't help feeling I should've done rather more research myself… He said you were a retired policewoman and Customs official who'd got too much time on your hands and couldn't retire gracefully, but had to go poking your noses into long-dead matters of no concern to you," observed Carlyle.

"Very well," replied Rosemary. "I think it's time for you to write a short statement and sign it. Then you can be on your way."

That done, we allowed him to pull up his trousers, but we chucked his belt into the back of his van, to restrict his mobility – just in case he'd got some desperate plan. Then we led him out to his van and Rosemary removed his handcuffs.

"One last thing," she said. "We don't expect to see you around here again… and if we do see you or if the listening devices have been removed from the Deal flat, you can expect an early knock on the door by the police."

"Believe me," replied Carlyle. "You are the last people I wish ever to see again."

As he drove away, I remarked to Rosemary that he was by no means the first to utter such sentiments. She gave a well-practiced smirk.

11. THE TUNBRIDGE WELLS CONNECTION

"Well, how much of that did you believe?" asked Rosemary. "You were watching him all the time."

"I think I believe most of it. He didn't strike me as a natural crook – or a good liar either. He's basically a man who installs sophisticated security systems and does a bit of this electronic eavesdropping as a sideline. And the fact that someone helped you out when some equipment was needed urgently is a perfectly valid reason for owing them some sort of a favour… and it didn't strike me as a rehearsed excuse."

"Do you think he'll tell Bent that he's been rumbled?"

"I doubt it. His only problem would be if the people using Bent wanted to use him for another week or two. Otherwise he can get out of it clean as a whistle by saying – truthfully – we've neither done or said anything that suggests we're continuing with our investigations. And he doesn't want to ruin his business by getting caught up with police… Would you want to use someone to install your security system if you knew he'd been caught planting bugs and listening in on private conversations? I wouldn't. I'd always worry that he might've been paid by a rival to plant a bug or two within my security system."

"So he's got a strong motive not to say anything. But if he gets hold of the evidence, it'd be his word against ours."

"We can do what we usually do – and there's plenty of space in the concealed safe."

"Which already contains enough evidence to see off quite a few prominent people… a lot more important than Captain Carlyle…"

"Several of whom are dead, of course, like Kenneth King."

"Whenever you mention that, it always sounds as though you regret his death."

"I wouldn't go that far. But even though he was a crook and undoubtedly got up to some very unpleasant things, he had a set of rules – not necessarily moral, or ones we'd agree with – and kept to them. At least you knew where you were with him… and if you understood his rules, you could deal with him. In many respects, he had rather more integrity than several senior Civil Servants I've had the misfortune to come across."

"I'm not sure that's saying much for Mr. King."

"Anyway… what did you think about Carlyle?"

"I think I agree with what you said about him… The question is what do we do now?"

"I was going to suggest we go to Deal and remove the bugs Carlyle placed there. But it seems to me one way we can check his good faith is to leave it a couple of days. If he's removed them, we know he can't be trusted and we can assume he's told Bent about what happened here this afternoon. But if they're still there, we can rest a little easier."

"And on the other stuff?"

"I'm inclined to do nothing until next week. Then, with any luck, Carlyle will've reported back that we're no longer doing any investigating and we could go to the Land Registry and wherever else we need to go with the reasonable prospect of not being watched."

"What about the man Bent? Shouldn't we be trying to find out who his contact is?"

"Of course. But we'll need to tread carefully. It's likely that he knows what we look like and we shouldn't rule out the possibility that Carlyle will've told him that we rumbled him. If I was Bent in those circumstances, I'd assume we'd start investigating him."

"I may be able to dig up a certain amount of info about his company... and can't you find out a bit about Army officers from published material?"

"I think they publish lists of Army officers annually. We should be able to check that out in Beckenham library... But when we don't know what name we're looking for, trying to see whether the person employing Bent is a military connection is going to be a very long shot... The connection could just as easily be school or even old family friends with no traceable link."

"Even so – it's likely to be more useful than digging around in the 1880s, I reckon."

"It's tying the two together that strikes me as the problem. It'd be easy if we found out that a Culpeper, Dromgoole or Rust was a director of Bent's firm or were fellow pupils at Sandhurst, but if any of the inhabitants of Sandown Terrace had daughters, presumably they will've shared in their inheritance, so the person we're looking for may be called Smith, Brown or Snodgrass... or whatever. And while you might be able to prove a connection between a Culpeper or Dromgoole of the current generation levelling threats at us, we wouldn't be able to do so if they appear to have come from a Smith or Brown, unless we could show that they stood to lose heavily from our investigations... and how and why. Since we don't even know who the dead man is, why he was killed and by whom, it seems to me that unless we can get a bit further with what happened in the last century we won't get anywhere, unless we're extremely lucky."

"OK. So, does that mean we've got to trace the descendants of all our likely suspects through to the present day? That could take months... and they're likely to find out what we're up to before we get anywhere."

"We might be able to cut down the number of suspects. What we've learnt from the letters and Carlyle's efforts to find out what we were up to and put us off is that whoever is bothered about this has something to lose – money or reputation. My feeling is that it has to start with the money. So if we could get to see the wills of the main characters – like Rust, Charles Culpeper, Dromgoole, possibly Barfoot and Gerald Culpeper – we'd know who managed to build up a large fortune in the late nineteenth century, which might've been built, at least partly, on concealing a murder..."

"Or the fortune would've been stopped in its tracks if the murder had been discovered... There's no particular reason why the murder was necessarily linked to someone acquiring their fortune..."

"Hmmm... I'm not so sure. If Charles Culpeper, say, had killed the man who could make his brother's speculation pay off, would Gerald's descendants have a right to the Culpeper fortune, always assuming there is one? But if Rust, say, had bumped off one of his maids' fathers, I can't see it'd have any implications for his descendants' wealth, would it?"

"I guess you're right. So, the first step is to see what Gerald Culpeper, Rust and the other possibles left in their wills."

"That – and taking a look at Major Bent. And that needs to be sooner than later, ideally before he gets any suspicions about Carlyle – or we get spotted doing something that makes him realise that Carlyle might not have been telling him the whole truth."

"So you believe Carlyle wasn't – isn't – the only person keeping an eye on us?"

"I don't know… I think the person who wrote the letters either met us or was tipped off by someone we met and, later on, they decided to employ someone like Carlyle, who'd both bug us and also do things to scare us off… So at the moment, I reckon we're probably not being watched by anyone… But, of course, we can't be sure once we start looking at wills or go to the Land Registry whether we won't get picked up by someone…"

"But unless they're very well connected, they could hardly have people in Somerset House and the Land Registry passing on information about who was looking into their ancestors. It must be illegal for staff at either place to do that. And they surely don't have someone hanging around anywhere we might turn up... just in case?"

"But..."

"But we should work on the assumption that once we resume our investigations, it may get picked up sooner rather than later."

"So who's going to do what? Are you the best one to have a look at Major Bent, while I go looking at wills?"

"Yes. You seem to have worked out what you're looking for... Though I think you need to check where old wills are kept... and don't make the obvious joke!"

"I thought I might ring the Public Record Office. They've usually been quite helpful and I don't want to go traipsing out to Kew again if I don't have to."

From a quick phone call the following morning, I learnt that I could look at the National Probate Calendar which would contain the information I needed, at the Family Research Centre. Though I had slight misgivings that my presence there might be passed on to whoever had sent the letters, it was certainly a much more straightforward journey.

Just as I finished, Rosemary was about to get the train to Tunbridge Wells. Her only attempt at disguise was to wear a light-brown, shoulder-length wig, which had belonged to Sarah at some stage – for what purpose, I'd never been clear – and had somehow escaped the clear-out when we moved to Manor Way. We walked up to the station together, Rosemary keeping the wig in her handbag.

"It'd be better to get no information about Bent, rather than put him on to us," I reminded her.

"You'd be surprised how inconspicuous I can be," she replied with a smirk.

We kissed. I headed for a Victoria train, Rosemary for one to Orpington, where she would change for a train to Tunbridge Wells. At Bromley South I changed to a Blackfriars train, which took an interminable time, but avoided an inconvenient tube journey once I got to London. I walked up Farringdon Street, subsequently Farringdon Road, and thence to the Family Research Centre. If anyone was following me, they were going to have to be quite fit, as I deliberately walked as fast as I could.

The information in the National Probate Calendar included the name of the deceased, the value of the estate and where the person died. I already had the date of death for the Culpepers and Samuel Rust, but neither Dromgoole nor Barfoot. I realised I was narrowing my search quite a lot. But for people like Hubert Jessop or the man Avram Groh, mentioned in the old postcard Rosemary had bought at the antiquarian bookshop, we'd have to start from scratch if we felt they were plausible suspects.

So, I started with the easier ones and discovered that Gerald Culpeper died leaving an estate valued at less than £100. Even in 1916, that wasn't much money. His brother Charles, in contrast, left an estate of just under £85,000 in 1926, a sizeable sum of money. But even that paled beside that of Samuel Rust who died worth a little under £250,000 in 1901 – in Tunbridge Wells.

That immediately set me thinking about Major Harry Bent, based in Tunbridge Wells. Did the Rust family still have property in the area? Or was this just sheer coincidence? And Rust couldn't've lived there long, as he'd been in Sholden Hall in the 1890s. And assuming he'd owned a large house in Tunbridge Wells, that was exactly the sort of property that got disposed of in order to pay death duties.

I returned to plough my way through the records for Dromgoole and Barfoot. I knew that Dromgoole had still been alive in around 1918. Otherwise, the only help I had was their unusual surnames. I hoped neither of them had emigrated, as I would have a frustrating and wasted day not merely looking for a needle in a haystack, but for one that wasn't even there.

Eventually I came across Percival Dromgoole who'd died in 1928 in Shrewsbury worth a tidy £97,000. For a man who reputedly had no money, he seemed to have done well for himself over the years. I added him to Rust and Charles Culpeper as someone whose descendants mightn't welcome the uncovering of a murder upon which the family fortune had been based. Though I recalled that it'd always been suggested that Dromgoole had something on Barfoot – or perhaps the man who'd bankrolled his purchases in Sandown Terrace – rather than carried out any murder himself.

I was on the point of giving up for the day when I finally turned up Jerome Barfoot. He'd lived to a ripe old age and died in 1935 in Richmond, in Yorkshire, with an estate valued at £33,000. That was rather more than I'd expected. Was it enough to constitute the basis for a family fortune? It was difficult to say. I supposed it would be worth ten or twenty times that amount now – and if invested by his children might've swollen considerably. But how would the knowledge that he'd killed someone remove their right to their inheritance? I added him to this list with a question mark.

It was late afternoon. I realised I'd had no lunch and I was also condemned to travel in the rush hour.

I walked down Farringdon Road, then Street, to Blackfriars, where I got on an already crowded Thameslink train which would take me all the way to Bromley South, but probably standing most of the way.

I stood up against the glass barrier and wondered whether what I'd learnt had told me anything. I'd always taken it for granted that Samuel Rust had left a sizeable fortune and assumed that Charles Culpeper had bequeathed his heirs a tidy sum. Dromgoole was more of a surprise, as no one had ever suggested he possessed much wealth of his own. But, as I'd already suggested to myself, getting rich through blackmailing someone for a crime they'd committed might be reprehensible – and your descendants might not welcome it being made public. But that was a seven days' wonder and aimed no threat at the family's wealth. And Barfoot? All I'd learnt led to further questions which probably couldn't be answered.

We stopped at Denmark Hill. A few people got off. As many got on. One stood next to me, his open copy of the *"Evening Standard"* almost touching me. He was one of those people who folded the paper, so I got to read the whole of the paper, rather than the front and back pages, which was more usual. To my great unease, the second time he turned over the page and folded it with great deliberation, glancing at me as though he suspected I was taking illicit advantage of him, I noticed a headline "Woman injured in car crash in Tunbridge Wells". I couldn't make out every word, without making it obvious to the man who'd bought the paper. But it seemed that a middle-aged woman had been knocked down by a speeding car, which had failed to stop, near Tunbridge Wells station. She'd been taken to the local hospital and was said to be seriously injured.

Inevitably the fear leapt icily into my brain that the woman was Rosemary, that she'd been spotted and that someone had tried to kill her. Of course, there was no solid reason to suppose that the woman was her, but terrible memories flooded back into my mind of that time in our flat in Copers Cope Road, when I thought Rosemary had been brutally killed by a rocket grenade. I now inwardly cursed myself for having chosen to take such a slow route – every station on the meandering Catford Loop line, but also a wait and a couple of stops back from Bromley South. Even as the train started to empty out – including the man with the newspaper – and seats became vacant, I couldn't sit down. I stood there, staring out of the window, silently urging the train to move faster and the passengers to get off and on faster at the various stations.

I was tempted to make my own way from Bromley South, but there was a stopping Victoria train in six minutes. So I waited – watching the seconds tick away on the illuminated timetable, seeming to go a half or a third of their normal speed. But the train came in, I leapt on and, having reached Beckenham Junction, ran from there to our house.

Of course Rosemary was there, as usual, preparing dinner – plainly unscathed by any car or other incident. I gave her a big hug and a long kiss.

"What was that for?" she asked with a smile. "Have you been doing something you shouldn't?"

"Not that I'm aware of… I saw an article in the *"Standard"* about a woman being run over near the station in Tunbridge Wells. I realised it was unlikely it was you, but after what happened before I'm afraid my imagination tends to get the better of me."

"Oh, so that's what it was! They were clearing up what looked an RTA, but there weren't ambulances at the scene, so I thought it must just have been two vehicles coming into contact."

"Apparently the car drove off without stopping."

"I can see why that got your imagination working. But I've been as cautious as you'd expect."

"Knowing you, I'm not sure that's quite as cautious as I might like."

"Possibly... But I'm confident no one I met in Tunbridge Wells knew my true identity... But you've also been busy ferreting around in old wills..."

"Not quite. But while we're there, let's stay in Tunbridge Wells... How did you get on?"

"Let me start from the beginning. I didn't put the wig on until I changed platforms at Orpington. I didn't have to wait too long for a train and I got to Tunbridge Wells not long before 11AM. I decided to try the local library first, to see what I could find out about Oak Heritage Ltd and Major Bent. The library is quite close to the station – inconveniently in the opposite direction from the Pantiles. I found a local business directory, which listed Bent among three directors of Oak Heritage Ltd. He is the Operations Director. The Chairman and Sales Director is David Hellier, and Donald Mustin is the Finance Director. I guess Hellier gets the clients, Bent gets the work done and Mustin makes sure the money gets managed properly. It seems that they have around ten regular employees – mostly doing garage sheds and conservatories rather than timber-framed houses. So no surprise there."

"Are they purely a local firm?"

"The stuff I read in the library suggested they covered pretty well the whole of southern and south-eastern England. Oak Heritage Ltd is about ten years old. There was a local Tunbridge Wells magazine with an advert of theirs in it. It was very conservative, boasting the traditional values of oak as the archetypal English building material. I assume they know who their potential customers are…"

"Yes… 'disgusted of Tunbridge Wells'… a dyed-in-the-wool Tory who only just tolerated Mrs. Thatcher because of what she did to the trade unions and regarded John Major as dangerously left-wing… And now they regard themselves as foreigners in their own country under a Labour Government, even one as right wing as Blair's."

"No hobby horses please! Actually, as I was walking from the library to the Pantiles, I did see a couple of rather stout women on tolerant horses. I've never been to Tunbridge Wells before… It's rather pleasant… Somewhere to visit, not to live. I couldn't see you fitting in there… You'd be 'disgusted about disgusted of Tunbridge Wells'…"

"With my background, I'd probably be blackballed."

"Sorry… I'll try not to digress. I walked to the Pantiles, which are really rather elegant. I discovered that Oak Heritage Ltd aren't actually in the Pantiles but at the end of the High Street that leads into the Pantiles. Not surprising, as I guess the rents on places in the Pantiles must be astronomical. I found about the cheapest place to eat in the Pantiles and had salad and apple juice… It was quite possibly a veggie place… definitely not your sort of place, Nick."

"I'd happily eat cheese and salad 'til the cows come home…"

"They generally serve fresh cheese, not stuff you've deliberately let dry out… Sorry, stop me digressing, please! While I was queuing for my lunch, I tied to spot anyone who might be local but who also might tolerate a stranger at their table. By and large the sort of women who frequent the Pantiles eateries don't appear entirely welcoming… Or was that just my prejudice? At any rate, I spotted a couple of middle-aged women who didn't seem too forbidding. They were a couple of places ahead of me in the queue and made the mistake of sitting at a table for four. When I'd paid, I took my tray over to their table. There was only one other vacant table anyway and I'd've felt a bit mean pinching from a mother and three young children just behind me in the queue.

'Do you mind if I join you?' I asked.

'Not at all,' replied one of the women, a lady in her early sixties with dyed blonde hair and quite a lot of make-up that made her seem older. 'I'm Cynthia.'

'Jenny,' I replied, using the first name that came into my head.

'Barbara,' said the other women. She was possibly in her late forties, possibly even Cynthia's daughter, though there was little family resemblance. Both had cut-glass accents.

'I'm sorry to accost you when you were hoping for a quiet lunch, but I'm a stranger here. I'm trying to get some information for my son and daughter-in-law. They're moving to a village between here and Tonbridge in a couple of months. They've both got jobs in the City and are moving down from Leeds. They worked in financial services there and had a lovely house in a village between Leeds and the Yorkshire Dales. One thing they particularly enjoyed was a really nice conservatory. The house they're moving into only has a shed, and Peter and I would like to get them a really nice conservatory as a moving-in present. We don't want one of those metal or pvc things that looks like some kind of lean-to, but a proper one that they can have dinner parties in. I'm trying to see whether there are any local firms who could put up something really nice... and you seemed to be the sort of people who might know.'

'Well, we're certainly local,' replied Cynthia. 'Been here all our lives. You're not local?'

'Oh no. We retired from Blackheath to Canterbury. Blackheath was convenient for Peter to commute into the City, but it's getting so frightfully crowded, noisy and dirty from all the traffic fumes.

Now we don't need to get to London quickly, we find Canterbury much nicer.'

'More than a few commute from here. Apart from the hospital and the insurance company, there's no significant local employer. But there are lots of shops and small businesses. We had a conservatory built about ten years ago by Oak Conservatories, a local firm. But one of the partners ran off with the money, so they went bankrupt. So much for our twenty-five-year guarantee! Colonel Hellier took over the premises and contacts, but not the guarantees regrettably… They're now called Oak Heritage. They're just round the corner in the High Street. Never heard a bad word said against them. But they claim to use only best quality oak, so they are at the pricey end of the range… the wood in our conservatory was evidently of a lower quality. If it lasts the twenty-five years of the worthless guarantee, I'll be astounded… but I don't blame David Hellier for not taking over his predecessor's guarantees… not at all…'

'Do you know him?'

'I wouldn't put it as strongly as that. We've met. Not least when we were exploring the possibility that he might take over Oak Conservatories' guarantee. See him at local events sometimes otherwise.'

'So he's local? It's always best, I say, if the work is done by someone local. If they live too far away, they don't really worry about having to face you if something isn't up to scratch.'

'Not a local family. Hellier came here after he left the Army. But Harry Bent has lived here all his life, like us. And Don Mustin comes all the way from Tonbridge. I've a feeling Hellier may have been at Tonbridge School. The other two definitely were... But it's possible Hellier and Bent met while they were in the Army. Certainly, when Oak Heritage started up, they were part of it from the start... along with Don Mustin.'

'They certainly don't sound as if they're going anywhere. But I suppose I ought to have a second string to my bow, if they turn out to be a bit too pricey. Is there anyone else you know of?'

'The only other ones I can think of are Wood and Son, on the corner of the High Street and Frog Lane. The actual owner is called Graham Richards and, as far as I know, there's no son. But they've been recommended to us as good people to fix our conservatory without costing the earth. They have a reputation for quality, but they also want business. We've occasionally debated whether there isn't some family money somewhere in Oak Heritage, as they seem to maintain high standards, even when there isn't much business about. If you really insisted on a pvc conservatory, Wood and Son would build it, even if they were gritting their teeth. Oak Heritage would pass you on to someone else.'

'Perhaps I should visit their premises after lunch and find out some more details. I imagine they'd need to survey the site before they could give me a proper estimate of what it'd cost.'

'I should hope so. But just you keep an eye on what they call ancilliaries. Oak Conservatories insisted on a deep concrete base for our conservatory. Virtually everyone I've ever mentioned it to has suggested that it was at least twice as deep as necessary.'

"We finished our lunch on the topic of the elegance of Tunbridge Wells," Rosemary continued. "Unsurprisingly they were keen to praise the place, but also to disparage recent developments, especially very rich people who'd descended from the outside – usually London – without respect for the culture and traditions of the town… It was at some point during this conversation that I twigged that they were a lesbian couple, which might account for the completely unwarranted and barely veiled hostility of Barbara, the younger of the two. She barely spoke a word, but evidently regarded me as an interloper, trying to befriend her partner… It takes all sorts, I suppose…"

"I assume she wasn't a Culpeper or a Rust who knew who you were, in spite of your wig?"

"I'm not a great believer in coincidences as great as that would've been. I could just imagine it if they'd recognised me and encouraged me to join them, but I doubt they'd even seen me before I forced myself on them... No that's several millions to one... and I don't believe that chances like that are real."

"So did you beard Major Bent in his oaken lair?"

"Not immediately. I decided I'd need to give these conservatory people a lot more circumstantial detail than I'd needed to give Cynthia and Barbara. So, having made certain they weren't in the vicinity, I went into an estate agents' and with their help, did quite a lot of research on suitable houses in local villages. As a result, I've got about two dozen sheets of details about houses in places like Bidborough, Speldhurst and Pembury... I've even got one for a house in a place called Frant. Obviously, everyone says the same thing when they first hear the name mentioned... Just as no doubt they say when someone asks what it's like living in Deal."

"I'm saying nothing."

"For once... At any rate, I got them to give me some details of houses in Bidborough and Speldhurst that'd been sold in recent months, so I could get some idea what property was like in these villages..."

"As a prospective buyer yourself?"

"As Mrs. Rosalind Carter-Browne, with an 'e'. I can do plummy accents with the best of them. Now my husband is cutting down on his directorships, we prefer to live a little further out of London than Keston, but with a decent train service on the occasions when you don't want to drive in."

"I assume all this deception got you the right property?"

"Yes. I reckoned that Oak Heritage Ltd and Wood and Son, if I went there, would be pretty clued-up on the local property market, as it must be one way they get their business. So, I thought I might well get into trouble if I made up a property or gave a tale that didn't fit facts they already knew... There was still a risk that they might've been in touch already with one or other of the properties I'd chosen. But both seemed a bit unlikely... But I thought I could work my way round it, if necessary. Anyway, I returned to being Jenny Carter... I decided I could lose the Browne... Then I wondered how many of these people met each other regularly, and decided I'd be Jenny Anderson, as it'd raise fewer questions if Cynthia and Barbara were to meet Hellier or Bent socially and ask about me... and Bent or Hellier meet someone from the estate agents I'd been in. Of course, the real problem was that I couldn't guarantee I'd meet Bent. Indeed, it was more likely I'd meet

Hellier or one of his salespeople. But I could just do the best I could. At least I'd get a feel for the place."

"As you might expect," she continued, "their office was set up like my idea of an English gentleman's club – all dark green leather and, inevitably, plenty of oak. There's a front office, with a couple of salespeople – a young horsey lady with long blonde hair and an even younger chinless wonder in a sports jacket. I guess he makes the tea, polishes the oak and hands out brochures. Fortunately, the young woman – calling herself Jacquie – met me. I explained what I was after and why, without being too specific at that stage… but consistent with what I'd told Cynthia and Barbara.

'Do you mind telling me who suggested us to you?' asked Jacquie.

'Certainly,' I replied. 'I met a couple of local ladies when I was having lunch quite near here. The café was quite crowded, so I had to join them at their table. We got chatting and my reason for being in Tunbridge Wells emerged and the name of your firm from that.'

'Do you think you'll want one of our standard model conservatories from our brochure or will it need to be customised?'

'The door which will lead out to the conservatory is on a sort of dog-leg wall, so I imagine the conservatory would have to be customised, as you put it.'

'Is it a brick external wall or is there rendering or beams or something like that?'

'That's a good question. I'm trying to remember… I think there'd be some rendering and the bottom of some wooden beams. It's a while since we've been there and it was very much a flying visit.'

'I think you probably need to have a word with my boss, Colonel Hellier.'

"She went off to a room at the back and within a couple of minutes, she emerged, following a tallish man, who, apart from his receding hair, looked much as I guess he did when he was a serving officer. He looked the sort of man who goes for a ten-mile run at the crack of dawn every day – carrying a twenty-five-pound rucksack!"

"I occasionally wonder what a masochist would look like!" I remarked.

"He grasped me by the hand in a vice-like grip… I often wondered if I'd ever be able to say that," Rosemary continued. "He was one of those people who put their faces about six inches too close to you when they engage you in conversation. As a sales technique, it leaves something to be desired… with me, at any rate. I explained a bit of the stuff I'd been telling Jacquie and he asked several more questions about the door to the proposed conservatory, the wall it'd be leaning against, the ground it'd be standing on, whether there was any drainage passing under the ground or from the roof. I wasn't able to answer all the questions, but I felt it was safer not to start making things up.

'A genuine oak conservatory on a proper base is likely to cost at least £20,000 in that location. But it could go as high as £30,000, depending on some of the unknowns,' he concluded. "We'd need to visit the site to make a detailed estimate... But you should realise that it'd increase the value of the property by at least that amount.'

'I understand,' I replied. 'It is a lot of money. For that sort of money, we'd need to be completely satisfied with what we were getting.'

'I can show you our brochures, of course. But I realise that things can be made to look better in brochures than they actually are... and prospective purchasers are rightly sceptical about them... Let me introduce you to Harry Bent, who's in charge of everything from getting the plans put on paper right through to tidying up the site after construction is complete.'

He went to a different room at the back of the premises and came out with a bear of a man – six feet four inches, I'd say, with a mane of thick, black curly hair, a broad, ruddy face with a slightly incongruous pair of old-fashioned round NHS spectacles. Perhaps less of a bear than a giant owl! He too shook me by the hand, but in contrast to Hellier, his grip was more like shaking hands with a dead flatfish.

He then took me through how the firm approached working out the plans, how they visited the site and undertook various tests and agreed the size and exact specs for the conservatory with the client before settling on the exact price. This wouldn't alter, even if they encountered unexpected problems. He also explained how they would operate during the construction phase – including bringing their own mobile latrine, to avoid causing any nuisance to the client – and afterwards, in terms of remediating the site to its previous condition.

'Harry was a Sapper,' explained Hellier. 'So he's got the very best grounding in carrying out projects like this thoroughly, on time and keeping the cost to its lowest level… You should understand that though the cost sounds a lot, much is down to the cost of the oak. Other firms use cheaper wood, but we use only properly matured oak that will last as long as the bricks in the walls of the house.'

'Oh! I would've expected oak to have been quite plentiful after the Great Storm? Didn't that make a lot of wood available?' I asked.

'Yes. Unfortunately, the Great Storm was shortly before we set up this business. Indeed, it was the exact cause of our predecessor's demise. He'd been hoarding oak which was worth a considerable sum of money and was, in effect, keeping the business solvent. But when all that oak suddenly became available after the Great Storm, the value of his stock plummeted and he ended up being made bankrupt. Regrettably, quite a lot of it had to be sold to pay off his debts. So we're almost entirely dependent on the available supply of oak – and English oak of a suitable quality is comparatively rare... and then must be allowed to mature over several years.'

'I understand... Well, you've given me plenty to think about. If I may take a brochure, I need to discuss this with my husband and I hope to get back to you shortly,' I said, taking my leave.

"I decided not to call into the other conservatory makers and made my way back to the station," Rosemary concluded.

"What did you make of Bent?" I asked.

"Of course, I only saw one facet of him. He seemed thoroughly knowledgeable about his work, and professional... I noticed in the brochure he's evidently studied for a number of relevant professional qualifications... There's an odd contrast between the huge man and the weak handshake and rather high, unassuming voice. Like Hellier, he's plainly quite upper drawer... My feeling is that – a bit like Carlyle – getting people bugged or setting fire to cars to warn them off isn't something that comes naturally to him. I'm just guessing, but I suspect this is all being done to help out a distressed relative or friend, who feels directly threatened by our activities."

"You don't think he might've worked out who you are?"

"I don't see how he could've done. Unless Carlyle blabbed to him almost immediately. I made sure not to ask any questions that weren't entirely relevant to my conservatory... and from what I could tell I fitted the part exactly in this 'wedding guest outfit'... Which reminds me, I must put something more comfortable on... While I do so, you can tell me what you learnt in darkest Clerkenwell."

I told her what I'd picked up there.

"I suppose we now have to decide whether we concentrate on Rust, Charles Culpeper, Dromgoole and possibly Barfoot and hope that if we can find out more about them – not least who their current descendants are and how much they've all be leaving in their wills – we might get a connection to Major Harry Bent somehow?" suggested Rosemary.

"As he's an officer, we might be able to find out more about him from the Army records. Don't all officers go through training at Sandhurst?"

"You know that sort of thing a lot better than I do."

"I think that's right. I wonder if their records would say what school someone went to. If Bent seemed rather upper drawer, as you said, he probably went to a reasonably posh public school. We might be able to get hold of information about people who were there at the same time."

"That might be OK if you find someone called Culpeper or Dromgoole. But what if the family money passed through someone who only had daughters? You'd never spot who the connection might be if the descendants are now called Smith or Smythe or Fauntleroy-Browne with an 'e'."

"So it looks like another famous two-pronged approach: check out a series of wills – and marriages, if necessary – as well as going through the military connection."

12. THE FAMOUS TWO-PRONGED APPROACH

We agreed that I would try and follow up the military and public-school side, while Rosemary would return to the Family Research Centre and try to follow a series of deaths and wills through several generations. One drawback immediately struck her. The National Probate Calendar didn't contain details of the heirs to the estate – and, of course, the executor was as likely to be the family solicitor as a member of the family. But we really didn't want to pay for a dozen or more wills and study them in detail. So she would look at wills from anyone called Rust, Culpeper, Dromgoole or Barfoot. If there appeared to be a connection with those we already knew, she'd assume for the time being that they were right and would see what had happened to the value of the estate, and then go forward to the next generation.

Meanwhile, I would see how I could lay my hands on records of cadets passing through Sandhurst and see whether there was any connection with Rust, Culpeper, Dromgoole or Barfoot there. If not, I'd have to try to dig further into where Major Bent had been to school and see if I could get hold of the relevant information and then see whether there were any straightforward connections there. Throughout,

I'd need to remind myself that the fact that there was a John Rust, say, at Eton with Harry Bent didn't either mean he was related to Samuel Rust or, even if he was, that was necessarily the connection that was currently being played on.

As I was doubtful whether our local libraries would have the records of cadets who'd graduated through Sandhurst, I decided to travel up to London with Rosemary, and visit the British Library, while she went to "darkest Clerkenwell", as she liked to call it, for the Family Research Centre.

I knew that the British Library had moved from Bloomsbury to a brand new – and to my mind rather plain – building on Euston Road, between St Pancras and Euston stations. I wasn't quite sure what I expected to find… Not least because I wasn't at all sure whether it had been opened for public use or not. When I got there, an attendant assured me it was open for business, even though it hadn't yet been formally opened by the Queen. However, being open informally did nothing to prevent the usual formalities of registration, for which I was better prepared than many queuing up in the entrance. Once I got inside, I had to admit that it was perhaps more impressive inside than from outside.

I had to ask my way to the right place to get access to the material I wanted. I was having to do a certain amount of educated guesswork. From what

Rosemary had said, it struck me that Major Harry Bent was between 45 and 55. That suggested he would've been at Sandhurst between 1964 and 1977, assuming he might've gone there after taking his first degree. So I asked for the published lists of Sandhurst graduates for those years. While I was waiting, I looked at the computerised records which suggested that Sandhurst had the equivalent of a year book, which would tell me a bit more about the antecedents of the cadets. So when the lists arrived, I asked for the yearbooks for the same years, in order to save time. In practice, if I could find Bent in the lists, I'd only need a couple of yearbooks, at most. But if I was lucky, I was going to have to get copies of yearbooks for whatever public school Bent had attended. All this took time and I was keen to complete my research in one day. For that reason, I took no interest in former Captain Carlyle – on the basis that there was no reason why he should've been at Sandhurst at the same time as Bent, as it seemed their paths had crossed while on active service.

After leafing through several graduation lists, I came across Henry Robert Grey Carlyle, receiving his commission in 1965. On the same and immediate surrounding lists, there were no Culpepers, Rusts, Dromgooles or Barfoots (or Barfeet, for that matter). This was disappointing, but perhaps not entirely surprising. If one of those families had a military background, I might well have expected them to know someone like Carlyle to contact directly, rather than go through Bent. Indeed, they would surely have gone to someone they knew and trusted… And doing it via Bent hadn't been a success – even if they didn't yet realise that. Whereas I was sure Bent would never reveal who'd asked him to bug our home and set fire to our car if necessary, Carlyle didn't have the connection born of being at school or military training together.

I needed to examine the yearbooks for 1965 and a few years before. I'd no idea how long it took to receive officers' training at Sandhurst, so I decided to start in 1965 and work back. It became clear quite soon that the course lasted a little under a year. So it took me less time than I expected to discover that Bent had been to Durham University, where he'd got a 2.1 in mechanical engineering, and previously had attended Haberdasher Aske's school in Elstree. I knew nothing about the school, except the name (and the fact that I'd attended school at its distant cousin in Brockley). I assumed they had school magazine's or yearbooks and asked for copies from 1960 and 1961.

Of course, it would've been highly convenient if there'd been a Rust, Culpeper, Dromgoole or Barfoot who was in Bent's year at the school. But – inevitably, I suppose – there wasn't. I decided to write down all the names of his contemporaries, in case that brought up someone who emerged from Rosemary's researches. As I tidied up my notes and headed out through the main doors of the library, I felt that my side of the two-pronged approach was decidedly blunt.

I'd agreed to meet Rosemary at Charing Cross station at 5pm, so we could decide whether to go straight home or perhaps wander around and have a meal somewhere. We decided to have a walk along by the Embankment gardens towards the Temple and then joined the crowds in Covent Garden, as we realised we hadn't really been there since it'd become a magnet for tourists, who apparently didn't mind being overcharged for practically everything. It certainly wasn't somewhere we'd eat a meal, we concluded, and headed for Chinatown, where, provided we went to a restaurant on one of the side streets off Brewer Street, we'd avoid the fate of the passing tourists… albeit at the price of being unable to read the menu, written entirely in Chinese.

"We could've gone to the 'Gay Hussar' in Greek Street, you know," I said, as we sat down. "I don't think the prices have got too astronomical."

"We've only been there once… and it's an occasion I treasure. If something wasn't right, I wouldn't really want to go back and blur the memory."

"I thought we'd avoid several Chinese restaurants with possibly fishy connections."

"That was a while ago! The fishy restaurants are probably different now. Who knows, me might just have chosen one being staked out by the Security Service, who'll be wondering why we've come in here."

"Perhaps if there's an MI5 agent in here, he or she can decipher the menu for us."

"I think if we just point, we'll get what we want… and chop sticks presumably… I'll probably go for roast duck and noodles with vegetables…"

"That sounds OK for me too… I normally go for soup in Chinese restaurants, but it's been a bit too warm today."

We ordered – hoping we'd get what we thought we'd asked for.

"So, what did you find out today?" I asked. "I can tell you now. I uncovered no relevant name either in the army, at Sandhurst or at school with Bent… I admit I didn't go back to his prep school, but I didn't get any information about that."

"It was thoroughly tedious. As you'd expect, all of these families have had both sons and daughters. The daughters have married. So we're not just looking at

Rusts, Culpepers, Dromgooles and Barfeet, but several other names, which I've put down in my notebook. I haven't got through to the latest generation, so there may be more names to add… Did you write down Bent's contemporaries at Sandhurst and school?"

"Yes. Quite a lot of names, of course. And it's always possible he had friends who weren't his exact contemporaries. But as we're simplifying a lot already, I thought I'd stick to contemporaries at this stage. Otherwise we'll need a computer to sort out all the names… Could you work out what happened to the money left by the original Rust and Culpeper and so on?"

"So far, yes. I've got up to the generation that were dying off in the fifties and sixties. They seem to have done well with the money and all but the odd one seems to have been careful with it, so that pretty well all of them were richer than their parents, even though the money was split as many as four ways."

Our food arrived. To our relief, it was what we ordered. I suspected that at least some of the waiters had a reasonable command of English, but spoke Chinese partly for effect and partly – and here the former Customs & Excise official emerged from retirement – to be able to claim ignorance when investigated by the dreaded VATman.

"I don't think there's any point me mentioning the names here," said Rosemary. "We really need to sit down with your list and see whether there are any overlaps... and we should enjoy this food... We really ought to eat out a bit more often."

A further advantage of enjoying a meal out was that we missed the worst of the rush hour. When we arrived home, I made us a mug of tea each and we settled down to compare the names which Rosemary had got from the various wills and the longer lists of names I'd collected from Bent's contemporaries at Sandhurst and school. What emerged was perhaps more than we expected, but also sufficiently inconclusive to be slightly disappointing.

From Samuel Rust we got Nigel Underwood, a contemporary of Bent's at Sandhurst. Charles Culpeper's great-grandson was Leonard Vinson, a contemporary of Bent's at Haberdasher Aske's. Finally, James Ormesby, grandson of Percival Dromgoole, was also a contemporary of Bent at school.

"Oh well," observed Rosemary. "We never thought it'd be easy... I felt we probably wouldn't identify anyone. Instead we've got three."

"I'm only surprised we didn't find a descendant of Jerome Barfoot lurking there too... But perhaps we can put him to one side for the moment. Even though he left a reasonable fortune, I can't see why a murder he committed could affect his descendants. Suppose he killed someone for some reason and hid the body in the attic of Number 3 Sandown Terrace… and Dromgoole learnt about it and attempted to blackmail him about it? Perhaps he didn't know the complete truth until the 1890s, which was why he was able to buy Barfoot out of the school. But he surely would've got a generous deal out of Barfoot. And in such circumstances, whatever money Barfoot made later on in life could hardly be seen as being directly connected to the body in the attic?"

"What if the reason Barfoot had the money to buy Number 4 Sandown Terrace in the first place came about as the result of a murder? Perhaps he robbed someone? Or he killed the real Jerome Barfoot and assumed his identity? Or he disposed of a wealthy relative who'd left him all his money in his will? All of those might well encourage him to hide the corpse, as otherwise the finger of suspicion might well be pointed at him."

"But unless there are some descendants of the dead man, whoever he was, who could lay claim in some way to the money which Barfoot's descendants have now, I can't see why they should be bothered about what we've been up to… But we could certainly check with the Land Registry to see how much Barfoot sold Number 4 Sandown Terrace to Dromgoole for."

"I agree, Barfoot has always seemed a slightly less likely candidate… And putting the corpse in Number 3 Sandown Terrace would be a bit odd anyway, as there'd always be a risk that someone might find it. You'd surely hide in the house you owned, not next door… And though there may be a link to Bent, I agree it's sensible to try and follow up those we've actually managed to identify. We can come back to Barfoot and anyone else if we get stuck."

"And what do we do about these others?"

"We find out what we can about them. We've got some initials with the surnames, so we can check things like phone books… If we knew whether they were company directors and of which firms, we could check up at Companies' House… But I suppose if we knew that already… And it really wouldn't be practical to try and look at every company registered with Companies' House to see whether they were directors of any… So we might just have to find out where they live and do a bit of sniffing around there."

"I realise they haven't got completely ordinary surnames, but I suspect we'll find more than one of each of them… In any case, there must be Army records which may give us a bit more information about Underwood… and I wonder if I couldn't get some info about the other two out of Haberdasher Aske's…"

"Well, if anyone can think up a plausible excuse, you can… But we need to think more about this… Why did whoever it was get in touch with Bent? He's not a security expert."

"Presumably they thought he'd be able to contact someone who was… Or he'd be an intermediary who'd hide who they were from the bloke who was going to bug our house and possibly set our car alight."

"Yes. But why him? If it was the man who was at Sandhurst with him, you'd think he might know people who could do security work who were more reliable and less likely to give way to pressure than Carlyle. And if you were living in Leicester, for instance, why would you contact your old school friend Bent in Tunbridge Wells? Surely, you'd know someone you could trust who lived a lot closer to you."

"So you're suggesting it was someone in the Tunbridge Wells area… or reasonably close, like South East London?"

"Yes. If we find a Vinson, Underwood or Ormesby in the local telephone directory covering Tunbridge Wells, we go straight for them… Is this perhaps a version of your famous Ockham's razor?"

"Probably… But if Underwood is living locally, we should also follow him up. If he's involved – possibly on behalf of one or more of his relatives – he'd have the same wish to avoid a direct link between any security expert and himself."

"I agree."

We agreed to continue with our two-pronged approach. Rosemary would go to Beckenham library the following day and look through telephone directories, while I would try to find out about the sale of Number 3 Sandown Terrace by Samuel Rust to Percival Dromgoole and Dromgoole's subsequent purchase of Number 4 Sandown Terrace from Jerome Barfoot. To check how these prices compared, I'd also try to find out about the sale price of Number 2 Sandown Terrace by Charles Culpeper in the late 1890s.

After Rosemary had gone off to the library and to have a swim at the next-door swimming pool, I rang the Land Registry. After I'd explained what I wanted, I was put on to an expert… who was both helpful and unhelpful – though not deliberately, I hasten to add. She explained that before the 1950s – in the case of Kent – deeds to properties didn't have to be registered. So there was no central record of sales of property before that time. Indeed, there was no particular reason why there should be any local records – and if there were, there was no guarantee

306

that they'd been archived at all. Though the Public Record Office held many deeds, they were generally those involving the Crown or court cases, but weren't indexed at all. She suggested that I might find something in the Kent County archives in Canterbury or Maidstone... and it was possible there might even be something in any local archives in Deal or Dover, but she had no idea whether such archives existed. I thanked her for her help and made myself some coffee, feeling frustrated.

I reckoned that there would be copies of the relevant deeds somewhere. But rummaging around unarchived records in Maidstone or Canterbury seemed to me both likely to be a waste of time – not least because I might be searching a haystack for a needle which wasn't there – but also potentially dangerous, if my unfocussed research alerted the person who might well have put the writer of the threatening letters on to us in the first place. This struck me as having all the hallmarks of a dead end. I just had to hope that Rosemary had done better.

She returned at lunchtime, promptly taking her swimsuit and towel out of her sports bag and putting them in the washing machine.

"I don't think we're going to get anywhere with the sales of the properties." I began. "There don't appear to be any archives of them before about 1950."

"Well, we always thought the main use for it would be to see whether Dromgoole had anything over Barfoot... and Barfoot has always seemed a little unlikely. If he had killed someone and wanted to conceal his body, I can't see how or why he'd use the attic of Number 3 rather than the attic of the house he owned himself. Either he had to break the attic wall down or he'd've had to get the body through the next-door house and then build a wall in the attic - all without being seen. It doesn't really add up."

"But I think when we are next in Deal, we should take a final look at the walls up there, just to make sure there isn't anything we might've overlooked. For instance, I'm not sure how hard I've ever looked at the dividing wall with Number 4... But more important than that, how did you get on this morning? I hope you did better than I did."

"I got some names. Whether they turn out to be dead-ends or not, it's too early to say, of course. There's an L. T. Vinson who lives in Tunbridge Wells, a J. W. D. Ormesby, who lives in Edenbridge. The nearest N. Underwood is a N. R. Underwood, who lives in Westerham. I glanced at a couple of the south-east London directories and found two or three of each name. But let's start with these three. It seems to me if you live in London, you'd look up someone rather closer than Tunbridge Wells... But I could easily be proved wrong."

"So what do we do about these three? We can hardly ring them up and invite them out for tea."

"We need to think more about that… We should assume that one of them knows what we look like… and may be put on alert by anything – even someone ringing them and claiming it's a wrong number."

"But there must things that don't make them suspicious. For instance, if I got myself dressed up as a jobbing gardener and went round the streets around where they live, not just asking at their house, but those all around, it could hardly look too suspicious. After all, we've already had a couple since Easter. A pair of old jeans, a green t-shirt and combat jacket and my native accent, I reckon I'd be pretty convincing."

"Don't forget, these men will probably be out working during weekdays. I know it's possible they're wealthy enough to be retired. But you'd have to assume they wouldn't be at home… and these garden people don't tend to come round at weekends."

"But I might be able to do a bit of gossiping, so I could find out a bit more what they were like."

"Hmmm… Women on their own tend to gossip more to other women than to passing middle-aged gardeners."

"Or young gardeners with large muscles and little vests?"

"I wouldn't know anything about that."

"But perhaps we need to think further. It seems to me we could go to Deal tomorrow and remove the bugs and have a final look at the attic. At least no one can see us doing that... It allows us to see how far we've got Carlyle bothered... If he's removed the bugs already, in spite of what we told him, we can reckon he isn't to be trusted and may well have told Bent what happened. And in case anyone is watching the Marine Buildings anyway, we could see whether it triggered another letter – or something happening... I have been checking to see if we were being followed or if there are any cars or vans in the neighbourhood at odd times..."

"Me too... But I reckon Carlyle didn't want to let on he'd been rumbled. So as far as Bent is concerned, we're not up to anything... and if we just go to the flat in Deal, it seems to me we've got to do something that stirs them up. We can hardly be expected not to make any use of the flat for the next couple of years just in case it gets someone all hot and bothered. If we keep away from libraries, archives and even antiquarian bookshops, I can't see anyone could take it we were still digging around."

We drove to Deal the following day. Though our car would be parked outside the Marine Buildings and be more vulnerable than at home, at least if someone did set fire to it, only the car would be damaged, not our garage as well. Besides, we felt that if anyone was following us, it'd be easier to spot them if they were following us in a car. As it was, we didn't believe we were being followed… Though, of course, once we'd set off eastwards along the A2, anyone who knew much about us could probably have guessed where we were heading. We arrived in time to have lunch in the café at the end of the pier and, with reluctance, avoided going into the antiquarian bookshop.

We settled ourselves into the flat, found and removed the bugs which Carlyle had planted, and checked that as far as we could tell, there weren't any others. Then we ascertained that Bill Joyner hadn't yet returned to flat 4 and made what we expected would be our final visit to the attic. There was already evidence that someone had started to tidy things up there, but, so far, no one had demolished the false wall. So we were able to look at that wall, as well as the walls between the adjoining flats on either side.

"As far as I can see, neither of these walls have ever been partly broken through," I observed. "The only one I can't be certain about is the false wall. It's possible it could've had a hole knocked in it and been bricked up again. But now all the rubble has been removed, we're never going to be able to tell either way… and I doubt the photos you took would bring anything out either, especially if any hole that might've been there was in the bit Bill Joyner knocked out in the first place."

"And if it was done a long time ago – by Dromgoole to blackmail Barfoot, for instance, he would presumably have replaced the bricks and I doubt whether anyone could tell the original mortar from mortar used on the 1890s, certainly not from any fragments that might be left lying around," Rosemary added.

"The only other thing to check is whether the adjoining walls look as though they're the same vintage as the other attic walls… It struck me that if you were really determined to hide the fact that you'd brought the body through from Number 2 or Number 3, you might feel it safer to replace the whole wall – even though it'd be more trouble and take longer . But these look as though they were built at the same time and the mortar is properly finished. I don't see how you could do that if you were building it back up from the other side… and I find it impossible to believe that someone from another building was able to sneak up to the attic of Number 3 and construct a complete wall."

Rosemary said nothing. As we made our way back down to flat 3, I realised she wasn't really listening.

Something was occupying her mind, but long experience told me to wait until she was ready to say what she had to say.

I wrote up what we'd seen in my notebook and made us both a mug of tea. Then I drank it, looking out of the window at the grey waves pounding the beach, growling as they did so, and muttering as they encountered the groynes. I could make out half a dozen grey shapes of container ships or ferries on the horizon, the far side of the Goodwin sands, and a couple of white-sailed yachts making slow progress through the Downs, the near side of the Goodwins.

"I've been trying to fathom something out," said Rosemary. "Let's go down to the box room… just in case."

"Oh… I thought that was the sound of the waves," I replied, as we made our way down the flight of stairs to the little box room, which Emily and Greg had set up as a sort of study.

"I could keep what I've been thinking about to myself," she remarked, smiling. "But as I'm sure you're only teasing, I'll tell you what I've been thinking about. I've been trying to work out the sequence of what we were up to and the letters we received. In particular, how did the letter-writer know what we were up to and whether we knew enough to be worth threatening. After all, if we appeared to be getting nowhere, there'd've been no reason to write to us at all… as it was likely to stir us up. Of course, the person who first notified the letter-writer might've done so entirely innocently… If you knew that X was a descendant of Y who'd been living in Sandown Terrace at the time the body was hidden there, you might just mention we were looking at it in passing conversation. After all, if you were Rowena Warnle, for instance, you almost certainly wouldn't know anything about the family's nasty little secret, but you might well think they'd be interested."

"But we might've come across someone who knew rather more… Hence the need to send the letter at all… After all, I assume you'd only want to send the letter if you felt there was a genuine risk we might stumble across something inconvenient."

"In theory… Of course, it's possible someone panicked and once they'd let the genie out of the bottle, couldn't get it back in again… But if you remember the original letter, there was a lot in it about it being unlikely we would get anywhere, but a slight suspicion that we might. Doesn't that suggest the letter-writer was advised by someone like Esmee Culpeper or one of the archivists we met? Of course, it could still be an innocent conversation, with someone like Esmee Culpeper mentioning what we were up to, but pointing out that we weren't likely to get far."

"You'd think that anyone who knew much about the subject would be fairly confident we'd hit a brick wall sooner or later. Indeed, if I was a professional archivist or local historian, I'd've advised the letter-writer not to write us. All it'd do would be to intrigue us more. Whereas if they just left us to our own devices, chances are we'd've given up by now."

"And that suggests that the letter-writer probably isn't any of these men we've identified. They're all likely to be still working at their age and this response seems too panicky, too querulous, to come from someone who's having to earn his living every day. It's more like the sort of thing you'd expect from an aged aunt... But actually I was thinking more about the car that was set on fire in front of the Marine Buildings and the second letter that was posted the same day in Beckenham. In between the first and second letters, we went to the Family Research Centre several times and then met Challenor and the antiquarian bookseller. But we met them on the same day the car was set alight and the letter delivered, so it couldn't've been them telling the letter-writer what we were up to..."

"So Carlyle must've bugged the flat and the car before then."

"Yes. It's the only realistic explanation. I realise it's possible someone spent their time hanging around the Family Research Centre, but it doesn't seem very likely. Which means that the letter-writer was so hot and bothered that he or she got their relative to contact Bent to get someone both to keep tabs on what we were up to and to set up some fireworks if we didn't seem to be desisting."

"And probably the second letter and the car fire in Deal was set up after Carlyle had picked up conversations we had in our car going to or coming back from Budleigh Salterton?"

"I reckon so."

"I'm not sure where this is taking us…"

"Mainly, it's showing that whoever has been writing the letters panicked… without really thinking through what we might be able to find out… But was so hot and bothered that they wanted to make sure they knew what we were up to… and also that they needed to set in hand the threats they'd made… I think this is someone who's absolutely terrified of losing their money and the comfort and security that goes with it, and they believe that if the victim and the murderer are identified, that's definitely what will happen."

"So we need to follow the money… Which probably means putting both the Barfoot and Dromgoole connections to one side…"

"Barfoot definitely... I wouldn't wholly discard Dromgoole yet. He may have got his money from blackmailing someone else... I guess that an elderly descendant might be worried that somehow that money could be clawed back somehow... though as far as I can see, I'm not sure how... But I suppose it's not the sort of thing you'd want to seek legal advice about."

"But that suggests we should start to find out a bit about Underwood who lives in Westerham and Vinson who lives in Tunbridge Wells."

"You'd better do Tunbridge Wells. I don't really want to reappear there as either Mrs. Rosalind Carter-Browne or Jenny Carter. There's too much risk I'd be seen somewhere where I didn't look right – or my two identities had to meet each other."

"OK. I can be a retired bloke who's doing a bit of gardening to pay for his holidays as easily in Tunbridge Wells as in Westerham... Who will you be in Westerham, Carter or Carter-Browne?"

"Carter, I think. On reflection, I don't think I should be using any name that anyone's likely to remember later... and double-barrelled names are always that little bit more memorable."

"And what's your reason for treading the streets calling at people's houses?"

"A sewing, darning and clothing repair service, I think. We need to get some business cards made… for both of us I reckon… Isn't there a machine at the service station on the M2?"

"I think so. I didn't take much notice of what was there – other than somewhere to get some coffee… and it wasn't really worth it, either…"

"We need to work out references that aren't spotted as fake the moment we leave. If I was suspicious, I'd try the phone number on the business card. If it didn't exist or was plainly a wrong number, I wouldn't want to find myself explaining that when I was just a few houses further along the street."

"That could be quite difficult with a phone number. You could hardly use ours… It's obviously an Outer London number… and even if we have a look at a Tunbridge Wells area phone book, I don't see how we could get hold of a number that couldn't cause us trouble if anyone decided to test it out."

"Didn't you have a mobile phone when you were in your last job? Or did it belong to Customs?"

"No. I didn't like the one they provided. It never seemed to work properly, so I bought one… But where on earth it is and whether I could still use it, I've no idea. I barely used it at the time… If nothing else its battery must be as flat as a pancake."

"Well, it looks like our best bet. So we'd better hunt for it when we get home."

We drove home that evening, unable to make use of the business card machine at the M2 services because of the lack of a suitable phone number. Once we got home we started searching and eventually found the mobile phone languishing with several ill-suited companions in an old leather suitcase that had once belonged to my father and, I suspect, his father before him. The phone, along with its charging mechanism, was accompanied by an old fake revolver which we'd had since 1964 and a "Stationery Office" black mahogany cylindrical ruler which I'd inherited from the late Neville Davenport in the same year. Both had been used for defensive, even offensive, purposes over the years, but hadn't seen the light of day for at least ten. The phone was, of course, as dead as a dodo, so I plugged in the charging device and hoped it would work its magic overnight. When we woke, I tried the phone. To my relief – and surprise – not only did the phone start up, but it also seemed to work. Being a tidy person, I'd written the number down in an old notebook, so we were able to check that the number was still in operation. Then all we had to do was to find somewhere in Bromley that did "print it yourself" business cards and we were up and running.

"Of course, we can't both go off at the same time," Rosemary noted. "One of us will have to be at home on the end of the mobile phone in case someone rings… and only one of us can have the phone."

"You've already done your undercover bit. I believe it's my turn to have a go."

"OK. You'd better make sure you leave one of your business cards with me, so I get the details right if anyone phones."

The following day I put on a pair of older jeans, a khaki tee-shirt and one of those travelling waistcoats with about a dozen pockets which I'd bought about ten years earlier and barely ever worn. Along with a plain fawn baseball cap, I thought I looked plausibly like a retired gent who was offering gardening services that didn't involve any heavy-duty stuff – like cutting down trees or laying new lawns. I got the train to Tunbridge Well and headed for the Calverley Park area. Vinson lived in Lansdowne Road, but I thought I should begin somewhere else. So, I went one way up Calverley Road and back along Calverley Park Gardens before going into Lansdowne Road. I got no answer at about a third of the houses and pretended to put a business card through the door, but I didn't really want a load of unnecessary phone calls about my non-existent gardening business. Indeed, putting lots of people off might mean word got around the

neighbourhood and suspicions being aroused…
Though when I came to think of it, people would be
more likely to suspect possible burglars than amateur
detectives… But the local police could probably tack
down who owned the phone and that would mean
awkward questions that Rosemary and I would prefer
not to answer.

About a third of the houses weren't interested.
The door was opened by a maid, au pair or cleaning
lady who informed me that they didn't take stuff from
itinerant tradesmen… or words to that effect. In the
other third, the lady of the house came to the door.
Mostly they saw no need for a jobbing gardener. They
either employed one already or it was their way of
keeping their husbands out from under their feet at
weekends. But several were chatty enough to tell me a
bit about the area and whether there was likely to be
anyone who might be interested.

Lansdowne Road was full of large white houses,
the sort that were built for larger families that'd been
common for the last fifty years and more, along with
servants who'd largely disappeared since the 1920s. It
struck me that if Leonard Vinson lived in one of
these, he might well have an aged aunt or granny or
two dwelling with him, possibly with sufficiently large
funds for him to wish to keep her/them sweet.

Next door to the Vinson house didn't answer the
door. This was a pity as I was hoping to learn more

from neighbours than I could from Vinson's family. Inevitably, when I pushed the rather fine old door bell, a middle-aged woman came to the door. I explained quickly why I was there.

"I'm afraid I'll have to disappoint you," replied the woman, in a cut-glass accent. "We already employ a gardener for the heavy work and Leonard does the rest to keep in trim."

"I'm beginning to realise there are too many men like your husband who keep their gardens in good shape as a way of keeping fit," I replied, maintaining sufficient of my native Woolwich accent to give the impression that I was the sort of person who needed to supplement my retirement pension, but equally that I wasn't a prospective burglar on the prowl. "I confess I was hoping this area had rather older residents who might welcome some help in the garden."

"You evidently don't know Tunbridge Wells as I do," she replied. "It's a haven for old people's homes. You'll find that most of the elderly have passed their properties on to their children – not least to try to avoid death duties – and lead a rather comfortable existence waited on hand and foot in a retired gentlefolk's home in rather splendid surroundings. That's where a couple of our elder generation have placed themselves... But I doubt you'll get any work there. These places are large enough to employ their own groundsmen."

I thanked her for her advice and moved on. The neighbour on the other side had no more use for my services and told very much the same story about "the elder generation". Of course, this did indicate that Leonard Vinson might've been put up to contacting Major Harry Bent by a querulous mother-in-law or aunt in a nearby old gentlefolk's home. But that was as far as my morning's work got me.

I found a cheapish café for lunch and then walked to the other side of the town centre and found a park and read a book, sitting on a park bench in the sun. There was no point giving out any more business cards… or being seen to tramp the streets for business. Apart from the fact that most the houses I'd visited were quite secluded, the general advice had been discouraging, so I was perfectly entitled to have taken the view that I wasn't going to get anywhere in Tunbridge Wells.

In theory, I could have gone home. But some of me hoped to get a glimpse of Leonard Vinson. I'd got a timetable at the station and I tried to work out what train he might catch. By and large, trains to and from London were half-hourly to Charing Cross direct. For Victoria, you'd have to change… but you'd end up on one of the Charing Cross trains anyhow. Middle-aged men with plenty of money, like Leonard Vinson, were going to be bosses, I felt. They wouldn't be getting in at 8 am. These were the blokes who would work the hours that the "blue-bloods" used to work in the Civil Service in the earlier days of my career. They'd get in between 9.30 and 10. Given that they probably didn't need to flog their guts out, especially after a decent (and longish) lunch, I reckoned people like Vinson would get a train between 6 and 6.30. The trains took just about an hour. There was one that left Charing Cross at 18.10 and another at 18.40. Would Vinson walk from the station or would his good lady go and pick him up in the car? Working on the assumption that if he needed to do light gardening to "keep in trim", he'd walk home from the station, I reckoned there must be a chance I could spot him. Looking at the town map that Rosemary had given me, I felt sure he'd walk across Calverley Park in the summer at least, emerging at the T-junction between Crescent Road, Calverley Road and Lansdowne Road.

I needed to do a recce of Calverley Park, to see whether there was anywhere I could position myself, without looking suspicious, where I could decide who might be Leonard Vinson and follow him home at around 19.20. Of course, if several middle-aged men came past, I'd be stuck. I might just have to pick one on a hunch. I found a phone box in use and rang Rosemary, explaining what I was planning to do. She didn't say it was a pretty desperate plan, which she might reasonably have done, but did confirm the mobile phone had remained silent so far. Since I'd only handed out half a dozen cards in the end, I wasn't wholly surprised.

It was a good job I'd brought a book with me. It didn't take me long to find a suitable place at the Lansdowne Road edge of Calverley Park where I could station myself later. But it was out of the sunshine – and it wasn't such a warm day that I wanted to spend the afternoon in the shade. So, I found a suitable bench in Calverley Park and read my book, with a short interruption for an excursion to a café for a cup of tea and use of the facilities. (One of the inconveniences I recognised age had brought was my increasing inability to sit around all afternoon like this without needing a pee).

There weren't many people going through the park during the afternoon. Between three-thirty and four, mothers with primary school children came through. After I got back from the café, gaggles of teenagers in school uniform were making their way along the paths, distinctly better mannered than their counterparts in Beckenham. From around five-thirty, the occasional commuter came past. At first it was the young women – secretaries or the equivalent I guessed – in smart "office" clothes, then the men, mostly middle-aged, invariably in dark business suits, looking hot. At 6.15, I closed up my book and made my way slowly to the bench on the corner of

Lansdowne Road opposite the park entrance. I felt the least suspicious thing to do was to sit there, looking as though I was waiting for a lift. I'd picked up a *Metro* on my journey to Tunbridge Wells and now held it, carefully folded, in my hand hoping people would assume it was an *Evening Standard*. From time to time, I peered up the road as if I was looking out for a car.

At just before 6.20, a middle-aged man in a smart business suit appeared. He crossed the road and went into Calverley Park Gardens. A minute or so later, he was followed by a similar type, who made his way down Lansdowne Road. I almost got up to follow him – but there was something about him, an air of tension, almost a cloud of anger, that made me halt. It seemed to me – quite possibly incorrectly – that someone born into money, as Leonard Vinson undoubtedly had been, wasn't likely to be carrying that degree of frustration or irritation around with them. And I felt that my hunch had been rewarded when a couple of minutes later, a slightly plump middle-aged man in a dark grey chalk-stripe suit emerged from the park and crossed the road into Lansdowne Road. I waited for a minute or so until he'd come past me, then followed him. He was walking quite slowly, almost meandering. The walk from the station might ostensibly be for his health, but I doubted whether at this pace it was doing him a lot of good. From what I could make out of him, he was plainly well-heeled, but a bit slow-moving, self-indulgent. I suspected his position in whatever firm he was employed, was due to his money and possibly a native cunning, rather than any get-up-and-go or leadership qualities. To my pleasure (finding one's hunches turning out accurately is always a treat), he turned into the Vinson house. I walked past. I knew I'd recognise him in future if I needed to follow him or, indeed, corner him at some point.

And that was as much as I was going to get. So, I made my way by a slightly circuitous route – mainly through a miscalculation from my memory of the town map rather than any concern about being followed – to the station and thence home.

"Either you didn't give out many cards or they're very trusting in Tunbridge Wells," remarked Rosemary after I'd got home, kissed her and taken a mug of tea from her. "I haven't had a single call on this... at least I got what I'm sure was a genuine wrong number... but I said it was your garden services thing, just to be on the safe side... and I reckon I did a fair effort at your London accent."

"I didn't really learn much," I confirmed. "If it is Vinson, at least I know where he lives and what he looks like... and that he has a couple of aged relatives in a local home for retired gentlefolk. One of them could, of course, be the person we think has been instigating and possibly even writing the letters..."

"Though if it was someone in an old people's home, they must still be quite robust, as the writing was definitely done with a steady hand."

"And judging by the house the Vinsons live in, there's still a fair amount of money in the Culpeper family. Charles may have died alone, if Esmee is to be believed, but even if she claims none of his descendants were so well off that they could afford to compensate Gerard Culpeper's heirs, the Vinsons at least have a house that must be worth at least twice ours... and can afford to keep at least two aged relatives in a home for retired gentlefolk... a description that I'm sure means the cost is double what you'd pay in an old people's home."

"Certainly nothing you've seen today suggests we should be ruling the Culpepers out at this stage. Let's see how I get on in Westerham tomorrow."

The following day, I sat by the mobile phone indoors. I'd hoped to spend the day doing some light gardening and reading, but it was one of those summer days of the old-fashioned sort that couldn't make up its mind whether to rain or shine, so it alternated between the two. So, I did some work on writing up notes from incidents earlier in my career, listened to a couple of CDs of music from the 1960s and read a bit of my book. My day wasn't interrupted at all by any call on the mobile phone, though I got several on the house phone from double glazing salesmen, etc.

Rosemary returned shortly after 7 pm.

"I wouldn't wish commuting from Westerham on my worst enemy," she remarked, as I handed her a mug of tea and gave her a kiss. "I decided our car shouldn't be seen in Westerham, so I found a convenient street in Biggin Hill and caught a bus from there. But the traffic from Biggin Hill there and back was horrendous… in the other direction fortunately. I don't know whether everyone from Westerham commutes via Bromley South, but it certainly seemed like it."

"I suppose it's a lot cheaper than Sevenoaks or Orpington… Otherwise it must be somewhere like Edenbridge or Oxted and I'll bet the fares will be dear and the journey slow from either of those."

"But there really isn't anywhere to park at Bromley South. I'm sure it must be commuters from Westerham and Biggin Hill that block up all the surrounding streets… Though I guess some get driven there and back by their wives."

"So what was Westerham like?"

"It's rather a nice place. When we've finished this stuff, we should both go there and have lunch. It's not very big – certainly nothing like the size of

Tunbridge Wells. But it's got a rather elegant centre with a sort of green and a lot of nice houses. I suppose you can get them quite a bit cheaper there because of the awful commuting from there."

"So what did you discover?"

"The Underwood residence is on Vicarage Hill. Like you, I decided not to start there, but on the other side of what they call Market Square, there was an odd mixture of houses, some looked more like former council houses and I couldn't see them wanting a sewing or clothes alteration service. There's not so much money about that most people don't do that for themselves... So I went through Market Square and found myself on Vicarage Hill almost immediately. It was a mixture of huge and very nice and elegant houses and smaller old cottages. The houses must be worth millions! I tried every one, but mostly they thanked me and said they weren't interested. I got no reply at several of the cottages... but there was always someone answering the door at the big houses – but usually it was the au pair or the cleaning lady, I reckon. They were reluctant to take a card. I got the lady of the house in a big white Georgian-style house. She was pleasant in a very posh way, but she already had someone who "did" for her."

"I guess there are plenty of serfs in the council houses."

"I'm sure your father would've agreed with those sentiments."

"But I'm sure they treat them very nicely… Sorry… Please go on…"

"The Underwood residence actually has its own name – Clarendon House. It was very nice, with sort of a brick Regency frontage on to Vicarage Hill and what seemed like a couple of houses attached to it at the rear. Unfortunately, I couldn't really go snooping around. When I rang the bell – which had a maritime air about it – an old woman came to the door. I guess she was in her eighties. She had a very refined, old-fashioned accent… like the old BBC announcers before the war. She explained that her niece-in-law was out, meeting friends for lunch at Hever Castle. But she was quite clear a sempstress wasn't required. She had a rather old-fashioned vocabulary, but there was certainly nothing querulous about her. She struck me as sharp as a tack… Which meant, of course, that I couldn't ask too many questions or hang around longer than seemed appropriate. I offered my card, but she declined it politely and I had to be on my way. I realise no one has ever suggested the Rust family were at any risk of poverty, but judging by what I could make out of the hall and the outside of the house, I'd say they're plainly worth millions."

"That pretty well confirms what Esmee Culpeper said."

"Don't remind of that woman, please! I realised I was going to have to be quite careful in what I said to the neighbours. But just as I was leaving the Underwood residence, I noticed an extremely fine brick house almost opposite. It had a couple of notices outside and I discovered it was called Quebec House and was owned by the National Trust. As Westerham is so small and didn't seem to have a convenient park like you had in Tunbridge Wells, I thought this might be the best place to observe Clarendon House... and possibly to pick up a bit of gossip about the Underwoods. Fortunately it was open, so I went in and bought a day ticket. I told them I'd like to look round the house, but if the weather cleared up I might quite like to sit in the garden and read my book for a bit. The lady at the desk was about our age and seemed rather bored. I doubt whether they get many visitors outside weekends... and not all that many then. I guess General Wolfe isn't particularly well-known, though you could argue his actions at Quebec were as decisive as Nelson's at Trafalgar... and of course, both died in the course of their victory. Before today, I knew practically nothing about Wolfe, apart from a vague idea that he'd captured Quebec and something about the Heights of Abraham. But that was pretty well it... "

"That's about all I knew... apart from the extra opinion that he was an agent of British colonialism.

Whether the fact that he was fighting agents of French colonialism made his actions better or worse, my father never said… Sorry, please go on…"

"After I'd got her to tell me more about General Wolfe than I really feel I need to know, I got her on to Westerham and its history and then on to some of the people who lived there… Naturally they claim Churchill as a quasi-resident, as Chartwell is pretty close. I got it all connected up with some of the grand houses – which do rather stand out in such a small town – after a while we got on to Clarendon House and I got the early history and then the purchase by Edgar Rust in the late 1920s. Apparently he had two daughters. One – Lilian – never married and still lives there. I guess she was the old woman I met earlier. The elder sister – Eleanor – married Jonathan Underwood and it's their youngest son, Nigel, who is the current master of the house. There were two other sons – both deceased - as is Eleanor Underwood, nee Rust. According to the lady in Quebec House, Nigel was a 'mistake', born when his mother was well into her forties.

'The Underwoods are an undistinguished family,' the lady told me. 'Jonathan Underwood was a local solicitor whose family were comfortably off. But the Rust family are much more notable. The MP for the Weald is a second cousin or something like that.'

'I don't think I've ever really heard of the Rust family,' I remarked.

'You probably don't remember Rust's pastilles or Rust's tonic,' the lady replied. 'You don't see them about much nowadays. When I was a child, we often had them when we had winter colds.'

'That was the Rust who lives here? For some reason, I always thought they were made in the North somewhere.'

'Oh no. They were a Kentish family through and through… Of course, they don't own the company any more. I believe an American company took them over, but the pastilles and tonic are still made over here, I believe.'

'They must certainly have done well if they can afford to live in a house like that.'

'Yes. When they sold the company, I'm told they invested the money sensibly… and kept some shares in the new company. Even so, it shows what inventing some cough pastilles can do for your fortune.'

"This was all quite useful, if not entirely new," Rosemary continued. "The icing on the cake would've been Nigel Underwood driving into his house so I could recognise him in future. But it was still only later morning and I couldn't see why he'd be going home at that time. So I did a lengthy tour of Quebec House. Almost every time I looked out of the window it was raining, so there was no point hurrying. Then I took advantage of a sunny spell to walk back into the centre of the town and have a salad in a little café. Some of the restaurants seemed quite pricey, but – as I'm sure you'd say – the serfs have to eat somewhere too.

"Afterwards, I tried the houses next to Clarendon House, but the people who came to the door were servants of one sort or another and I felt they were possibly more likely to detect nosiness than the mistress of the house. So I was finished quite quickly. Unlike some of us, not only was there nowhere to sit and read a book without it being evident to all and sundry I was just hanging around, it would've looked particularly silly whenever it rained, which seemed to be about every half hour. So, I went back to Quebec House and the lady was content for me to sit in the little tea room and read there – provided I had a pot of tea and some home-made cake. Unfortunately, the choice was between date and walnut and carrot cake. I had the carrot cake, and though it may have looked as though I was devouring a molecule at a time in order to make the minutes pass less slowly, I was actually hoping the taste might improve with age. Quebec House closed at 5pm and there wasn't really anywhere I could go to watch Clarendon House without it being blindingly obvious, so I decided I'd got all I was going to get. Inevitably, I'd just missed a bus back to Biggin Hill and I had to wait ages for the next one. Then I made the mistake of driving back through Bromley rather than West Wickham, which is why it's taken so long… I'm afraid I've no idea what Nigel Underwood looks like… and I'm not sure how we could find out without making it obvious that we were staking out Clarendon House."

"Apart from sitting around reading, I've also been looking at my notebooks and thinking. What you've just been saying confirms the conclusion I've reached… provisional, of course. But I think I've reached the point you get to in a game of 'Cluedo' when I should write down who killed Mr. X, where and with what. Though in this case it's who was killed, who killed them and why… Rather more than we did with Goronwy Rees that time in Wales…"

"You're well ahead of me. Are you sure you aren't making some great leap which happens to fit what we know rather than taking account of the massive amounts we don't? But please don't tell me… Apart from wanting to think it out for myself, there's a risk that I'll get caught up in your reasoning and then I can't get back on track properly afterwards."

"Well, if you'll allow me to give you directions as to where we should drive tomorrow, you may be able to see how I've got to where I've got to."

13. THE SKELETON IN THE FAMILY CUPBOARD

Rosemary said little for the rest of the evening or the following morning. I knew that she was trying to work out how I'd reached a conclusion and what it was. When we set off, I began the journey in a way that gave nothing away. We could've been heading for Deal, Tunbridge Wells, Westerham or even Edenbridge, where James Ormesby lived. But fairly soon, it became clear that we were heading for Westerham.

"I can be a bit slow sometimes," she remarked, as we headed past Keston Ponds, "but I think I've finally caught up. Have you worked out how you're going to play this? I doubt whether it'll work if you just play it by ear and hope you can wing it, as you did that time in the squash club in the City."

"There are just two things I want out of today. The first is the intellectual satisfaction of having worked out what happened. The second is to make absolutely certain that no one has any reason to harm us… or Emily or Sarah for that matter. There's no reason why we should ever make public who the body in the attic was or why he was killed. It's not our job – and, in any case, we could never prove it. If the police wanted to investigate it, they could've done so. All those concerned are long dead. So nothing would be served by dragging it into the full light of day."

"Apart from the descendants of the victim. We should perhaps try to achieve something for them, don't you think?"

"I guess so… Is there somewhere convenient to park in Westerham? Or do you want to park in their drive?"

"In the drive. That's the right psychological move, I believe."

We drove through the town and down Vicarage Hill and into the pebbled drive of Clarendon House. We got out and went to the front door. We had got ourselves smartly dressed for the occasion, so we certainly didn't look like an itinerant gardener on sempstress. A middle-aged woman opened the door. She was dressed in a dark blue twinset with a string of pearls round her neck. I could hear the deeply-buried voice of my father wishing to make a comment, but I kept it to the back of my mind.

"Good morning," said the woman in a plummy accent. She had short hair, dyed a medium blonde, I would've said. "Do you have business here?" She had evidently spotted our car in the drive, but was sufficiently cautious, or just good-mannered, not to make an issue of it.

"We would be grateful for a few words with Miss Lilian Rust, if she is here and willing to see us," I replied.

"And who may I say wishes to see her?"

"Mr. and Mrs. Storey from Beckenham. I believe she'll know what it's about."

"If you will just wait there, pray, I'll seek her opinion."

We continued waiting at the front door while she evidently went through the hall and along a corridor to a room at the rear of the house. I thought I could hear voices in the distance, but I quickly realised it was either a TV or, more likely, a radio. The lady returned after about five minutes.

"I'm sorry to keep you waiting," she said, unsmiling. "Aunt Lilian says she's prepared to meet you. But she would like me to be present as a witness. I take it you have no objection to that?"

"None whatsoever," I replied.

It was plain that her brief conversation with "Aunt Lilian" had reduced the tepid warmth of our initial welcome to several degrees below freezing. But one thing you can say about the rich bourgeoisie, when they're not in command of a situation, they are generally cautious enough to maintain the rules of civility. She led us through a large hall panelled in dark wood, with a fine wooden staircase leading off it. But we went behind the staircase and several doorways to a square room of no great character apart from a large square window with diamond-shaped leaded lights and a Regency-style fireplace made of black marble, with a log fire burning merrily away in the grate. I guessed Aunt Lilian suffered from rheumatism of some sort, as it was a fairly warm day outside, although not particularly sunny.

Lilian Rust was white-haired, elderly, with a thin, pallid face and a pair of half-spectacles sitting on her long nose. She was dressed in a plain greyish-purple dress with a gold brooch. She was sitting in an armchair and turned to examine us as we came into the room.

"I've seen you before," she remarked, pointing a long, bony finger at Rosemary.

"We met at your front door yesterday," replied Rosemary.

"Spying," retorted Lilian Rust.

"Confirming what we'd already surmised," I replied, not wholly accurately. But I didn't want her to turn the conversation in the direction she wanted.

"I suppose you'd better sit down," said Mrs. Nigel Underwood, indicating a two-seater chesterfield covered in dark green velvet. She sat on a curious high-backed chair covered in dark crimson velvet with patterns of flowers made out of dozens of tiny glass beads. It was evidently Victorian and, I would have thought, extremely uncomfortable to sit on, certainly for any length of time.

"You'd better commence what you have to say," said Lilian Rust.

"You evidently know who we are," I replied. "Does your niece-in-law?"

"No. She knows practically nothing about these matters."

"Very well. We are Nick and Rosemary Storey from Beckenham. Rosemary is a former Chief Inspector from the Metropolitan Police and I am a former Commissioner of HM Customs and Excise."

"Why on earth should you require to have dealings with Aunt Lilian?" asked Mrs. Underwood.

"Be quiet, Margaret. Unless there's something you really don't understand, all I require of you is to listen so that you can recall what was said, if necessary," ordered Lilian Rust.

"Just so we're accurate – you are Miss Lilian Rust, grand-daughter of Mr. Samuel Rust, formerly of Number 3 Sandown Terrace, Deal, Sholden Hall and other residence?"

"You are correct. You have plainly adopted a thorough approach to your investigation."

"As far as records allowed. You are aware, of course, that after a corpse was found in the attic of the flat above that of our daughter in what used to be Number 3 Sandown Terrace and is now Number 3 Marine Buildings, we obtained the agreement of the local police to see if we could discover who the dead man was and how he had died. As he'd plainly been walled up in a small space in the attic, it was evident he was murdered and we hoped to identify the killer. As the corpse had been dead for well over 50 years, the police had no intention of investigating. Indeed, we discovered early on that the body had been in the walled cavity for a hundred years or a little more. But our intention all along was to see how far available records and evidence would take us. It was a purely academic exercise – to see whether it was possible to find out. At that stage, we knew virtually nothing about censuses, genealogy, the Family Research Centre or any of that. We've investigated several crimes during our careers and since, and we've always had an interest in evidence, how it's obtained and what you can learn from it. So this posed an interesting new challenge. But I repeat, it was purely academic. We had no interest in publicly naming the dead man or his killer. Plainly, they were well beyond the reach of British justice."

"It occurs to me that you should have made that considerably plainer," remarked Lilian Rust.

"We didn't think we needed to. We were digging away in lots of old records…"

"And talking to local historians in Deal. Both are troublesome busybodies who, even if you were prepared to be silent, would be only too happy to blacken the names of the dead to gain a few more pence for their miserable books and pamphlets. Esmee Culpeper has been trying to find a way to blacken the name of the Rust family for the whole of her adult life."

"I take your point. But you should perhaps be aware of two things. First – we don't believe it's possible from the evidence which remains in archives and so on to prove who the body in the attic of Number 3 Sandown terrace was or who killed him. Second – until you started writing your threatening letters, we were getting close to reaching a dead end in our researches. The reason why we know who the dead man was, who killed him and why has resulted largely from the evidence we've gathered as a result of those two letters… and as you might've guessed, making arrangements to damage our property and getting someone to plant listening devices illegally in our house and car and our daughter's flat made us a good deal more determined to discover who was behind it."

"Regrettably these days one cannot employ reliable people, I see."

"When you wish to set up a lengthy chain to distance yourself from such activities, inevitably you lose some control over the individuals at the end of the chain... But let me continue: There were certain things about the dead body and where he'd been placed and the time period. Your letters gave us additional valuable information, even though that wasn't what you intended. Why was the body placed in that cavity in the attic of Number 3 Sandown Terrace? There could be plenty of reasons, but one stood out. The body was placed there because the killer didn't want the body to be found... at least, not for a very long time. Why was that? Because the dead man would be immediately or very rapidly connected to the killer. The killer must've had a sufficiently great motive for killing the man that the local police would've been bound to suspect him. With any luck, the body wouldn't be found for a very long time and at that point it might well be unrecognisable. The second thing that followed from this was that the man who was killed was unlikely to be missed – certainly not in Deal or thereabouts. For instance, there were Coast Guard and Excise officers living in Sandown Terrace. If they'd gone missing, it would've been noticed quite quickly... and you'd expect the local constables to check where they lived, when they were last seen, etc. Other men living in Sandown Terrace at that time would've had wives and sweethearts, mothers, families – mostly nearby. It'd be difficult to dispose of someone like that without too many questions being asked."

"But there's a flaw in that reasoning, which I confess it took me too long to get past," I continued. "There was no reason why the body which was found in the attic necessarily had to have been anyone who lived in Sandown Terrace. It just had to be someone whose presence in Sandown Terrace – particularly Number 3 – would've passed unnoticed. Though there were times when Number 3 was unoccupied – not least after Samuel Rust sold it to Percival Dromgoole, while it was being converted for use as a school – there appears to have been no event at that time which would explain the body being walled up at that point. In any case, as you're aware, Miss Rust, the body had already been placed in the cavity some years before then. And though to an extent it runs against logic, the body did belong to someone who lived in Sandown Terrace. Using our flawed logic to search various records and archives, we identified several men of the approximate age of the dead man for whom there were no death certificates. But in practice, we couldn't have got much further.

"But then you wrote to us, demanding that we desist from our research. That told us that there was at least one person alive who knew what had happened, who the body was and how he'd come to be in that cavity in the attic. But you mentioned that if we found out what'd happened, it'd cause untold harm – I think those were the words you used weren't they, Miss Rust? – to people living blameless lives today. It seemed to us there were two reasons why our finding out what had happened should damage people alive today – either it'd damage their reputations or their wealth. Try as we might, we couldn't see how the descendants of anyone who lived in Sandown Terrace could have their reputations seriously damaged by a revelation of a hundred-year-old murder. Naturally, we thought about Mr. Nicholas Rust, the MP, but we couldn't for the life of us see how his reputation could've been seriously damaged if it emerged his grandfather had killed someone over a hundred years ago. It'd be inconvenient – but no one would blame him and we've long got past the stage of believing that evil blood gets passed from one generation to another. So, the only other explanation had to be that if our research was successful, it'd put the killer's descendants' wealth at risk. And since you had seen fit to investigate us, threaten us, get bugs planted in various properties and were prepared to damage our property, quite possibly putting our lives at risk, it seemed to us the wealth of these descendants must be quite considerable.

"But the most important aspect was that the killing must've played a highly significant role in the creation of this family wealth. Alongside that, the descendants of the dead man would have a claim on the killer's wealth – even though it'd passed into the hands of numerous descendants. And we followed up various possibilities, but once you strip away the various intriguing possibilities, one thing stares you in the face. Rosemary will tell you that I've been over-fond of using Ockham's Razor as a posh description of stripping something to its basic elements. But that's essentially what I've been doing. The first thing is that the body was found in Number 3 Sandown Terrace. If you're trying to hide a body in such a way that no one is likely to find it for a very long time, would you really carry a dead body from another part of Sandown Terrace or from elsewhere unless you absolutely had to? You'd conceal it as close to where you killed the man as you possibly could. Even in the 1880s and '90s, you couldn't guarantee not to be seen dragging, carrying or carting the body of a dead man around. And in Number 3 Sandown Terrace, there were children and servants about. Could you guarantee to get a body through the front door and up to the attic and then brick up a wall without someone noticing? Especially if you weren't living in the property already?

"So the first place to look must be the people who lived in Sandown Terrace. Now you might suggest that perhaps a servant killed another servant and managed to brick them up in the attic without anyone being aware of it. But where did the bricks and mortar come from? How did they get them up to the attic? In any case, had we come across any suggestion that any of the servants in Number 3 Sandown Terrace had subsequently become so wealthy as a result of a possible murder that a descendant might be the author of the letters to us? It seemed utterly implausible. So, we were left with the two occupants of Number 3 Sandown Terrace during this time – Samuel Rust and Percival Dromgoole. We know that Samuel Rust made his fortune from his tonic and pills. Dromgoole was reputed to have no money of his own, yet he was able to buy Number 3 Sandown Terrace from Samuel Rust. Did he steal it from someone who he'd murdered and put in the attic? But the timing doesn't fit. I doubt whether Samuel Rust would've allowed him to move in and start converting the building to be a school before he got his hands on the money. Besides, even if the unknown dead man had provided the wherewithal for Dromgoole's wealth – such as it was – it's inconceivable that any descendant could seriously expect to make a claim on his descendants.

"So I was led inexorably to Samuel Rust. From what we'd been told, I wondered whether the dead man mightn't've been a brother, father or lover of one of the maids who Samuel Rust had made pregnant. Might that mean that there were descendants of his bastard child who could lay claim to his descendants' wealth? That seemed plausible –

but from what we'd been told, the family had maintained and built on the wealth inherited from Samuel Rust. So it seemed to me that another claimant or two might be accommodated and wouldn't warrant the concern evident in the two letters sent to us. But it was something Esmee Culpeper said – 'if it wasn't for his discovery of the formula for the pastilles and the tonic, he'd just have been a successful local chemist' that finally got me there. I wrote it down in my notebook at the time. I should've thought harder about it. As I'm sure you're aware, Samuel Rust didn't discover the formula for the tonic and pills that were named after him. Matthew Stowe did. And if it was shown that the body in the attic of Number 3 Sandown Terrace was that of Matthew Stowe, who was known to be employed by Samuel Rust as his researcher, at the very least some very awkward questions would be asked… and the descendants of Matthew Stowe – or heirs, I suppose – might seek to make a claim on the wealth of Samuel Rust's descendants.

"It'd be simple enough for Samuel Rust to get Matthew Stowe into Number 3. There could be any number of plausible reasons. He might even have invited him to dinner from time to time. And the one person who could make sure that no servants or children were around at a particular time would be the master of the house. If he arranged for bricks and mortar to be taken up to an attic room which he'd be sure was vacated – perhaps for redecoration – no one would question him. The servant who'd previously been using that room could easily be sacked or given a different room and a new servant would have the room, not knowing it was a couple of feet smaller than previously. And would anyone question Samuel Rust if he said that he'd got rid of Matthew Stowe because his work wasn't up to scratch and Stowe had left the district right away?

"The only thing I'm not sure about is whether Percival Dromgoole knew – or guessed? Or whether Samuel Rust funded his purchase of Number 3 Sandown Terrace in order that Dromgoole would be so grateful he'd keep his mouth shut, even if he did make an inconvenient discovery in the attic?"

"I can understand how you've come to this conclusion," said Lilian Rust. "But it's scarcely evidence that would stand up in a court of law. What are you planning to do with it? Blackmail us? Or would selling the story to the newspapers or television make you more money? Or are you intending to track down Matthew Stowe's heirs and make some arrangement with them?"

"We weren't intending to do any of those things. But perhaps we could come on to that later. First, I'd be grateful if you could confirm what I've just said."

"I can. I've sometimes considered it was unwise of Grandfather Samuel to have insisted that this knowledge was handed on from generation to generation. I can but assume he expected us to arrange matters so that if and when the body of Matthew Stowe was ever discovered, the family wealth would be beyond the power of his heirs to retrieve. Some have adopted his plan and been cautious. But others, not least those who have had control over the bulk of the family's wealth, have been greedy. I believe that if the heirs of Matthew Stowe made a successful claim for what is rightfully theirs, well over two-thirds of the family wealth would flow to them. It may have been a sensible move from a certain perspective to retain so many shares in the companies that bought Grandfather Samuel's original company, but it is all vulnerable to a claim by the Stowe heirs…

"But yes, I can confirm that it was as you indicated, Samuel Rust didn't discover the formula for making the pastilles and tonic. Matthew Stowe did. From what I was told, it was a question of longevity, what I believe is known these days as shelf-life. It was imperative that the pastilles and tonic could last for at least a year. Stowe developed the chemical agents that achieved this. But he was a greedy man and though Grandfather Samuel had been employing him for the best part of ten years, provided him with excellent accommodation, and had developed the basic ingredients himself, Stowe insisted that he would establish his own company to make a tonic and pastilles using the formula he had discovered, while denying use of it to his employer. In spite of offers of money, even a partnership, he was adamant. So Grandfather felt he had no alternative. I don't believe I can usefully add to what you have surmised about how the matter was carried out. Fortunately, Stowe wasn't local and had been of an itinerant nature before coming to work for Grandfather. But he had a widowed mother in London somewhere, a brother and a sister. From my researches, I'd say he has about half a dozen heirs who could make a plausible claim, if they knew what you know."

"And was Percival Dromgoole involved in any way?"

"Percival Dromgoole was a deeply unpleasant man, according to Grandfather Samuel. He was both charming and utterly unscrupulous. But he was also clever and greedy. By the later 1880s, Grandfather was making so much money that he wished to move to more distinguished premises... and Sholden Hall became available at the right time. But, as you may imagine, he was concerned that the new owner of Number 3 Sandown Terrace would discover Stowe's body. What he required was someone greedy and pliable enough to take over ownership without asking any awkward questions or doing any inconvenient exploration of the attics. Jerome Barfoot, who'd just established the preparatory school in Number 4 Sandown Terrace was a prig and a pedant, one of those stiff-necked self-righteous little men who was completely unsuitable as the future owner of Number 3 Sandown terrace, even though he sought to buy it. But Percival Dromgoole was one of his assistant masters – and a very different kettle of fish altogether. Grandfather Samuel agreed that he would lend him the money to purchase Number 3 Sandown Terrace on certain minor conditions, which, if breached would require the immediate repayment of the loan. So in practice, Grandfather never really lost control of Number 3 Sandown Terrace, as he was well aware that Dromgoole would be unable to repay the loan from the money he would make from his school. So he could foreclose on him at any time. Dromgoole was well aware of that, naturally. Grandfather Samuel was convinced – or certainly, convinced himself – that Dromgoole didn't attempt to discover for himself what the secret of the attic was. Doubtless he had a look round, but perhaps the risk of tearing the wall down was too great…"

"Or possibly he didn't realise there was a false wall," remarked Rosemary. "No one who lived there for the best part of a hundred years seems to have realised that attic room was a couple of feet narrower than it should've been."

"That may well be the case," remarked Lilian Rust, giving Rosemary a sharp look. "But to be on the safe side, Grandfather Samuel loaned Dromgoole the money to purchase Number 4 Sandown Terrace from Jerome Barfoot, in order to keep him even more under his thumb, financially speaking. Though you might believe that he did it because Percival Dromgoole had uncovered his secret and was blackmailing him, Grandfather Samuel assured my father that such was not the case. As he became wealthier, he felt it safer to increase Dromgoole's debt to him considerably. In that way, Dromgoole got rid of a rival and the closest competition and almost certainly would have less use of the attic rooms, since between them the schools had never secured a sufficient number of pupils to require the use of every room in both Numbers 3 and 4 Sandown Terrace… In the event, Dromgoole paid off his debts when the military took over the whole of Sandown Terrace in 1915. He made sufficient profit on the sale to set himself up elsewhere."

"Wasn't your grandfather – sorry, your father and his brothers, concerned at what the military might discover?" I asked.

"They were concerned, naturally, but not unduly so. By 1915, it was 30 years or so since Stowe had died and Dromgoole had occupied the house for considerably more than half of that time. Besides, they considered it unlikely that the army would have the time or the interest to discover such a small cavity in the attic. Indeed, my father told me that their biggest worry was the possibility that one of the enormous German guns which they used to shell across the Channel during the last war might inadvertently disclose Stowe's final resting place. But by that stage, many owners, tenants and lodgers had come and gone, so the likelihood that anyone would point the finger at Grandfather Samuel seemed increasingly remote."

"Thank you. I assume that the delicacy of the subject meant that you couldn't ever seek legal advice as to whether Matthew Stowe's heirs had a claim to your grandfather's wealth as it had been handed down over the years? Or, indeed, what sort of claim they might be able to make?"

"As you suggest, it was seen as being too delicate. Indeed, it was a family rule that only the family should know. My sister Eleanor felt obliged to inform Nigel Underwood and her other sons – but I doubt whether her husband knew anything… and certainly the first time Margaret has ever known anything about these matters has been this morning… But now I've confirmed what you managed to surmise, what are you intending to do with this information? Before you do so, I believe I require both some coffee and a couple of Rust family witnesses, if that won't inconvenience you?"

"Not at all. May I ask who you have in mind?"

"My nephew Nigel. He may be ineffectual and as bland as plain junket, but he is a qualified solicitor. And my cousin Nicholas, the MP for the Weald, as you undoubtedly know already. Both are within half an hour of this place at this time of day on a Friday. So, if you are content to bide your time here, we might have some coffee."

"As you wish."

Margaret Underwood, who appeared completely dumbfounded and not a little furious, was despatched to summon the two men and arrange coffee. She returned with a face of thunder, announcing that both her husband and his cousin would be present within forty minutes. She was followed about five minutes later by a servant, who looked to be of Mediterranean origin, bringing a tray of coffee and biscuits. This being a somewhat old-fashioned household, the coffee came in an ancient electric percolator, of the sort that in my experience invariably produced stewed, foul-tasting coffee. And so it proved – and the accompanying arrowroot biscuits did nothing to mask the taste of the coffee.

"Am I correct in my understanding that if Aunt Lilian hadn't written certain letters to you, it's unlikely that you would've worked out that Samuel Rust had murdered this man, Matthew Stowe?" asked Margaret Underwood, sharply, looking at Rosemary.

"Yes. That's correct," replied Rosemary, looking straight back at her. "The letters showed us that there were descendants of the murderer who believed that their wealth was potentially at risk if the truth came out. That suggested that the heirs or descendants of the murdered man must have some sort of claim on their wealth. From there, knowing who was living in Sandown Terrace during those years, it was possible to narrow down the field of suspects quite a lot."

"And you say you were doing this largely as an academic exercise?"

"That's so. Our children are grown up, but as yet we've no grandchildren. It seemed like an interesting challenge. But even assuming we were able to work out who the dead man was, who'd killed him and why, we expected it to be purely of historic interest. Suppose it'd been one of the Excisemen who lived in Sandown Terrace who'd been killed and we found out that he was killed and his body hidden by some smugglers, named Smith, Brown and Jones. It would've cleared up a mystery – both now and presumably then. But there was no way we could've foreseen that our research would cause problems for people a hundred years later."

"I can see that. So why did you persist when you got letters telling you to stop what you were doing?"

"During our careers, we've been threatened several times by crooks of one sort or another. We've been shot at and someone once tried to blow me up with a rocket grenade. You may think this stupid, but we don't like being threatened and it usually has the opposite effect to what was intended. We've also never liked the idea that there was criminal activity going unpunished when we might be able to do something about it... and that has continued after our retirements."

"I imagine if someone had done as thorough research on you that you appear to have been doing on this family that might've become apparent?"

"I suppose so. It'd depend on who you spoke to, of course."

"There's such a thing as being too clever by half... or do I mean so over-cautious that your caution has the opposite effect to what you intended," remarked Margaret Underwood acidly, staring at Lilian Rust. I guessed that she'd had to put up with being under the thumb of the old woman all her married life and this was the moment when the worm finally turned.

Lilian Rust looked at her rather as she might look at a fly that had just settled in her cup of coffee, but said nothing. Having obtained from us what she wished to know, Margaret Underwood lapsed into silence. Both Rosemary and I were well practiced in holding our tongues when we didn't need to speak. So silence reigned.

Eventually we heard the sound of a car drawing up in the drive. Rosemary had parked sufficiently to one side to allow several cars to park as well. We heard the front door open and Margaret Underwood went to meet whoever it was. She returned with a fairly tall, plump man, with thinning hair and a face that was bland and elephantine at the same time. The dark, conservative suit, blue-striped shirt and old-school tie suggest to me that this was Nigel Underwood. His wife confirmed it.

"What's all this about?" he asked, with faint tones of irritation. "And who are these people?"

"Wait until Nicholas arrives, if you will," replied Lilian Rust. "I don't want to go through all of this three times over."

Nigel Underwood shrugged his shoulders. Evidently, he was used to being ordered around by his aunt. I wondered whether he'd be quite so compliant when he realised what her meddling had achieved. He sat on the remaining comfortable chair. His wife resumed her seat on the long-backed Victorian chair.

Ten minutes later there was the sound of another car, followed by the doorbell. An unseen servant went to the door and ushered a tall, lean, silver-haired man into the room, Nicholas Rust MP. He was dressed in what would be called "country casual" - a checked green tweed jacket, a checked shirt with plain green tie, a brown moleskin waistcoat and russet-coloured cord trousers.

"Well, Lilian," he began in a very upper drawer accent. "What's the reason for this urgent summons? I do have constituency business on a Friday, y'know."

"Allow me to explain, Nicholas," replied the old woman. "But first, allow me to introduce Mr. and Mrs. Nicholas Storey. You may recall I mentioned them briefly that last time we met."

We rose and shook hands with Nicholas Rust and with Nigel Underwood. I had a feeling I must've come across Rust when I attended a House of Commons Select Committee at some time, but other than recognising his face, I had no recollection of any contribution he'd made. Rust rested against the table, looking as though he was about to hold forth.

"Now we all know who's who, an explanation is in order," Rust continued.

"Mr. and Mrs. Storey arrived at our door this morning and explained that evidence they'd gathered pointed to Samuel Rust as the killer of his assistant

Matthew Stowe. Their reasoning is unassailable and I have confirmed that their suppositions are accurate," explained the old woman.

"I suppose it was necessary to do so?" remarked Rust.

"In the circumstances, it seemed to me that the more honest we are, we have a better chance of avoiding what Mr. and Mrs. Storey could do with their information. The more difficult and unhelpful we were, the more likely that they would feel no compunction about passing their suppositions on to the newspapers and television… and there's no law to prevent them from doing that."

"So you brought me here as a matter of extreme urgency to tell me that! Couldn't it have waited?"

"You need to understand that Mr. and Mrs. Storey have not clarified what they intend to do with this knowledge. I hasten to add that is because I asked them to await your arrival and Nigel's."

"You mean… they are seeking some form of compensation for keeping what they have uncovered out of the public arena? That's tantamount to blackmail!"

He turned and started at us with a practiced air of righteous indignation. I was sure he was one of those backbenchers in the House of Commons who regularly boomed "resign" at Ministers of the opposing party, very much like the foghorn on the Woolwich ferry in my childhood.

"Don't be so stupid, Nicholas! You always were a fool, even as a child. Mouth first, thoughts later. No wonder you ended up as an MP."

I could sense that Margaret Underwood was itching to say something, but perhaps a desire not to put marital harmony at risk kept her silent.

"So what do Mr. and Mrs. Storey intend to do with this knowledge?" Rust turned to glare at us.

"Almost certainly nothing," I replied, looking him in the eye. "We are retired public servants, not blackmailers. Indeed, the only people who've broken the law are members of the Rust family. It was you, I presume Mr. Nigel Underwood, encouraged by his aunt who asked Major Harry Bent, his old school friend, to employ someone to plant listening devices in our property and car and a device in the petrol tank of our car which would've set it alight, had we not discovered it beforehand. This individual also stole and set alight a car as a warning to us. Because we aren't amateurs in this sort of thing, we now have a signed statement from this individual, as well as the devices he used. The statement names Major Harry Bent as the person who employed him, but I'm confident that, faced with the possibility of the damage to his reputation that would ensue if we took the matter to the police, Major Bent would disclose that the person who asked him to get this done and who actually paid for it all was Mr. Nigel Underwood."

"I take it what he says is true?" demanded Rust of Nigel Underwood.

"Aunt Lilian can be extremely persuasive. She was genuinely deeply troubled by what Mr. and Mrs. Storey might uncover," replied Underwood, shamefacedly and limply.

"As a result of utterly misreading the situation and panicking, she achieved the complete opposite of what she intended," broke in Margaret Underwood, seizing her moment. "Mr. and Mrs. Storey have made it quite clear that not only did Aunt Lilian's interventions put them on the track of the murder, but also stiffened their resolve to find out what'd happened in Deal all those years ago."

"It's easy to get it right post facto," observed Rust, with an urbane wave of his hand. "I'm sure Lilian did what she considered the safest course of action at the time… Nevertheless, if illicit means were employed, we can but apologise and hope that Mr. and Mrs. Storey will be prepared to let the matter rest, as it appears no harm was done."

"As I said," I continued, "there are certain conditions. The most obvious one is that you plainly believe that you have an immense amount to lose if this matter were to become public knowledge. We have no particular interest in it becoming public knowledge. It happened over 100 years ago and all those involved are long dead. Much as we might feel that both Matthew Stowe and Samuel Rust deserve justice, it's far too late for both of them. However, you know we have this knowledge. You've already shown you were prepared to act illegally to prevent us getting to the truth. We need your assurances that you won't try to do anything to expunge this knowledge… in other words, by getting rid of us… And before you protest that you wouldn't dream of such a thing, remember you had no idea of the sort of man who you'd entrusted scaring us off to. The device placed in the petrol tank of our car could have been set off while we were in the car. I believe you stipulated that no harm should come to us personally, Miss Rust, but when you operate – as you necessarily have to – at arms' length, you lose control over such things. So you should be aware that, along with material relating to other matters during our lives, this information will be held securely and you should expect that it would become public knowledge in the event of anything untoward happening to either or both of us. I hope that is plainly understood?"

"I believe you can have our full assurance on that score," replied Rust. "It strikes me that in such matters you have a considerable professional advantage over us… and considerably greater experience in this sort of affair… But is that your proviso? Or are there more?"

"There is a second condition. You are plainly aware that Samuel Rust stole Matthew Stowe's formulas for the pills and tonic when he murdered him. I accept that Stowe might well not have had the opportunity to develop those formulas without Samuel Rust's facilities and assistance. Nevertheless, as Miss Rust was so acutely aware, there are heirs of Matthew Stowe who have as legitimate right to the large amount of money made by Samuel Rust as a result of Matthew Stowe's discoveries. Miss Rust, you mentioned that Stowe might have around half a dozen heirs living at present. I believe that they are rightfully owed compensation for money which the murder of Matthew Stowe deprived them…"

"That is making the assumption that he would've been able to market and sell the pills and tonic as successfully as my great-grandfather," observed Underwood.

"I'm not proposing that Stowe's heirs should get the two thirds of the family wealth – that's tied up in stocks of GMR Inc. – as Miss Rust indicated to us earlier. What I am suggesting is that you should find a way to ensure that each of them gets a fair measure of compensation – say, £100,000 – in any way that you like. I imagine you'd want to keep it anonymous and hard to trace, but I would ask that this should be done within six months and that Mr. Underwood should meet us subsequently and explain – with any necessary documentation – that it has been done and how… And though I'm sure you wouldn't think of pulling the wool over our eyes for an instant, you'll be aware, I'm sure, that Rosemary is a trained accountant who spent most of her career in the Met in the Fraud Squad… But those are the only conditions."

"That'll take some managing… and six months will be required, but it can certainly be done," observed Nigel Underwood.

"And we shall do it," added Nicholas Rust.

"There's no surprise," remarked Lilian Rust acerbically. "When self-interest and lack of other options coincide with making a belated moral stance, it takes a politician to nod his head vigorously… We have no choice. We'd prefer not to do it. But our circumstances could conceivably be much worse."

"It's easier for you to say when you don't have any children or grandchildren," retorted Margaret Underwood. "If it wasn't for your meddling, this need never have happened. It shouldn't have taken two complete strangers to force this family to do the right thing. And if we weren't prepared to do the right thing, we should take no pleasure in doing it now. We must accept this condition, of course. But I have a condition of my own. The so-called family money that is locked into that shareholding with GMR Inc. must now be parcelled out to each of those who benefit from it. We cannot have money we hope will come to our children and grandchildren be dependent on the vagaries of old people whose fears outweigh their common sense."

The atmosphere in the room, already chilly in spite of the log fire, descended several degrees further. It was time for us to depart and leave them to their family quarrel.

"I realise that you know where we live," I said to Nigel Underwood. "So when you're ready, please write and we'll arrange to meet somewhere convenient."

"But if we don't hear anything by six months, we'll most certainly be in contact with you," added Rosemary.

14. LAYING A GHOST TO REST

We left the house, got into our car and drove back towards Beckenham, before deciding to make a detour to a garden centre which did a decent lunch at a reasonable price… and where we could get a couple of plants for our garden, which had too many spring and summer flowering plants and not enough to brighten autumn and winter days. We'd occasionally wondered whether our predecessors had spent a month or six weeks in Spain every winter, as the garden we'd inherited from them seemed particularly drab and despondent from December through to March.

"I realise that wasn't quite in the category of your Houndsditch squash club performance," remarked Rosemary, as she made her way through a cheese salad. "But there was some thinnish ice you were skating on out there. It's a good thing 'Aunt Lilian' didn't try to deny everything."

"I'm going to wave Ockham's Razor at you again. What other explanation could possibly fit with what we knew? While I agree someone in Number 3 Sandown Terrace could've killed a passing stranger or Dromgoole could've killed Matthew Stowe in order to blackmail Samuel Rust, the letters about the threat to the family's wealth could realistically only have come from one of Rust's descendants. They were the ones who'd made all the money. Rust transformed himself from an ordinary chemist into the manufacturer of pills and tonic and made a mint from them. Matthew Stowe was one of his researchers – and disappeared. That postcard you got seemed to me to confirm that his relatives were concerned he'd gone missing… and we never found a death certificate for him. He was there at precisely the time Rust seems to have discovered the formula for making his pills and tonic. It all seemed to me to go well beyond coincidence… and nothing came together in quite the same way with the Culpepers or Barfoot and Dromgoole, it seemed to me. And, in any case, the ones who might've carried out a murder lived in the wrong building. Once we were certain that no one had broken through the walls between the attic of Number 3 on either side, it always seemed far more likely that whoever put the dead man in the cavity lived in Number 3. So I didn't really feel I was on particularly thin ice at all."

"I'd just about got there… but with a lot more hesitation and reservation than you evidently had. I felt there was so much we didn't know. For instance, anyone who lived in those buildings between the censuses, but wasn't there on the night of the census… which could've included another researcher for Samuel Rust… and actually the one that he killed, not Matthew Stowe…"

"I confess I hadn't really taken sufficient account of that. I suppose I felt that we should've been able to find a death certificate for him... and there was that postcard..."

"Which might or might not have been about him..."

"Someone writing to Eleanor Stowe about Matthew? I suppose there could've been more than one Matthew Stowe who'd been living in Deal at that time, but it seems a bit unlikely."

"And Avram Groth and the man he met called Percy – from the other postcard?"

"Almost certainly nothing to do with anything. I reckon the chances of there being more than one Percy living in Deal at that time are a lot higher than two Matthew Stowes. But it could've been Percy Dromgoole. From what we've heard of him, he doesn't seem averse to borrowing large amounts of money... Presumably he knew he didn't actually have to pay Samuel Rust back until such time as he sold Number 3 Sandown Terrace, so if he was making enough from the school, he might wish to borrow money to make sure his school seemed better than Barfoot's, if nothing else."

"It's an explanation..."

"I'm not suggesting it's the only one, just that I didn't see it was relevant. It always seemed to me that, if anything, Dromgoole was a blackmailer, not the murderer… and even if he'd killed someone who he owed large amounts of money to and concealed the body, I can't quite see that his descendants would feel that their wealth was threatened if it was disclosed. And the money that was critical in Dromgoole getting on and leaving a fair-sized estate to his heirs was what Samuel Rust lent him, not anything he borrowed for desks and books and so on."

"OK. But admit it, you were lucky that the old woman was prepared to confirm your supposition so easily."

"Yes… and no. From the moment it came to me that it was Samuel Rust who'd murdered Matthew Stowe, I felt fairly confident that whoever wrote the letters would admit it."

"Why?"

"Because if they were difficult, we might feel completely free to publish our suppositions. Since all those concerned are long dead, there'd be no question of libel. But if they were helpful, there was a greater chance they might be able to persuade us of the damage publication would do and seek to make a deal of some sort."

"And you got to 'Aunt Lilian' being the letter writer after I met her yesterday and found out about her at Quebec House?"

"Exactly. If Nigel Underwood was Major Harry Bent's contemporary at school and he had an aged aunt, as sharp as a tack, living with him, I felt I could safely put two and two together and come up with four."

"I'd got that far… But, as I said, I wasn't as certain as you that the dead body had to be Matthew Stowe… I was certain that Samuel Rust had murdered A. N. Other for the formula for the pills and tonic, but the evidence it was Matthew Stowe wasn't sufficient for me… But that's water under the bridge… And I thought you did a nice job in laying it all out so that there was practically nothing for Lilian Rust to challenge."

"Well… If I'd thought a bit harder about whether Samuel Rust's victim wasn't Matthew Stowe but A. N. Other and I'd got it wrong, it would've been a deeply embarrassing moment… Though I wonder what she would've had to say if I'd got it all right apart from the identity of the victim? Do you reckon she'd've tried to bluff it out?"

"I doubt it. I think once you'd shown you'd got enough evidence to point the finger conclusively at Samuel Rust and the reason why his victim was killed, the precise identity of the victim would be less important… Especially since her overriding concern was to keep this out of the public domain to avoid a lawsuit by the victim's heirs."

"I suppose so… Still I'm relieved that when I was skating on thinner ice than I realised, it didn't give way underneath me."

"I'm surprised you didn't ask her who her informant was?"

"I wanted to keep on the front foot. If nothing else, I thought it might confuse matters… and it didn't really matter. For what it's worth, I suspect it was Esme Culpeper… Not because she suspected Samuel Rust was the murderer, but because she liked to show off to another old lady with a bit of shared history just how much more she knew about what was going on."

"That's pretty thin ice too. A good job you didn't try it out on Lilian Rust."

We finished our lunch, bought some plants and drove home. Within a day or two, we'd pretty well forgotten about the whole matter. There was plenty to do and a holiday to prepare for. It was only after we'd come back from Brittany when Emily and Greg called in on their way back from a long weekend in Deal that we were reminded of it.

"Whatever happened to that research you were carrying out about the body that was found in the attic for flat 4?" asked Emily. "Didn't someone connected with it threaten you… or something like that?"

"We found that the records couldn't tell us who the body was or how he got there. So we've had to finish our research," replied Rosemary, being, in the current phase, economical with the truth. "As for the threats, it seemed as there'd be nothing we could make public, the threats ceased."

I wondered how much of this Emily believed. But she was canny enough not to press us – and was probably relieved that her visits to Deal would not have some vaguely menacing shadow cast over them.

"Has the bloke above you moved back into his flat yet?" I asked.

"Yes. He got a couple of friends to do up the attic rooms, but even if he wanted to sell the flat, I can't see many takers until everyone has forgotten about the dead body he found there."

"You'd better give him back the key he lent you. We've certainly no further use for it."

"Though we don't ever plan to go researching dead bodies, why couldn't you find out who the man was?"

"The problem is that records are based largely on names… and to a lesser extent places. But if you don't know someone's name and have no way of identifying it from the corpse, especially when you can't pinpoint when the person died, you may have a list of names from the censuses or even electoral registers, but unless the murder took place on the night of a census, there are likely to be people who've lived in a property between censuses and may not have been on the electoral roll. Indeed, for much of the nineteenth century, a lot of poorer people wouldn't have qualified for the electoral roll. And then you can't assume that the victim actually lived in or near the property where they were killed. And there are plainly a lot of people who've died without death certificates. So you'd have to be extraordinarily lucky to find out who someone like that dead man was, when they died such a long time ago."

"It must've been frustrating for you not to be able to find out who it was."

"We're retired. And though it would've been interesting to know who the man was and why he was put there, no one can be brought to justice now for whatever they did… It was an interesting piece of research and I've learnt a lot about old records and where you can find out things about your ancestors… But I'll let your mother continue with the genealogical stuff… I think I'd find the gaps and unknown bits too frustrating if I was looking into my own family history."

"But if you're going to stay in Deal, you really should learn about its history and get to know all the interesting buildings there," added Rosemary. "The man in the bookshop by the Royal Hotel, The Golden Hind, is very knowledgeable and helpful and you can spend your money on old maps and engravings of Deal."

"Well, we may be going to Deal less often over the next year or so. I really wanted to call in and tell you that I'm pregnant – eleven weeks – and Greg and I are planning to get married at the end of October!"

We congratulated them both. Our surprise was only surpassed when we got a phone call the following evening from our younger daughter, Sarah, telling us that she and Adam were going to get married in October... fortunately at the same registry office and with a joint "wedding breakfast" afterwards. We were forbidden to pay for anything – though eventually Rosemary persuaded them that we would pay for the booze.

Preparations took up a lot of our time between then and October.

We'd totally forgotten about the body in the Marine Buildings until a letter arrived from Nigel

Underwood suggesting that we meet so that he could show us what'd been done to meet the Rust family commitment to Matthew Stowe's heirs. We agreed to meet at a garden centre in Keston, which had a small café. I mostly observed, while Underwood took Rosemary through what they had done. She pronounced herself satisfied and Underwood left, no doubt hoping never to see hide nor hair of us again… a feeling which was entirely mutual.

"Well, unless you've got some urgent and deeply necessary investigation to complete in the next few weeks, I believe we're going to have to pack away our investigators' notebooks from now on," observed Rosemary. "As grandparents, I suspect we're going to have less time for ourselves and we need to be responsible and not take risks – for the sake of our grandchild… and possibly grandchildren, as I can't imagine Sarah will delay long starting a family now Emily is having one."

"I suppose we had to grow up eventually," I replied. "But I wouldn't've done anything differently…"

"Sometimes it hasn't felt like it, but overall it's been fun… and I wouldn't have missed any of it, not least because we've done so much of it together…"

"But now we can file away Ockham's Razor and the two-pronged approach…"

"But make sure you keep writing it all up... I don't know what our daughters may think, but our grandchildren may find it interesting what those two old people got up to in their heyday."

So I have... But sometimes there are promises you make to yourself or to each other that you find difficult to keep!

****

Glossary

Back-Ullaging   A Customs & Excise term, loosely used to mean working backwards from the evidence available

Blackballed   Excluded

BT   British Telecom

C&E   Customs & Excise

DC   Detective Constable

Junket   A milk pudding

MI5   British security service

FRC   Family Research Centre

Okham's Razor   The idea that the most straightforward solution to a problem is the most likely

PC   Police constable

RTA   Road traffic accident

SOC	Scene of crime
SOCO	Scene of crime officer
VAT, VATman	Value Added Tax, VAT Inspector

About the author

Richard Hernaman Allen spent his early years in Loughborough, got a degree in History from Merton College, Oxford, and joined Customs & Excise as an Assistant Principal (fast stream trainee) in 1970. After working on the introduction of VAT, he was Assistant Private Secretary to Maurice MacMillan (Paymaster General at the Treasury) and Harold Lever (Chancellor of the Duchy of Lancaster). On his return to C&E in 1975, he worked on VAT, excise duties, customs, planning, budget work, legislation and EEC negotiations, before being promoted to the Board in 1990 where he was responsible for indirect tax policy (1990-91), finance and IT (1991-4), compliance operations (1997-8) & personnel & finance (1998-2001). He also worked as Director in the Department of Social Security (1994-7) and Department of Environment, Food and Rural Affairs (2001-5). After early retirement, he worked in various jobs as a consultant, including in Georgia and Kosovo, while completing *"Through Fire"*, which he began in 1976. He lives in Petts Wood and has a flat by the sea in Deal. He divides his time between writing, running (insofar as his right hip allows) and grandparenting. He has a wife, Vanessa, two daughters, Jo and Kat, and two grandsons, Joshua and Jasper.